GHOSTS
of the
COVE

To Carol –
Hope you enjoy !
Vicki –

Victoria Bennett

NEWMAN SPRINGS PUBLISHING
320 Broad Street
Red Bank, NJ 07701

First originally published by Newman Springs Publishing 2019

ISBN 978-1-64531-336-6 (Paperback)
ISBN 978-1-64531-337-3 (Digital)

Printed in the United States of America

To the writer's group, Nola, Dana, Gina, Myrna and Lee (our token male). Thanks for keeping me going.

Prologue

1862

HEAVY BOOTS HIT THE CABIN porch with a hollow thud.

"Jacob, is that you?" The young woman stood from where she stirred the kettle on the hearth and tucked a strand of honey-colored hair into place. Abigail wasn't expecting her husband for several days but turned to the door, her blue-green eyes smiling at the prospect of his early arrival. Like many other able-bodied men of Cades Cove, Jacob now spent most of his time in the surrounding mountains. Although his sympathies lay with the Union, this war was not his doing, and Jacob chose not to join either army. Born and raised in this remote valley, he wanted only to remain on his small farm and work the land. But the cove's fertile fields and plentiful livestock made an enticing target for Confederate guerillas from North Carolina. When the bushwackers began raiding the farms and homesteads, stealing livestock and food, and killing the menfolk, Jacob's plans changed. Abigail, like many of the other wives, sweethearts, and mothers, finally convinced her man to join his friends and kinsmen and go into hiding.

She glanced quickly around the cabin Jacob had built for her. Everything in the single large room was in its place, and not a speck of dust had escaped her cleaning rag. Their home was nearly a mile from their nearest neighbor and even farther from most of the other residents of the cove, but they found contentment there with little but each other and the wind in the trees for company. The forest crowded close around the clearing that held a cabin, springhouse, and small barn. After the raids began, Jacob moved their mule and extra grain to his father's barn for safekeeping. Later he took the horse with him into the mountains.

Left with only the cow and a few chickens for company, Abigail felt the isolation for the first time.

When he agreed to go with the others, Jacob urged his wife to go down into the settlement and stay with kin. Abigail would have no part of it. Hands on hips and small chin held high, she stood toe-to-toe with her much taller husband. "I'm not going to leave our home for those thieving marauders," she'd said and quite literally stuck to her guns. The musket that hung above the fireplace was longer than she was tall, but she demanded that Jacob teach her how to use it, as well as a pistol. Neither his protests nor a bruised shoulder from the musket's recoil weakened her resolve. Crossing to the door, Abigail wondered how Jacob had fared since she'd last seen him.

Living off the land meant little hardship for the men with no farms or families of their own, but the married men chafed to return home. There were crops to tend and repairs to be made before the first snows. When scouts reported no sign of an impending raid, Jacob stole home. On these infrequent visits, he worked their small field of corn and mended whatever was broken around the homestead. Abigail worked alongside him, asking questions and learning something new with each task. As the war dragged on, Abigail grew accustomed to Jacob's prolonged absences, and without the larger animals to tend, she could run the farm by herself. But she missed her husband—now more than ever. What she had suspected for several weeks, the granny woman confirmed. She was pregnant, and their first child would be born around Christmas.

Reaching for the door latch, she blushed at the thought of Jacob's reaction to the happy news. She threw open the door, ready to tumble into his welcoming arms. Rosy cheeks turned ashen when she saw not her husband but three rough-looking men in gray.

Chapter 1

THE STORM HIT WITH AN unexpected ferocity. Abby paused over her half-packed duffel bag to watch. When she'd left her apartment that late September morning, humidity hit her in the face like the damp face cloth she'd left hanging in the bathroom. By midafternoon a large mass of cold air swooping down out of Canada ran smack into an equally large mass of warm, moist air over east Tennessee. Abby left her office in time to see leaves turn their silver underbellies toward the boiling clouds. As she reached her apartment, large raindrops dashed themselves against the hot pavement and created mini-geysers of steam.

The storm gathered strength, cooling the asphalt and sending tiny rivers coursing toward storm drains. Lightning danced across the firmament and made occasional forays to the earth below. Mother Nature was showing off. Wind-whipped rain and bits of leaves slapped against her windows as the tempest passed over the city taking with it the day's heat and mugginess. As she watched the last of the storm clouds race eastward toward the Smoky Mountains, Abby thought of her brother and glanced heavenward. "You would have loved this one, Steven."

As kids, the first crack of thunder sent Steven and Abby racing to the highest point on their property to watch as the wind-driven rain marched up the valley toward them like Sherman to the sea. This drove their mother to distraction. The sensible daughter of an Indiana farmer and a veteran of everything from twisters to blue northers, she could not understand why her children were determined to stand in the face of the storm and dare it to do its worst. It was a wonder they hadn't been struck by lightning where they perched under a tin-roofed shelter to watch the weather drama play out before them. Somehow both survived the follies of childhood, but in the waning days of the Gulf War, the plane Steven was piloting went down over the Persian Gulf. There were times when Abby almost forgot that he was gone. Times when she got as far as dialing the telephone before she remembered, and hurt replaced the funny story she meant to tell him.

Abby gave herself a mental shake and got back to her packing. She'd finally managed a few days off from the Knox County District Attorney's Office and really needed it. Most of the time, she found it difficult to believe she'd been there for five years; but at others, it seemed like her life had always been an endless parade of the worst the city had to offer: pushers, pimps, prostitutes, thieves, and murderers. She hadn't even started out to be an attorney, much less prosecuting alleged felons.

* * * * *

For as long as she could remember, Abby wanted to be a doctor. She brought home an assortment of strays, both two- and four-footed, and did her best to repair what was broken, be it a hurt paw or hurt feelings. Medical school was a foregone conclusion by the time she was twelve. But a virus that struck a few weeks before the end of her internship derailed her neatly laid plans. The resulting meningitis left her weak and unsteady on her feet for months. The white coat she wore so proudly became a blanket of lead, and each day seemed to last longer than the last. Sheer force of will pulled her through finals but left her with no energy reserves. A few days after graduation, she tearfully wrote a letter rejecting the offered residency at Vanderbilt. As in the old adage, the spirit was willing, but Abby knew she would not be able to perform at the level she demanded of herself. "Next year," she said as she squared her shoulders and watched the envelope and her future slip into the mail slot.

Strength and balance were slow to return. She awoke each morning determined to write letters and complete the paperwork required for late admission to another residency program. But by noon, a giant unseen hand forced her back to the sofa, her medical career just out of reach amid the papers scattered on the coffee table. August came, and with both her bank account and chances of getting into another quality program dwindling, Abby took a position with the Knox County Coroner's Office. It was only temporary, she told herself, something to earn a living until she figured out when and how she could complete her medical training.

Although her med school curriculum included pathology, Abby had never considered forensics as a career choice. Anatomical pathology in a hospital setting was, for the most part, a tidy process with the patient's medical chart pointing to the cause of the patient's orderly, if not always peaceful, demise. Death was a decidedly messier affair on the coroner's table. Most who ended up here did not go peacefully into that good night, and each case brought new mysteries to unravel. Always a puzzle fan, Abby found the work engaging. Working among the recently dead on a daily basis also required a strong stomach and an odd and often dark sense of humor. Fortunately, she'd developed the first in medical school and soon gained the second, usually with the assistance of the police officers and other emergency personnel involved.

Like the time the EMTs brought in the body of a man shot by a jealous husband.

"What have you got for me?" she asked.

"Uh, thirty-seven-year old...uh, white male, uh, GSW to the chest," the first EMT barely managed to get out between snickers.

"Yeah, uh, DOA at the scene," said his partner, also smothering a laugh.

As the new kid, Abby took her duties very seriously and was a bit perturbed at the behavior of the officers involved. She'd also heard tales of practical jokes being played on morgue neophytes and figured it was her turn to be the mark.

"Okay, guys, what is it?" Abby asked.

"Nothing, Doc. Just a GSW," they said in unison and fled before she could ask more.

Abby read their written report as she moved to the body. It looked like a straight-up domestic homicide and simply said the victim had been caught in the act with the shooter's wife. However, nothing she read explained the odd shape of the body bag. Where the body's feet should have created only a modest peak in the rubberized canvas, it rose nearly eighteen inches from the table. At the other end, a decidedly unhead-like form created a mound above the shoulders. Still wary, Abby went to the table, unzipped the bag, and let out a yelp when a gaudy red flower jumped out at her. Apparently, the cheating wife had unusual tastes.

The body before her was dressed in full clown regalia, makeup and all. He wore an oversized bowler hat complete with spring-loaded flower, a mismatched suit with plaid jacket and polka-dot pants, and finally a pair of what had to be at least size 20 shoes. Abby heard barely muffled tittering from her coworkers and the EMTs in the hallway. Thinking the joke was over, she set about making an inventory of the deceased's effects. In a pants pocket, she found a tin of Altoid mints. It looked like the real thing, and she opened it without hesitation. When a two-foot snake jumped out, her startled scream set off a round of unrestrained guffaws from the hall. Strange cases were not unusual in a county morgue, and after the initial shock, she joined their laughter, knowing she would eventually have an opportunity to exact revenge on her tormentors.

A few months into her forced but now comfortable exile from residency, an assistant district attorney asked her out. Abby hesitated. Her last romance as a sophomore in college had ended badly. Now, after four years of books and being on call, she likened her social skills to those of her current patients—stiff and cold. During med school, there simply hadn't been time to think about dating. Now the prospect was a bit frightening. But he was bright and funny and persistent. After his fourth request, this one in writing and delivered with a single red rose, she gave in. Somewhat to her surprise, she enjoyed the evening. For the first time in months, her mind shifted from her stalled career. He was definitely charming, but Abby found herself more drawn to the work he did. Most of their dates consisted of a rehash of his most recent cases. Whenever the case was circumstantial and based primarily on forensic evidence, her ears really perked up. They had many lively debates about the value of various techniques for identifying both perpetrators and victims. Like her work in the morgue, criminal cases presented puzzles to be solved, and many called for medical expertise. Six months later, she was hooked—on the law, not the lawyer. She sat for the medical boards and obtained her license, but instead of applying for another residency, she took the LSAT and enrolled in law school. Abby told herself (and anyone else who would listen), she was not giving up on medicine; she was just going to use her medical background in a different way. And most of the time, that worked…most of the time.

Law school had its challenges, but not like medical school. Even with a full-time job and ample time devoted to her studies, Abby still managed a semblance of a social life, something she'd only dreamed about in med school. She didn't feel the same sense of urgency she'd felt before. The law was important, but was it really life or death? When she allowed herself to dwell on it, Abby had the vague feeling she was selling herself out but usually banished such thoughts to the far reaches of consciousness.

And then during her last semester of school, she met Kerry Michaels.

The thirteen-year-old appeared on the medical examiner's table after being tortured, raped, and murdered. Just three months earlier, the accused had been arrested on a similar charge but released for lack of hard evidence. Abby slammed instrument pans around the morgue and wailed her protests to the stiff and silent witnesses on the other tables. This time, the investigators found trace evidence that conclusively linked the killer to Michaels. The prosecution was flawless, but a shrewd public defender and a credible psychiatrist persuaded the jury that he was insane. When the defendant was found innocent by reason of insanity and sent to the state hospital, Abby consoled herself with the thought that at least he was off the streets.

When she graduated, her old beau, now an assistant district attorney, offered her a job. Remembering Kerry Michaels, Abby found a passion she hadn't felt in a long time—a chance to make a difference again. Now five years later, the fire that initially fueled her enthusiasm was burning low. She was no longer certain that anything she did or didn't do made a difference; and worse, there were days when she found it difficult to muster the determination to try. No matter how many thugs they locked up, there were always more of them out there, and they seemed to be getting younger and more violent every day. And to make matters worse, Abby saw the same names with an alarming frequency—the jails, it seemed, had revolving doors instead of bars.

* * * * *

Abby finished loading the car and pulled out of her driveway. Leaving the noise and traffic of Knoxville behind, Abby headed for the peace and tranquility of the Smoky Mountains. Originally from the Midwest, her parents moved to Tennessee when Abby was six and Steven was ten. Steven was always happy to go back to Indiana for school vacations and holidays and even returned there for college. But Abby quickly fell in love with the hills of Tennessee and, as soon as she was old enough, made it clear that this was going to be her home. When Steven died, her parents returned to Indiana to grieve among family and old friends, but Abby found her solace in these gentle old mountains. There was just something about the Smokies, especially Cades Cove. Here, unseen forces worked to heal her soul and bring her peace when nothing else could. The cove was her refuge from all the ugliness of the world; it was, very simply, home. If Abby could have, she would have lived in the Cove; unfortunately, the National Park Service had a prior claim, and she had to content herself with visits whenever time permitted.

Chapter 2

THE COVE WAS PART OF the Cherokees' hunting grounds and first settled by the white man in the early nineteenth century. Abby understood why people chose to settle in this remote place. It was as if God
had scooped a big oval bowl out of the mountains and lined it with
everything needed to sustain those who found their way in from the
outside. The fertile valley provided rich soil for crops and abundant
game for the table. She'd been here in every season but to this day
couldn't decide which time of year she liked best.

The winter air could be so clean and cold it hurt to breathe, but
when the sunshine made a field of snow sparkle like a carpet of diamonds, it didn't matter. Some summer mornings, the mist clung to
the hillsides and hung in the trees like Spanish moss, giving the cove
an otherworldly appearance. The fall color was spectacular for those
up to fighting the crowds and with spring came an abundance of
wildflowers and new life all around. Despite its ever-changing pan-
orama, Abby found the cove like the pages of a favored and well-read
book, bringing new wisdom with each rereading. No matter how
long she stayed, she always wanted to stay longer.

Cades Cove had been home to over 650 people in the mid-
1800s. By the time the Park Service took over in the 1920s, most of
the remaining residents chose to sell out rather than fight eminent
domain. A few accepted less money for their land in exchange for
the right to stay and tend their farms. This right was on the con-
dition that their homesteads remain unchanged. No steel towers
strung with wire would bring power to this remote valley. Public
utilities such as water and sewer were luxuries enjoyed by outsiders.
Generators provided whatever electricity they might need and water
had to be pumped from wells. As time passed, the younger gener-

ation, yearning for modern conveniences, gradually moved away. With the exit of the human residents, the Park Service removed most of the "modern" houses and other structures and allowed the cove to return gradually to its natural state. Only a few primitive homesteads were preserved to show what life was like when Cades Cove was a thriving little community.

For Abby, the only less-than-perfect thing about the cove was the number of tourists it attracted. Millions of people visit the Great Smoky Mountains National Park annually, most between June and September. Abby was certain that each and every one of them, by choice or by chance, managed to find Cades Cove. From sunup to sunset, an unbroken line of cars, trucks, and RVs circled the floor of the basin like an enormous snake. Fortunately, from Abby's perspective anyway, most didn't linger and returned as quickly as possible to the shopping and other attractions of nearby Gatlinburg and Pigeon Forge. Many of those who took the time to leave their air-conditioned cocoons left their marks in the form of graffiti on rocks or buildings. Because she feared encountering one of these vandals would give her an unbearable urge to commit bodily harm, Abby usually stayed away during the summer months. Later she would endure another self-imposed absence when colorful autumn foliage turned the road around the cove floor into another slow-moving parade of cars. Leaf jams, Abby called them. They were like bear jams, only worse.

The park had its fair share of bear jams during the summer— cars stopped for miles because some would-be nature photographer with a brand-new Nikon just had to get a little closer to a poor bear who simply wanted to get across the road. It was amazing that so few people were injured. When provoked, black bears, while not as fearsome as their grizzly cousins, can do serious damage to the human body. In the autumn, the problem was not bears but trees. The forest of hardwoods and pines became a kaleidoscope of red, green, orange, and yellow against the misty blue backdrop of the mountains, drawing thousands of visitors from far and near.

Today, with school already in session and the height of the fall color still weeks away, Abby hoped that she and whatever wildlife hadn't been scared up into the hills would get a taste of nineteenth century peace and quiet.

A small tent, sleeping bag, and provisions for her four-day respite were stored neatly in the trunk, her bicycle secured in its rack. Clean, fresh air blowing through the open sunroof swept away the remnants of stale office air that clung to her skin like cobwebs. By the time she reached the Townsend entrance to the park, Abby no longer felt like a watch too tightly wound. She prayed the campground would not be too crowded.

As she drove past on her way to check in, Abby grinned broadly when she saw that it was practically deserted. One of the benefits of playing hooky in the middle of the workweek, she thought to herself. At the building that served as an open-air chapel with attached camp store, Abby was greeted by George Martin, the manager.

"Well, I see you're back," he said. "Time off for good behavior?"

"Not exactly. I just escaped when they weren't looking."

George was in his mid-seventies with thick thatch of white hair and deep blue eyes that missed little. His wife, Jenny, passed away a few months before his projected retirement; and without her to share his plans, George decided to keep on working. Younger Park Service employees did the heavy work required to maintain the campground, leaving George to mind the store. Visitors from all over the world passed through his little domain, and as a naturally gregarious old gentleman, he said he couldn't imagine a better way to spend his golden years.

"What's it looking like for the rest of the week. Am I going to have company?" Abby asked.

"Not much. Take your pick of the sites. Just let me know where you light. Nice German couple down at the other end. Great hikers. Otherwise, day-trippers. Troop of Girl Scouts due in next week. Don't expect you'll be wanting to hang around for that!"

She laughed and shook her head. "No thanks. For some reason, when you get a bunch of little girls out in the woods, all they want to do is giggle and scream all night long. Remember last spring?"

When Abby came up for a weekend the previous April, she found every campsite but one filled with Girl Scouts. They were generally pretty good little campers, and the evening was quiet aside from the sometimes off-key strains of Kumbaya. But about three in the morning, one of the more intrepid Scouts decided she couldn't wait until morning to use the bathroom and trekked down to the restroom alone. Returning to her tent, she saw two beady red eyes staring back at her out of the darkness. A raccoon, making his nightly foray through the campground in search of food, had innocently wandered into her flashlight's beam. Whether the raccoon was particularly large or the camper particularly small, Abby didn't know, but the child immediately shrieked at the top of her lungs, "Bear!" She kept on screaming until she set off a chain reaction of squeals from every tent. As Abby scrambled to opening of her own tent to see what was going on, the terrified raccoon beat a hasty retreat past her, chattering all the way. The Scout leaders quickly quieted the girls, but after that, every little noise set them off again. No one, including Abby and the raccoon, got much sleep for the remainder of the night.

"Yep. It was weeks before that poor old 'coon dared to come back. Saved on cleanup, though, without him digging through the trash cans. No one yet has been able to design a trash can those critters can't get into."

"Why don't you work on that, George? Make your fortune and retire."

The old man gestured expansively. "What, and leave all this?"

"Can't blame you for that. Guess I'd better set up camp if I want to get a ride in before dark. I'll take my usual spot," Abby said, heading for the door.

"You gonna ride this evening?"

"Of course."

"Maybe you should wait 'til tomorrow."

Abby suppressed a smile. "Why?" she asked, although she knew the answer.

"After the rain and with the mists to hide them, the haunts will be about."

But for this one quirk, George was not a man given to flights of fancy. He scoffed at the tabloid tales of alien abductions and other paranormal experiences and seemed firmly rooted in common sense.

"Oh, George, you don't really believe in ghosts, do you?" Abby had teased the first time he mentioned this.

"Well, I can't say as I've ever met up with one myself, but I heard my granddaddy tell about strange happenings on misty evenings, and I just don't take any chances."

As he told it, most were benevolent spirits who just wanted to return to the familiar surroundings of their homesteads—to till the soil or tend to other daily chores.

"The spirits know that most folks won't admit that they've seen a ghost. They're all too happy to tell themselves it was just the mist playing tricks on their eyes."

He never said exactly how he came to acquire his information about these supernatural comings and goings. But given the earnestness of his warning, Abby suspected that he might have had a personal encounter with a more restless and less benevolent spirit.

"If I run across any, I promise I won't disturb them."

"I just hope they don't disturb *you*," grumbled George, shaking his head as he watched Abby pull out of the parking lot.

Abby drove up the hill to her favorite campsite. George said most campers didn't like the site because it was so far from the store, restroom, and shower facilities, but it suited Abby to a T. If she placed her tent properly, it blocked the light from the parking lot below and gave a sense of being truly alone in the woods.

Her ideal site would have been somewhere near Abrams Falls or any of half a dozen other isolated spots in the cove, but since that wasn't possible, Abby made do. And with the sound of the wind in the pines and the gurgle of a nearby creek as a lullaby, it was not bad. Not bad at all.

Chapter 3

ABBY QUICKLY MADE CAMP AND set out for a ride around the cove. After the storm, the air smelled of ozone and wet dirt. Just as George had said, the mist pooled in ethereal patches in the fields and draped the trees like freshly washed bedlinens. Here and there, the white vapor flowed over the road where her passing made it swirl and eddy like curtains in a breeze.

Abby reveled in the clean air and pedaled hard for the first couple of miles, enjoying the burn of muscles too long unused. Her opportunities to ride in the city were limited to a stationary bike at the gym, a poor substitute at best. Feeling the road under her tires and the wind in her hair, she fought the urge to throw back her head and shout. Slowing down after the first sprint, Abby realized that she had not stopped to visit with John and Lurena in a long while and turned her bike down a lane leading into the woods.

John and Lurena Oliver, the cove's first permanent settlers, were buried in the churchyard of the Primitive Baptist Church. Abby liked to wander through the graveyard and imagine what life must have been like when they were alive. Since her first visit as a child, she had read as many stories as she could find about the cove and the people who came to call this place home. She knew their family stories so well that stopping here among the headstones was like a visit to old friends. Abby admired the pioneer spirit and strength of will it took to settle here in 1821 when John, Lurena, and their baby came alone to a wilderness. Even though their lot could not have been an easy one, she often envied the Olivers, the simplicity of the times in which they lived.

The old clapboard church was almost as primal as its surroundings. Spare and purpose-built, plain wooden benches and a raised dais at the front were its only furnishings. Behind it, the old cemetery told many stories of times past. Abby meandered among the markers, stopping here and there to read the names.

Any spirits here must be amiable, she thought. With no sign of the modern world to say otherwise, the sense of the past was overwhelming. She could almost see men in homespun shirts and broad-brimmed hats escorting women in long calico dresses and bonnets up the stone steps and into the church. Standing near a tiny headstone, she could imagine the soft weeping of a mother as the men lowered a tiny casket into ground; from beside another, the sobs of a young girl whose soldier would not come back from a war that turned brother against brother. Clusters of markers with dates close in time bespoke an epidemic of some sort; still others told of later wars. Abby walked about lost in the stories told with only a few words and dates. The prickling of hairs rising on the back of her neck interrupted her reverie. Abby suddenly felt that she was not alone. Looking around, she discovered the surrounding woods shrouded in fog. She peered intently into the murk, hoping the dark forms that punctuated the whiteness were merely trees.

Although she didn't really believe in George's "haunts," Abby couldn't shake the sensation that she was being watched. "Don't be silly," she said aloud, her voice muffled in the heavy air. She'd been here dozens of times, often in the evening, and never felt uncomfortable amid the sleeping residents. Now she couldn't wait to get away. She reached her bike and found it lying on the ground instead of propped up against the tree where she'd left it. A twig snapped nearby, and Abby let out an involuntary squeak. Peering into the gloom, she still saw nothing out of the ordinary. Anxious to be free of the oppressive feel of the mist, she mounted her bike and sped away.

Once back in the open, Abby felt sheepish. It wasn't like her to get spooked so easily. *Guess I've been hanging around George too long,* she thought. Determined to enjoy the rest of her ride, she dismissed the incident and continued on. Daylight was fading quickly, and Abby realized she'd been musing in the churchyard for quite some time. She took a shortcut on one of the dirt roads that bisected the cove floor. A low haze had settled into the entire valley, but Abby no longer sensed the odd presence she'd felt in the churchyard.

By the time she got back to her campsite, it was nearly full dark, and the air had taken on the chill of early autumn. Abby used the kindling she gathered before setting out and soon had cheery fire blazing. She tried to eat sensibly most of the time, but camping always gave her a yen for junk food. There was nothing much better than a hot dog cooked over an open fire and washed down with an ice-cold Coke. She would have preferred a Killian's Red Ale, but liked to keep her wits about her when camping, lest a bear come wandering through looking for leftovers. And because no self-respecting ex-Girl Scout could go camping without making s'mores for dessert, she finished her meal with the gooey concoction of marshmallows, chocolate bars, and graham crackers.

When she finished cleaning up after her meal, Abby sat back in her chair watching the fire. She thought again about her experience in the cemetery. Had there been someone out there among the trees? When she started around the cove road, Abby had seen only a few cars and only one or two other riders. None of them had been near the church. People hiked around the cove as well, but most hikers kept to the trails, and there were no hiking trails running through the woods adjacent to the church and cemetery. "You really are getting dotty in your old age." She laughed. "There was no one there. You just let George and his talk of haunts spook you." Abby yawned and stretched. The exercise and the dancing flames made her drowsy. Even though it was still early, she decided to turn in and read for a while.

* * * * *

Abby walked around the church and opened the gate to the old burying ground. She was determined not to let the previous evening's events rob her of the tranquility she found in this place. *I don't know why I let George's ghost prattle get to me*, she thought. The morning dawned clear, so she was a little surprised to see mist still swirling among the headstones. Undeterred, Abby moved deliberately to where John and Lurena rested amid family and friends. She was leaning down to right a fallen jar of flowers on Lurena's grave when she heard the woman scream.

Abby jumped up and surveyed the cemetery. The scream sounded like it came from nearby, but she couldn't tell from which direction. As she stood, the cry came again, only closer. Now she also heard the sound of running feet and a man's voice. A woman clad in a long dress ran into the clearing, paused, and peered back toward the woods behind her.

"Are you all right?" Abby called.

The woman didn't respond but turned and ran toward Abby. Before the woman had taken many steps, a large man appeared out of the gloom. He grabbed the woman's arm and swung her around in an effort to pull her back into the surrounding forest. Although her attacker towered over her, the woman used her free hand to claw first at the fist that held her arm and then at his face. As the two struggled, Abby shouted to the woman again, hoping her attacker would back off if he thought there was a witness. Instead, he raised his arm and struck the woman a forceful blow to the head. She crumpled at his feet.

As Abby stood horror-stricken, the man gazed across the clearing toward her. Like the woman, he did not acknowledge her presence. He looked around the clearing as if to assure himself that he had not been seen then stepped back into the woods and disappeared. Abby ran to the woman and knelt beside her. As she reached down to feel for a pulse, her hand struck the wall of the tent, and Abby woke up.

Chapter 4

ABBY SHIVERED DESPITE THE WARMTH of her sleeping bag. A few birds twittered overhead, and in the weak predawn, she could just make out the outline of objects in the tent. She yawned and stretched. *What in the heck woke me up?* she wondered. She tried to pluck the dream back from the dark realm of slumber, did so, and wished she'd let it be. Abby wriggled out of her sleeping bag and into her biking shorts. She was not about to let the episode at the church or the dream destroy the peace of the cove. Poking her head out of her canvas shell, she found the world still slightly out of focus in the lingering fog. When another tremor passed through her, she paused. "No," she said defiantly, then scrambled out and got on her bike.

Dawn came slowly here in the valley. The sun was still behind the surrounding peaks when Abby arrived at the gated entrance to the road that curled around the cove floor. Two mornings a week, the loop remained closed to vehicular traffic until 10:00 a.m. This gave hikers and bicyclers the chance to walk or ride without dodging cars and RVs whose drivers were paying less attention to the road than to the scenery. Abby smiled when she saw only a few other early risers at the gate. Sharing the road with only those souls intrepid enough to make the trip on two wheels or two feet was a rare treat well worth getting up for.

The delicious coolness beckoned her to ride hard and fast, but Abby kept her pace deliberately slow. Daybreak and twilight were the best time to see the cove's four-legged and two-winged critters going about the business of life. The road slowly meandered down a long gentle grade with a field off to the left and a steep forested ridge to the right. Low haze still hovered just aboveground, turning the field into a calm white lake. Abby paused to gaze out on the landscape. A frisson of fear passed through her. Something was moving about just below the surface of the thin misty pool.

Without warning, a wild turkey poked its head up, looked around, and disappeared. She watched as the sight was repeated, two, three—six times, each in a different place as the large birds feasted on insects on the ground and clinging to the tall grass. Abby laughed, realizing that there must be a whole flock of the wily birds hidden there.

As her eyes followed the stately birds, she returned in her memory to a long-ago trip with her brother. Midsummer sun and a soft but steady breeze off the peaks made the cove the perfect place to while away the afternoon. The tourists had temporarily abandoned the area for livelier pursuits, and Abby and Steven had the road pretty much to themselves. They drove slowly, stopping whenever it suited their fancies to poke around this old house or that old barn.

As they neared one of the old churches, Steven punched her in the arm.

"Ow! What the—" she began.

"Shhhhh," he hissed, "turkeys."

Certain that he was hallucinating, she nevertheless slowed the car. Abby knew there were wild turkeys in the cove, but like lots of critters in the cove—fox, beavers, and bobcats, for example—she never expected to see them. But there in a field at the edge of the churchyard was a flock of ten to fifteen of the large birds appearing for all the world like hens browsing in a barnyard.

"Pull over up at the church. I want to get some pictures," Steven directed. "I think I can sneak up on them."

The tract was an acre or two in size with a large solitary cedar tree squarely in the middle. As they crept through the woods, Steven explained his plan.

"See that tree? If I stay behind it, I think I can get close enough with the telephoto."

Abby rolled her eyes. "Yeah, right. You just keep thinkin' that way, Butch. That's what you're good for," Abby said, quoting a line from an old Paul Newman-Robert Redford movie. "Don't you know those birds are smarter than you are?"

"Just hush and stay here. You'll see."

Abby settled down on a convenient log to watch. Benjamin Franklin once proposed that our national bird should be the turkey since they were a noble and intelligent species. Abby wasn't sure about the noble part, but they certainly got the better of her big brother that day.

When Steven first spotted them, the turkeys were feeding midway between the big cedar tree and the woods at the back of the field. When he left the shelter of the trees, the birds seemed to take no notice of his presence; and for a moment, Abby thought he just might get close enough to get his pictures. However, it soon became apparent that these wily creatures were not fooled by Steven's efforts at stealth. As she watched, all Abby could think of was a *Peanuts* cartoon strip in which Snoopy tried to slither up behind his prey like a snake. Steven would take a step or two and then freeze, always keeping the tree in his line of sight. She could almost hear him thinking, *If I can't see them, they can't see me.* But for every step he took, the turkeys sidled a bit closer to the trees, never in a panic and never giving any indication that they noticed him. By the time her brother reached the cedar, the turkeys had faded into the tree line. To this day, Abby swore she'd heard them giggling along with her.

Still chuckling over the memory, she rode on. Here, the pavement ran around the edge of the flat cove floor, the peak of Thunderhead Mountain barely visible on the far side of the basin. A bit farther on, the roadbed wound its way back into the forest and up the steep sides of the surrounding hills where sun had finally risen above the mountains to the east. As the trees closed around her, Abby felt none of the apprehension of the previous evening and was at ease in her surroundings. The sun filtering through the trees created an ever-changing mosaic of light and shadow on the ground as she pedaled up and down the hills. The woods were alive this morning but held no threat—she heard only the movement of the cove's natural denizens.

Halfway around the circuit, Abby stopped at the park interpretive center at the Cable Mill. When the cove was a thriving community, there were a number of water-powered mills used for sawing logs or grinding corn or wheat. John Cable's operation was different in that the same wheel was used to power both grist- and sawmills. It was the only mill remaining in the cove and the focal point of an outdoor museum at the center. Here, visitors could catch a glimpse of what life was like in the Cades Cove of the 1800s. The area also included an early frame house, blacksmith shop, log barns, smoke- house, and a mule-powered sorghum mill. Abby loved to listen to the rangers relate the history of the cove and its early inhabitants, but today her reason for stopping had nothing to do with educa- tion. Stomach growling, she stopped at the visitor center just long enough to purchase some honey and a bag of the cornmeal that was still ground daily at the mill. Mouth watering at the thought of the feast she'd have for breakfast, Abby quickened her pace on the second half of her ride.

Making spoon bread in a Dutch oven was not the easiest way. When she first bought the medium-sized pot with short legs, she had to do some research to find out how to use it. As a sidenote, one of the articles she read said that Lewis and Clark prized their Dutch oven over many other seemingly more valuable possessions on their search for the Northwest Passage. After a number of failures, Abby finally perfected her technique and was inordinately proud of the fact that she could cook a traditional mountain dish in much the same way that Lurena Oliver must have.

Once back at camp, she set about building a new fire in the firepit. She was pleased to find the rocks surrounding the pit still held some warmth from last night's fire. Her concession to the pres- ent day was to use charcoal instead of wood for her fire. While she waited for the coals to reach the proper temperature, Abby tidied up around the campsite. She'd been making spoon bread since she was a Girl Scout and no longer needed a recipe or measuring cup as she mixed together a batter of cornmeal, milk, and egg yolks on the cookstove. As it came to a slow boil, she beat the egg whites into the stiffest peaks she could manage without benefit of an electric mixer and then gently folded them into the cornmeal mixture. After noting that the coals were ready, she poured the fluffy concoction into the Dutch oven and made sure the lid was on securely. Using a small shovel, Abby pushed the coals around until they resembled a red-hot bird's nest. She then placed the pot in the middle and covered the lid with coals.

With nothing more to do for the hour or so it would take for the spoon bread to bake, she strolled over to the store to visit with George.

Chapter 5

As SHE ENTERED THE STORE, a man was just leaving. Calling back over his shoulder to the storekeeper, he nearly ran into Abby.

"Sorry," he said. "Guess I should watch where I'm going."

"No problem," said Abby as she gazed up into a pair of incredible blue-green eyes. He was handsome in sort of a mountain man-cum-college-professor sort of way. Despite the bookish look created by horn-rimmed glasses, he was dressed for the out-of-doors in jeans, flannel shirt, and hiking boots. She got the feeling she should know him but had no idea where they might have met.

"Hey, Jake," George called. "Forgot your sunglasses."

As the stranger and Abby approached the counter, George continued, "Abby Edwards, this is Jake Bartlett. Jake...Abby. Jake here spends as much of his off time roaming around the cove as you do."

"Nice to meet you." The man nodded to Abby as he reclaimed his sunglasses and headed for the door.

She turned to George. "Not much of a talker, is he?"

"Oh, Jake's all right, but he's sorta got a one-track mind. Surprised you two haven't met. He's always poking around looking for the roots to his family tree."

"Maybe that's why he looks familiar. Must have run into him at the visitor center or something."

George's eyes twinkled. "Or maybe it's because he's such a handsome devil. You still dating that lawyer fella?"

She grinned back at the old man and shook her head. "Couldn't stand the woods, so I had to throw him back."

Two years ago, Abby had a brief relationship with one of the other assistant district attorneys. Tim was fine in the city—they went to movies and the symphony and generally had a good time together.

But when she brought him to the cove for a weekend camping trip, he was totally out of his element, and it was not pretty. He hadn't the faintest notion about anything that wasn't electronic or automatic. He didn't like sleeping on the ground and wasn't too keen on food cooked over a campfire. And that was the good part of the weekend.

"Remember the day I took him to Abrams Falls?" Abby asked.

They'd set off early. It was only two and a half miles back to the falls, and Abby thought it would be just about right for a tenderfoot. The clearing around the waterfall would be a good place to rest and eat before returning to the trailhead. Tim was in good shape, and the trail was not strenuous, but he was just not a hiker. He groused and grumbled every step of the way. To make matters worse, he fell in the creek at the falls and had to slog back in soggy boots and jeans. Saying he was not a happy camper would have been an understatement of the highest order.

"Yep. Never did see the like. Looked like a drowned rat. Still see him?"

"Well yes, he is the district attorney, so our paths do cross. But I just couldn't imagine spending the rest of my life with a man whose idea of roughing it is a hotel without turndown service and mints on the pillows."

"We just need to find you a mountain man."

"Like your Jake, I suppose."

"Oh, Jake's not a mountain man. He's a professor at the university down in Knoxville. Knows how to walk across a creek without getting his boots wet, though."

"Now don't start sounding like my mother. She always wants to know when I'm going to settle down and start producing grandchildren."

"Well, you're not getting any younger. And you don't seem to be as enthusiastic about that job of yours as you used to." George peered at her closely, waiting for her reply.

His perception brought Abby up short. Was she that transparent? In her mid-thirties and attractive with an unruly mane of golden-brown hair and dark-brown eyes, Abby was still unmarried. The brief social life she enjoyed while in law school evaporated when she began working at the district attorney's office. She knew none of her neighbors in the apartment building where she'd lived for the past five years. Her closest friends were her college roommate and her study partner from law school. But even these relationships were fading. Judy, her college roommate, married a doctor and became a stay-at-home mother of three. All she could talk about was Sean's soccer game or Jenny's school play or the baby's latest tooth. Not that Abby could blame her, they were cute kids, but Judy's life was as foreign to Abby as Abby's was to her. With Marianne, Abby at least shared the common bond of the law. The two had been close during law school, but Marianne rode the fast track from associate to partner in a prestigious firm and now spent her days defending doctors and hospitals in malpractice cases. Marianne drove a new BMW and rarely wore the same suit to court. While Abby's old Mazda was paid for, it was on its last legs, and many of her suits had also seen better days. Abby wasn't jealous of her friends—it was just that their lives had all taken such different courses she now felt out of touch with both of the other women.

Abby shook her head but avoided the old man's gaze. "Of course I am, George. I'm just a bit tired. Besides, it's all I know how to do," she finished weakly.

"That's not true, and you know it."

George knew that she had never completely given up medicine, and even now she volunteered one weekend a month at a free clinic in the city.

"I know, but it's too late for that."

But George, who had known Abby since her high school days, was not convinced. "Hogwash!" He thumped the counter for emphasis. "It's never too late. I know you're good at what you do, but it's not the same. *You're* not the same." He paused before administering the coup de grâce. "And I don't think your brother would approve either."

Abby winced at the mention of Steven and knew George was right. The day after she got the news that she had been accepted into medical school, he showed up at her dorm with a gift-wrapped box. Inside she found a stethoscope and medical bag with her name engraved on it. From that day forward, Steven rarely referred to her as anything other than "Doc," and he was her greatest source of encouragement for the next four years. What would he think of her career change, Abby wondered? When he left for the Persian Gulf, she was working at the coroner's office and still planning to complete a residency. Steven's last words to her when she dropped him at the airport were that he expected her to be back in school when he returned.

"Maybe. But my work is important, and I'm happy enough." But her tone lacked conviction. Eager for an escape from this conversation, she said, "Hey, I've got to get back! I only came up to see if you wanted some fresh spoon bread."

"Always, 'specially if you got honey too. But you think about what I said."

She wouldn't admit it to George, but she'd been thinking about those things for several months. The previous Saturday, as she sutured an eleven-year-old's skateboarding wound, Abby caught herself thinking about a recent case that was a prime example of what she most disliked about her job. The defendant was a sixteen-year-old who'd spent more of his teenage years on the inside of correctional facilities than on the outside. Weldon's problem was that he just loved cars. Unfortunately, the cars he loved always belonged to someone else. His trouble with the law began when he was barely tall enough to see over the dashboard. He told the police he didn't mean any harm; he just wanted to take his girlfriend for a ride. But her father, the owner of the car, was not amused. For this, Weldon spent a year in juvenile detention. After his release, he went to work for the owner of a local garage, the perfect job for the young car lover. Unfortunately, the owner made his real money chopping up and selling the parts of the cars and put Weldon back to work stealing cars with several other young hooligans. A raid on the chop shop by the police department's grand theft auto division garnered Weldon another stay at the state's expense. One thing about Weldon, though, he didn't waste any time; less than six months after his release, he was picked up again. Only this time, the charge was felony murder. Weldon decided to try his hand at carjacking, and his first job went off without a hitch. Or so he thought until he discovered the three-year-old daughter of the car's owner asleep in the back seat. When the little girl woke up crying, he said he didn't know what to do. When the cries turned to screams, Weldon panicked. He said he didn't mean to kill her when he hit her in the head with the butt of his gun. "After all," he said, "I didn't shoot her. I just wanted her to stop crying."

Later, watching the boy proudly showing his stitches to his waiting comrades, Abby smiled for the first time in weeks. As she completed the boy's chart, her thoughts returned not just to Weldon but to the others who were even worse. Was this how she wanted to spend the rest of her career and her life? But then again, after spending the last five years moving up through the ranks at the district attorney's office, did she really want to go back and start over? And that was assuming she could get accepted in a residency program after all this time. Four years as an assistant to the medical examiner and the time she spent in the clinic kept her basic skills honed, but was she sharp enough for the demands of specialty training? That day, the intercom announced the arrival of her next patient and provided an escape from the mental debate. Today she just shoved the thoughts to that place where she kept the painful memories of her brother and muttered, "Darned old man, you know me too well."

1862

The smile died on Abigail's lips. Bushwackers!

The men reeked of alcohol, and their gray uniforms were patched and dirty. In a throat suddenly dry, she managed to find her voice, "May I help you?"

A large man with a grizzled beard and cold gray eyes stood closest to the door. "Wull looky whut we got here?" he said and slid one mud-caked boot across the doorjamb. He made no move to enter the cabin, but neither could Abigail close the door.

"Ain't she a purty little gal. 'Spose we jes' come in an' sit a spell?" asked another. Short and thin with close-set eyes and a wispy mustache, his eyes darted back and forth between Abigail and the larger man reminding her of a weasel.

Mustn't turn my back on this one, *she thought.*

The third man appeared only a bit older than Abigail's nineteen years. His clothes revealed an element of care absent from those of his companions. The patches on the elbows and knees were obviously sewn by one not used to needlework, but his jacket and pants showed signs of recent brushing, if not actual cleaning. His manner was almost deferential as he touched his hat and nodded in her direction, "Ma'am."

"Somethin' sure smells good," said the first man. "That stew you got cookin'?"

Abigail did not want the men in her house. She looked down at the boot blocking the door and then back up at its owner. The big man's gaze slid slowly down her body and he licked his lips. Fear mixed with anger clawed at her chest, making it difficult to breathe. Her mind swirled as she sought a means of escape. Even if she could get to the musket over the fireplace, it was still three to one. Perhaps she could convince them that Jacob was nearby, but failing that, she must find a way to get away from them. The cabin's back door was hidden from view in the large room that served as an all-purpose living area. Maybe, if the men were distracted...

"Yes, and spoon bread in the oven." Abigail forced a smile as she lied. "My husband will be home soon. Nothing fancy, but you're welcome to share our meal. You gentlemen soldiers?"

She moved aside, and as the men shuffled into the room and sat down around the table, the stench of their unwashed bodies filled the air in the warm cabin. Abigail's days of being sick in the mornings had passed, but fear and their smell sent a new wave of nausea washing over her. She clenched a handkerchief to her nose and willed the bile back out of her throat. You have to be strong for the baby, *she told herself.*

"Where's your man gone?" asked the big man.

"Down to the settlement helping his kin clear some land," she replied in the most convincing tone she could muster.

Seeking a distraction to avoid being caught in her lie, she spied the jug of corn liquor Jacob kept "for snakebites." When he first brought it home, Abigail hadn't wanted the potent brew in her home, but her husband was true to his word and never drank to excess. She went to the shelf and hefted the jug. Nearly full. Would it be enough to incapacitate all three men? Unable to think of anything else, Abigail tried to sound solicitous. "You look weary. My husband keeps a jug for medicinal purposes. Would you favor a small drink with your stew?"

"Been ridin' a long spell," drawled the man Abby thought of as Graybeard. "Reckon you best jes' bring us the whole jug."

The weasely man smacked his lips. "Yeah, the whole jug," he echoed.

The boy shook his head when she handed him a glass. "No, thank you, ma'am. I don't drink much."

"Ne'er be a man you don't learn to hold your likker, boy! Drink up. This here's fine stuff." Graybeard thumped the table.

The younger man took a sip and choked. The big man laughed and clapped him on the back. "You'll get the hang of it. Now drink up and have 'nother."

Abigail refilled their glasses and set about putting a dinner of stew and spoon bread on the table. As she busied herself, her thoughts turned again to flight. Out the back door, of course, but then where? Since running to Jacob's mother would only put another household of women in harm's way, she had to find some of the menfolk who remained in the cove. Maybe the church, *she thought. Although services at the Baptist Church had been halted the previous year, most days a few of the elders still gathered there to talk and make plans for after the war. It was a long way from their cabin, but the only place she might find some help.*

As she moved around the table to ladle stew into their bowls, the Graybeard grabbed her by the waist. "C'mere." He leered, pulling her close.

Wriggling away, Abigail willed strength into her voice. "Why, sir, I'm a married woman! Let me get you some butter for your spoon bread…just churned this morning, so it's fresh and sweet. My husband says I make the best butter in the cove."

"S'prised he'd leave purty thing like you here all alone-like," he said. "When'd you say he's comin' home?"

"Oh, any time now. I thought it was him when I heard you on the porch."

"Meantime, where's that jug? Mighty fine stuff."

Abigail poured more liquor and watched as they drank it down. How long before she dared try to escape? The men were drinking steadily, but the strong liquor didn't seem to be having much effect. She went to the fireplace and added more wood. Perhaps the warmth of the fire and full bellies would force the men to let down their guard.

"Thought you were gonna git us some butter," whined the Weasel as Abby had begun to think of him.

"It's out in the springhouse. I'll run fetch it."

"Luke here can go," said the large man gesturing to the youth. "You bes' stay here with us. Might get lonely-like."

"There are a lot of crocks out there. I can find it quicker."

He scratched his stubble of a beard thoughtfully. "Awright. Luke, you go 'long 'n' see she comes right back."

Now what? How could she get away from the boy? As they walked toward the springhouse, Abigail's gaze fell upon the length of wood used to keep the door closed.

Chapter 6

AFTER CHECKING ON THE SPOON bread, Abby puttered around the campsite, simply enjoying the out-of-doors. The sun's warmth chased away the last wisps of fog and promised another warm Indian summer day. The sky peeking through the leafy canopy created a collage of green and blue overhead. Halfway up a tall oak, a squirrel chattered noisily. On the ground, a pair of curious chipmunks scurried back and forth around the site in search of a dropped morsel of food. Apparently, she had invaded their plot of ground when she established her temporary home. Abby was, for the most part, a strictly law-abiding camper—she didn't try to feed the deer, always hung her food bag away from her tent, and took other appropriate precautions to avoid an unexpected encounter with the park's many black bears. But when it came to feeding the little critters, she bent the rules. What harm could a piece of apple or a few raisins be, she wondered? By the time her meal was ready, her three furry neighbors were munching contentedly on little bits of trail mix. The campsite was quiet except for the murmur of the stream and the wind in the trees.

After delivering a bowl of spoon bread and honey to George, Abby considered her options for the remainder of the day. Should she take a hike or while away the afternoon in camp lost in the pages of a good mystery? The lure of the cove tugged at her, and she finally found a compromise. The Elijah Oliver cabin, just a short hike off the main road and a site often overlooked by the casual tourist, would satisfy both her urges. She could poke around the homestead for a while and then sit on the porch and read—the best of both worlds.

Elijah's place was one of Abby's favorite sites in the cove. A son of John and Lurena, Elijah married and moved out of Cades Cove before the Civil War. Following the war, he brought his family back to the cove and built this cabin. Situated part way up the mountain, its isolation was also its appeal for Abby. Although she had no way of knowing, she imagined that after the turbulence of the war years, Elijah came back to the cove in search of the same peace and solitude she found here. The cabin's placement seemed to support this. Elijah built his home facing across the slope rather than toward the valley below. Visitors entering the clearing were met with a blank wall rather than the welcoming front porch. When she first visited the cabin, Abby thought it seemed as if this branch of the Oliver family hadn't wanted to turn its back on the community below, but neither did they want to encourage casual visitors. Later she learned there was a very practical reason—the house faced west, and the windowless southern wall provided protection from the prevailing winds and summer heat. Whether for practical or fanciful reasons, it pleased Abby.

The cabin had a wide front porch with a room at one end, separate from the rest of the cabin. Such rooms, Abby learned, were known as "stranger rooms," meant to accommodate overnight visitors. She also thought they'd also be handy for a less-than-welcome mother-in-law. The main cabin had one large room, perhaps fifteen by twenty feet. A large fireplace took up most of one wall. Near the front door, a small staircase led through the ceiling. There, under the steep roof, was enough space for a bed but little else. A tall man would not have been able to stand upright.

Out the back door, a steep set of wooden steps led down to and through a passageway to a smaller room that served as the kitchen. The homestead also included a corncrib, smokehouse, and barn—all constructed of logs. But it was the springhouse that most intrigued Abby. It was a small log building, no more than four feet across and eight feet long, built against the ridge where a spring bubbled out of a cleft in the rocks. Neatly placed rocks formed a channel directing water through a hole in the back wall and into a trough. There, even in the heat of summer, the cold spring water would have chilled crocks of milk, butter, and eggs. During the winter, it was said, the water was cold enough to crack your teeth. Most of the mortar between the logs had long since fallen away, but even on hot days, the temperature in the springhouse remained lower than ambient; and when properly sealed, it must have been a pretty efficient refrigerator.

Abby made an almost proprietary survey of the area to assure herself that the graffiti writers had not been at work. Finding little new damage, Abby pulled her book and an apple out of her daypack and made herself comfortable on the porch and was soon immersed in a Sharyn McCrumb mystery set in the mountains of Southern Virginia not far from where she sat.

"Abigail!"

Abby looked up from her book. Who could possibly be calling her up here? Besides, except for Steven—who only did it to aggravate her—no one called her by her given name. She looked around but saw no one. Was her mind playing tricks on her again? She listened intently, but the call was not repeated. With a shrug, she returned to the pages of her book.

"Abigail! Where are you?" The man's voice sounded strangely familiar.

"I'm here," Abby replied instinctively before it occurred to her that anyone calling could not possibly be looking for her. This time, she came down off the porch and looked around the clearing. Still no one around. "Hello? Is someone there?"

No reply. *Okay, I'm really losing it*, she thought. First, the strange unsettling feeling of being watched at the church, then the dream, and now this. *What is going on here?*

"Abigail."

She tried to get a fix on the direction of the voice, and it seemed to be coming from the high side of the clearing where the ground rose up sharply behind the springhouse. Only a mountain goat could get up there. Maybe some foolhardy rock climber attempting to scale the steep slope had taken a fall. Moving toward the sound, Abby called again, "Hello. Do you need help?"

Again, no answer.

Abby shivered in the late-afternoon sun. She didn't want to leave an injured hiker out here alone, but years of dealing with the city's criminal element made her wary. And she didn't like the fact that the man kept calling her name. After gathering her belongings, she headed down the trail toward the parking lot. The visitor center at the old mill was just few minutes away, and she could turn the whole matter over to the rangers.

Once on the path, she heard the call again, "Abigail, please answer me. Where are you?"

This time, the voice was nearer, but not from behind, as she would have expected—but off to her left. Abby turned and glimpsed a man walking away from her down a narrow track leading to the ruins of another cabin. Again, the voice sounded familiar, and something about the man's stride struck a chord in her memory. Realization washed over her like an unseen wave—it was Steven's voice.

"Steven, I'm here," Abby called and turned to follow. After a few steps, logic and the sound of her own voice pulled her up short. It couldn't be Steven. But something that defied common sense tugged at her sleeve. Even though she knew pursuing a strange man deeper into the woods was not a good idea, Abby could not resist. She quickened her pace to catch up, but the man remained almost out of sight in the gathering dusk. Although he kept calling her name, he didn't seem to hear her replies. As Abby approached the cabin ruins, the man simply vanished. She was close enough to see him clearly as he entered the clearing, and then he was gone.

"Steven," she called, "come back." The sound of Steven's name brought her up short. As if to convince herself, she repeated the mantra of the months following his death, "Steven is dead, and I have to accept it."

Am I chasing ghosts now? she wondered. *And why am I so calm?* Her earlier feelings of dread were now replaced with frustration. "This is ridiculous!" she cried and turned on her heel. A low moan from the rubble of stones and decaying logs in front of her stopped her.

"Help me," a man's voice called weakly.

Abby wheeled and saw a head barely visible amid the debris. When she reached the wall, she recognized the stranger she'd met in the store earlier that day. She reached for his name "Jake?"

"Huh? Who are you?" the man asked as he struggled to sit up. "Oh, George's friend."

"I'm Abby. What happened?" She saw a thin trail of blood and a darkening bruise on the side of his head. He winced as Abby gently touched it. Her doctor self took over, and she peered closely at his pupils and took his pulse. Pupils equal, pulse strong and steady. Good, she thought to herself, no obvious signs of serious head injury or impending shock. "Are you hurt anywhere else?"

"Mostly my ankle. Hurts like the devil," he said. "Uncovered a timber rattler."

"Did it bite you?" Abby shifted her gaze to his legs.

"Nope. Guess I scared him as much as he scared me. I jumped and caught my ankle in those rocks. Heard it pop."

"How long have you been here?"

"Don't know. What time is it?"

Abby glanced at her watch. "Going on five. Have you been unconscious?"

"Guess so. I came up right after I saw you at the store. Things are sorta fuzzy."

"Let's see if I can get you up. We need to get you out of here and have your head looked at. You've probably got a concussion."

Abby moved one of the large rocks trapping his foot, causing another wince of pain. One look at its odd angle told her that Jake's ankle was indeed broken. "Yep, if it's not broken, you've got one whale of a sprain going here. If I put a splint on it, think you can make it to the trailhead?"

"Sure don't want to wait for that old rattler." Jake laughed. "Might not be so timid when he finds out I can't move."

Abby worked quickly. By her calculations, he'd probably been lying here for at least three hours. She found a couple of sturdy sticks and then rummaged around in her pack to find something to bind his ankle. She carried a small first aid kit, but it was geared more for cuts, scrapes, and snakebites than fractures. She found a bandana and some spare bootlaces. A start, but not enough. "I don't suppose you have an Ace bandage or an inflatable splint handy do you?"

"No, but would some bungee cords work?" He pointed to a pack on the ground nearby.

She retrieved it—and amid several notebooks, a half-eaten sandwich, and an odd assortment of other items,—she found a pair of the stout elastic cords. Abby fashioned a makeshift splint out of the tools at hand and helped Jake to his feet. She hadn't really noticed his size when they met at the store. Tall, yes, she'd had to look up to see his face, but he was also solid. When he was finally upright and leaning heavily on her to keep the weight off his injured ankle, Abby was glad that the trail was both short and fairly level. By the time they made it back to her car, the sun had dropped below the mountains, and both were perspiring despite the chill of the evening.

She tucked him into the front seat of her car. "We'll stop and let George know what's happened and then head for town. You need that ankle set and a full skull series."

"Whatever you say, Doc." Jake sank gratefully into the car seat. "Think I'll take a nap."

"What did you say?" She flinched at the pet name Steven used, and her words had an unintended edge.

"Gonna take a little nap," he said, drowsily unaware of her tone.

"Oh no, you're not! Not 'til we see what that blow to your head has shaken loose. Keep talking, sleepy or not. George said you're a professor. What do you teach?"

As she drove, Abby learned that Jake taught cultural anthropology with a focus on Appalachian studies. She only half-listened as he told her about the various theories about the evolution of culture in remote communities such as Cades Cove, more intent on keeping him talking than on what he was actually saying. Back at the campground, they found George locking up for the night. Abby quickly explained what happened and where they were going.

"I'm going with you," George said and peered in at the younger man. "Sure you didn't break some rocks with that hard head of yours, son?" His face grave despite his joking tone, he pulled Abby aside. "How bad is it, gal?"

"Probably a concussion and a broken ankle, but I think he'll be okay."

An hour later, Abby and George delivered Jake into the hands of the emergency personnel and settled themselves in the waiting room.

"Now. Details," George ordered. "Where was he, and how did you happen to find him?"

Since finding Jake, she'd had little time to think about the events of the afternoon—the voice calling her name and the man she glimpsed on the trail. Until she had things sorted out in her own mind, she was hesitant to discuss them with George. Perhaps she had imagined the whole thing. "I was up at Elijah's place and decided to do a little exploring. Found Jake down a little side trail. Said he scared up a rattler and fell trying to get away from it. Do you know what he was doing?"

"Probably some of his genealogy stuff. Sometime back, he found a letter that seems to link his great-great-grandmother to the cove."

"What in the world did he expect to find in those old ruins?"

"Hard telling. He's been making a map of all the old homesteads in the area."

They lapsed into a companionable silence, and Abby was soon lost in her own thoughts. Had she heard Jake's calls for help and simply been mistaken in the direction from which they came? But she distinctly heard someone calling her name. And what about the man she'd seen? Until he vanished before her eyes, she'd been certain that she was chasing a real, live human being. Now she wasn't so sure. She had never seen another man with Steven's distinctive gait, but although improbable, it was not impossible. *This is just not like me. What is going on?*

George's nudge put an end to her musing.

"What?"

"The doctor says we can take Jake home as soon as the cast dries," he said. "Where have you been? Didn't you hear?"

"Sorry, guess I was daydreaming. What's the diagnosis?"

"Your friend has a slight concussion and a couple of broken bones in his ankle. He can go home as long as there is someone to stay with him tonight," the doctor said. "Afraid he'll be on crutches for several weeks."

"He can stay with me tonight," George said.

Once back in the car, the old man was soon snoring softly in the rear seat. Jake tilted his own seat back and closed his eyes. "Hey, Doc, now that my brain's been thoroughly photographed and pronounced at least nominally intact, mind if I snooze? Been a long day."

Seeing that his sense of humor was also intact, Abby laughed. "I guess so, but we'll have to wake you periodically all night to make sure you're still with us."

"Yes, ma'am. Whatever you say, ma'am," Jake said with a mock salute and left Abby to return to her own thoughts.

Who, or what, had she seen? Surely, if it had been another hiker, he would have stopped to help Jake. But then again, if he hadn't called out, she would not have seen Jake in the rubble. Perhaps the man she followed was simply trying to get off the trail before dark and unwilling to stop and talk to a fellow hiker. Not a likely scenario, Abby thought; but at the moment, it suited her better than the alternative theory that kept creeping into her thoughts.

"Jake, did you see anyone else while you were out there today?"

"Huh, what?"

"Did you see anyone else around that old cabin?"

"Think I would have stayed there all afternoon waiting for my scaly friend to return if I had? The reason I like this time of year is because it's just me and the trees." He paused and grinned. "Guess that sounds a bit antisocial, doesn't it?"

"Not really. If I had my druthers, it would be like this all year round. Seeing tourists race in, shoot a picture, and scrawl their names on the cabin walls before heading off to the next attraction really irritates me. Maybe the pilgrims had the right idea with the stocks and pillory—wish we could use them on the graffiti writers," she finished heatedly.

Jake's laugh was deep and melodious. "Well, gee, tell me what you *really* think. Seriously, though, the thought of some clod scrawling 'Bubba was here' on my great-great-grandma's kitchen wall makes me want to take up target shooting."

Abby smiled. She liked this man. As he settled back into the seat and closed his eyes again, she took a closer look at her companion in the dim glow of the dashboard lights. He had a nice profile—a long straight nose and a strong chin covered by neatly trimmed beard of salt and pepper. His black hair was also shot through with a good bit of gray, but he didn't look that old. All that combined with those blue-green eyes made an enticing package. Abby found herself wondering if he was married or otherwise entangled. She glanced into the rear-view mirror to George dozing in the back seat. How could she elicit that information from her old friend without actually asking? She was not about to give the old man an opportunity to try his hand at matchmaking.

Chapter 7

As THEY PULLED UP IN front of George's cabin, Jake bolted upright in his seat. "Hey, did you pick up my glasses?"

Abby shook her head.

"Must have knocked them off when I fell. Sure you didn't see them?"

"'Fraid not. How badly do you need them?"

"Only to see." He shrugged. "If I'm going to be laid up for a while, I won't be able to get them replaced."

"No problem. I'll go back up tomorrow and see if I can find them."

"Sure you don't mind? I'll go bonkers with nothing to do. Reading would help pass the time."

"No problem. But reading should be the last thing on your mind at this point."

Abby helped Jake hobble up the steps while George went ahead to light the way. The cabin was spare but cozy—one bedroom and living area below and a loft above where George kept a small office. Jake settled gratefully onto the couch as George started pulling bed-linens out of the closet. "You can have my bed, and I'll take the couch."

"No way. This couch will do fine."

"Right. And that long frame of yours will hang over the end by about six inches. Don't argue with me, boy. Besides, you'll be closer to the bathroom."

Jake grinned down at the older man. "Okay, you win. You sure can be a fussy old hen. And since you're bent on babysitting, suppose you can give me a lift back to town tomorrow?"

44

"Can you manage here 'til the after I close up? I don't have any help tomorrow. There is plenty to eat in the fridge, and I have a good stash of magazines."

"Sure. But the magazines won't do me much good—lost my glasses."

"If you're in a hurry, I guess I could take you after I find your glasses. I have no real plans for the day," Abby said.

"Thanks, but there's no sense in ruining your weekend too. I can wait for George."

"Then if you gentlemen will excuse me, I'm going to head back to camp. Don't know 'bout you, but I'm pooped!"

It was well after 2:00 a.m. when Abby left George's cabin and going on four when she crawled gratefully into her sleeping bag. Her last conscious thought was to wonder if she had remembered to hang the food bag away from any nocturnal visitors, but she was asleep before she could get up to check.

In spite of her late night, Abby awoke just after dawn to the sound of rain. She stretched lazily and considered going out to make coffee. Thinking better of the idea, she burrowed back into her sleeping bag and dozed off to the soothing pitter-patter of water on canvas. She awoke later to a weakly lit morning and glanced at her watch: 9:00 a.m. Although the rain was now just a fine mist, the sun seemed unable or unwilling to penetrate the thick cloud cover. A sodden chill replaced the warmth of the previous day. Pulling on jeans and a waterproof jacket, Abby set about making a breakfast of coffee and leftover spoon bread. Not exactly the breakfast of champions, she thought but it beat the freeze-dried packets in her food box. After cleaning up the campsite, she headed off to the shower house.

Clean, if not entirely refreshed by the lukewarm shower, Abby stopped to see George. "How is our patient?" she asked.

"Had a rough night. Wouldn't take anything for pain until just before dawn. But sleeping like a baby when I left. What about you?"

"You know me, I sleep better on the ground than in my own bed. Woke up, heard the rain, and snuggled back down for another nap. What happened to the sunshine?"

"Don't know. Weatherman said this rain was supposed to hold off 'til Monday. 'Course, you never know here in the mountains. You still going to look for Jake's glasses?"

"Headed there now. I'll take them out to the cabin and check on him when I get back."

"Oh, he'll be okay. I made some sandwiches and left some soup for him. No sense in spoiling another day of your vacation. Just bring them back to me."

"I don't mind. Too wet for hiking anyway. Maybe he could use some company." As soon as the words left her lips, she regretted them.

George peered over his glasses at her and grinned. "That Jake's a nice-looking fella, ain't he? Reckon he would like a bit of company. And some male companionship wouldn't do you any harm either, gal."

Abby felt the red rising in her cheeks. "Don't get any ideas, old man. He'll be bored to death since he can't see to read. You don't even have a TV. And what if he fell or something..." Her string of excuses trailed off weakly.

"Uh-huh, sure. He's been alone all of about two hours. Bet he's not even awake yet. Besides, the phone's handy, and he seemed to handle the crutches pretty well."

Flustered and unable to think of a comeback, Abby was relieved to see some customers entering. To her chagrin, she heard George chuckling behind her as she fled through the open door.

1862

Abigail swung the stick as hard as she could, striking her captor on the side of his head. Luke fell to his knees, and she hit him again across the back just for good measure. Then she ran—into the woods, just as hard and as fast as she could. The church was about two miles away as the crow flies, but the crows didn't have to contend with the hills and underbrush. Still it was the closest place she thought she might find help. Their nearest neighbor had moved down into the cove when the raids began, and the next closest was nearer to three miles away. Although there was a good trail leading there, Jenny had a new baby and was still feeling poorly. Abigail knew where Jacob and his friends were hiding out on the mountain, but it was much too far, and she wasn't sure she could find the hideout alone. No, it was the church or nothing. She prayed that the men would be there.

"Wonder whut's takin' 'em so long to fetch that butter," said Josh, the one Abigail called Graybeard. "Matt, git on out there and see. Send that little gal back. Ah need some more of that corn likker."

"Aw, they be back in a minute, Josh. Luke's prob'ly just stealin' a kiss. Leave him be. 'Sides, I wanna finish my stew."

Crashing a beefy fist down on the table, Josh shouted, "I tell you to do somethin', you do it! Now git!"

Matt scurried out the door but was back almost instantly. "Come quick! Luke's daid, and the gal's run off."

Josh jumped up, knocking the chair over in his hurry. He strode out the door and across the yard to where Luke was lying by the springhouse door. He shook the younger man and slapped his face.

"Wha...what happened?"

"Where's the gal?"

Luke looked around and shook his head. "W-we were talkin' 'bout her garden, and she leaned over to open door. That's last thing I r'member."

"She cain't be far. Look 'round. Don't want her warnin' the others," Josh ordered Matt.

Matt hurried to the edge of the clearing and held up a piece of cloth. "Looks lack she went this away. Ain't this a piece a her dress?"

"*Maybe this wasn't such a good idea,*" said Luke. "*Let's just let her go and head on back home.*"

"*Came for food and guns, and I ain't gonna to let some sprig of a gal warn the menfolk here 'bouts afore we git 'em. You'uns see what you can find 'round here, and I'll go git 'er.*" With that, Josh took off through the woods behind Abigail.

There was no trail where Abigail ran, but she knew that if she kept on, she'd come to the trail leading to the church. Vines and briars tore at her dress and skin as she ran headlong through the trees. She didn't dare slow down to pick a better way, so she paid them no mind. An exposed root sent her sprawling and knocked the wind from her lungs. As she lay there, gasping for air, she heard the sounds of someone crashing through the brush behind her. Abigail couldn't see which of the men was following her but instinctively knew it was Graybeard, the leader of the group. She struggled to her feet and prayed again that she would reach the church before the man caught up with her.

By the time she reached the trail, Abigail knew if she turned around, the man would be in sight. She could hear the pounding of his feet on the ground behind her and his angry curses as tree limbs whipped at his face. Fear clawed at her like the brush that caught and tore at her clothing, but in her fear she found strength. Now she could see light through the trees and knew she was nearing the burying ground that lay behind the church. "Help me," she cried. "Help me, please."

As she entered the clearing, rough hands grabbed her and spun her around. And then it was dark.

Chapter 8

ORDINARILY, ABBY DIDN'T MIND THE rain; and because it kept most people away, she welcomed an opportunity to have the cove to herself. But not today. Where yesterday's sun made light and shadow mosaics on the ground, today she saw only mud and dead leaves. Low-hanging clouds reduced visibility to a few dozen yards. As she headed down the dark trail, she rolled up her collar against a chill more imagined than real. To her chagrin, she caught herself looking around for the mysterious man of yesterday. Where had he gone, and why hadn't Jake seen him?

"This is ridiculous! I'm not going to let George's ghost tales get to me," she said out loud, hoping the sound of her own voice would calm her jitters. She quickened her pace and soon reached the ruins of the old cabin.

She hadn't had time to look around much yesterday and now took the time to survey the area. This homestead was smaller than Elijah's, but in addition to the cabin foundation, Abby could also see remains of what she supposed was a small barn. The sound of water drew her to the back of the clearing where she found another ruined structure. The few remnants of logs and small rectangle of stones with the stream running through the middle suggested more than stated that it had been a springhouse. The cabin had fared little better. While the Park Service had preserved and, in some cases, even moved some of the cabins typical of the period, this one had been allowed to fall where it stood. An interrupted outline of stones, a half-buried hearth, and few steps were all that remained of what had once been someone's home.

Mindful that the ruins held at least one reptilian resident, Abby began cautiously casting about in search of Jake's missing glasses. She didn't remember seeing them when she helped free him from the rocks that tripped him and suspected that they must have gone flying when he hit the ground. After making a cursory look around where he had fallen, Abby began a systematic search. Finally she caught a faint glint in the corner of the ruins several feet from where she thought the glasses should be. And as she reached to pick them up, her glance fell upon on etched lettering on one of the large stones. Slipping the glasses into her pocket for safekeeping, Abby knelt to take a closer look. After brushing away the moss and lichens clinging to it, she found the letters *JC* and the number *186* chiseled into the surface. The stone had been broken after the 6, but she was certain that it has once been a date, 1860-something. She looked around, but the remainder of the stone and the inscription were nowhere to be found. Abby wondered if Jake had seen the writing. Maybe it would offer him a clue as to the cabin's former owner.

Her task complete, Abby headed back to the car. Despite George's teasing, she was going to take the glasses to Jake. Unexpectedly, she found herself thinking of him as her patient, and she was determined to make sure he was all right. Rather than subject herself to any more of George's musings, she bypassed the store on her way out of the cove and was soon headed across the mountain toward Townsend. She expected to find Jake resting on the couch or maybe in a rocker on the porch. When he didn't answer her knock, she was alarmed. Trying the door, she found it unlocked and entered, calling, "Jake, it's Abby. Are you okay?"

No reply. She quickly checked the bedroom and the loft, but he was nowhere to be found. Going back outside, she was relieved and aggravated to see Jake making his way slowly down the hill behind the cabin. "Are you out of your mind? Didn't the doctor tell you to stay off that ankle?"

Jake looked sheepish. "I got bored. I couldn't see to read, and there was nothing else to do, so I thought I'd take a little walk. I used my crutches, Doc."

This time, she didn't flinch at the nickname. "That's not the point. What if you had fallen again?"

"But I didn't, so what's all the fuss? You're as bad as George. He fussed around here like an old woman all night. I finally pretended to be asleep so he'd go to work this morning."

"That's not the way George tells it." Abby laughed, her anxiety dissipating. "He said you had a pretty rough night. How's the pain today?"

"Oh, it's not too bad. Besides, I don't like the way those pills make me feel."

"Ooh, a tough guy, huh? Did it occur to you to take an aspirin or Tylenol instead? Or do you just like suffering?"

"Not really, and yes, actually, that thought did occur to me. I'm not a masochist. The only thing remotely resembling a pain remedy I found was a jug of what I suspect is the local snakebite remedy. Didn't figure that was a good idea on top of a concussion."

"Okay, okay, point taken. I think I have some Tylenol in my purse. I'll leave them for you. Have you had lunch?"

"George left a pot of soup on the stove, but I haven't gotten around to it yet."

"Well, if you've had enough adventuring, why don't you sit down and prop your foot up, and I'll fix you something to eat."

"Does that mean you're done fussing at me?"

"For the time being." Abby handed him a couple of pills and a glass of water and continued, "But only if you take these and promise to behave yourself."

"Whatever you say, Doc. Hey, did you find my glasses?"

"Yes, I did." She retrieved his glasses from her shirt pocket. "And for the record, I'm an attorney, not a doctor."

"That's not what George tells me."

"What do you mean?"

Her tone made Jake look around from his bed on the couch. "Just that he said you went to medical school before you became a lawyer. Was old George telling another of his tall tales?"

"Well, no. It's just that it was a long time ago. George has a big mouth."

"Didn't mean to touch a nerve. You were just so dead on with your diagnosis that I asked George if you were a nurse or something."

"No problem," she said, softening her tone. "George just thinks I made the wrong decision and never lets me forget it. Besides, it's odd to hear someone call me 'Doc' again." She didn't want to discuss her career choices with a stranger, even one she was beginning to like.

"What do you mean 'again'?"

"The only person who ever called me that was my brother, Steven. He was killed in the Persian Gulf." She wasn't in the mood to discuss Steven with a stranger either and changed the subject. "Didn't I tell you to prop that foot up? Do you need some more pillows?"

Jake shook his head, made a face, and settled down onto the couch with his leg resting on one of its arms. Abby busied herself in the kitchen heating soup and retrieving sandwiches from the refrigerator. She handed him a tray with his sandwich and a bowl of soup. "By the way, do you know who that old cabin belonged to?"

"Not for certain. The land and census records for the cove are pretty complete, but there are a few odd cabins that don't seem to be on any of the plats I've found. It was common practice back then for families to share their land. When a son married, he might build a small cabin on his father's land and help with the farming until he could afford to buy land of his own."

"Do the initials *JC* mean anything to you?"

"Maybe, why do you ask?" Jake sat up abruptly, nearly spilling his soup.

"Well, I found your glasses way over in one corner of the cabin, and the letters *JC* were scratched into one of the big stones. It looked like there had been a date there too, but the stone was cracked, and all I found was *186*. I figured it was 1860-something, but I'm not sure."

"Are you sure?" he demanded.

"Well, pretty sure," Abby replied, surprised at his tone. "The light wasn't very good, and there was a lot of lichen on the stone. Does it mean something to you?"

"It might. Since George has told me all about you, I assume he's done the same about me, and you know I'm looking into my family tree."

"Yep. There's telephone and telegraph and tell George." Abby laughed.

He grinned back at her. "Anyway, there's this old family story about my great-great-grandmother being from Cades Cove. I've been trying to figure out how she got from here to North Carolina but keep running into dead ends."

"But what does that have to do with *JC*?"

"Maybe nothing. But my great-aunt Sarah lived to the ripe old age of ninety-eight. When she died, she left my mother a locket that had belonged to her mother, and it has the initials *AM* and *JC* engraved on it. So far, I haven't been able to find out what it means."

"Do you suppose the cabin and the locket are connected?"

"I have no idea. I guess it's possible, but so far I haven't been able to find anyone with the initials *JC* that I could link to someone with the initials *AM*." Seeing Abby stifle a yawn, he said, "I didn't mean to ramble on. Most people don't find this stuff nearly as fascinating as I do"

"Sorry. It's not the company or the subject. I guess I didn't get enough sleep last night."

"And I'm to blame for that, as well as boring you with my hobby. Guess I've wasted a chunk of your vacation. I'd apologize, but I'm really glad you found me out there in the woods. Will you let me make it up to you with dinner some evening when I get back on both feet?"

"That would be nice. I really would like to hear more about your great-great-grandmother—I just love a good mystery. Did you get enough to eat?"

"Yes, thanks. Just put the dishes in the sink, and I'll wash up later."

"Down, boy! I think you've been up long enough. You don't want your foot to swell." She washed and dried their dishes and yawned again. "Think I'll head back to camp and take a nap."

"Thanks for finding my glasses. At least I'll be able to see to read this afternoon. Suppose George has a stash of books around here somewhere?"

"Didn't you know our George is quite the Renaissance man? He has everything from Isaac Asimov to Shakespeare up there in the loft. What's your pleasure?" she asked as she started up the stairs.

"I'm like you. I love a good mystery. Do you suppose he's got anything good?"

"I know he does. We swap books from time to time." She leaned over the loft railing. "Okay, we've got Dick Francis, Robert Ludlum, and half a dozen others, you name it."

"I'll trust you to pick out a good one. I like a writer with a good sense of humor."

Abby came back down the stairs with a stack of books. "I brought you several so you won't be tempted to try the stairs. There's a pretty wide variety here, and I've read most of them. I thought this one by Carl Hiaasen was a real hoot, but his humor is a bit macabre."

"Thanks, I'll start with that one. And cross my heart, I'll stay put this afternoon. My ankle is beginning to throb. Guess I overdid it a bit this morning."

"Ya think? I'll leave you this bottle of Tylenol," Abby said as she turned to leave. "But if it gets really bad, take one of the pills from the hospital." Seeing him wrinkle his nose, she went on, "I don't care if they do make you sleepy—you're not going anywhere anyway."

"Okay, Do—er, Counselor," he said, ducking the pillow Abby tossed at him as she went out the door.

Chapter 9

THE INTERMITTENT RAIN FINALLY SLOWED to a misty drizzle and stopped altogether as Abby headed back across the mountain and into the cove. While a nap was enticing, she really hated to waste the day and decided to take a brisk ride to shake off the lethargy. But as she crawled into her tent to change into her biking shorts, another wave of sleepiness washed over her. *Perhaps I'll just stretch out for a few minutes*, she thought. *And then I'll take that ride.* Instead of dropping off to sleep, she tossed restlessly for half an hour or so and finally decided the ride had indeed been the better idea. As she rode, her thoughts drifted back to the man she had followed in the woods the day before. There was only one way to prove that she had not imagined the whole thing, and that was to go back as see if she could find evidence of his presence. Abby held little hope of finding footprints after the night's rain, but maybe he left something else behind.

She secured her bike to a tree at the trailhead and started up the trail. When she reached the side trail, she hesitated and then turned resolutely toward the old cabin. If the stranger left any sign, she was determined to find it and lay all of this silliness to rest. Surprisingly, there were still plenty of footprints on the trail. Looking up, Abby realized that the canopy of trees had prevented the rain from washing them away. She quickly recognized her own boot prints. They were clear both going in and coming out. Next to her small prints heading back to the main trail, she saw the single print of a larger boot and the occasional drag marks that Jake must have made as she helped him back to the car. She didn't see any of his prints headed into the cabin but realized that he could have entered the clearing from another direction. What Abby didn't see made her decidedly uncomfortable. There were no other prints on the trail.

Abby stood in the middle of the trail, unable to decide whether to go forward or back. The man she had seen was a big man. If her prints were clearly visible on the trail, his should have been too. Her mind raced as she tried to find a logical explanation for what her eyes told her. But none came to mind. She was certain the man had walked down the trail just as she had; there should have been tracks. As she tried to decide on her next move, she heard a familiar voice calling, "Abigail, where are you?" The call came from behind her on the main trail up to the Oliver cabin. Suddenly more angry than afraid, Abby turned on her heel and ran back toward the sound. She was determined to get to the bottom of this.

When she reached the junction with the main trail, she looked both ways to see if she could see the caller. She saw no one, but the call came again from the direction of the Elijah's cabin, and Abby turned and strode toward it. "Hello, is anyone there?" she called as she walked. "Who are you looking for?"

Again the voice called her name.

"I'm here. Who are you, and what do you want?"

As she entered the clearing at the Oliver cabin, she saw a man on the steps of the cabin. "Hello, there. I'm Abby. Are you looking for me?"

But by the time she crossed the clearing and rounded the corner of the cabin, he was gone. "Is anyone here?" she called as she climbed the steps. The cabin was also empty, but from outside, she heard the call again.

"Abby, are you there?"

This time, the call came from right outside the tent, and Abby realized with a start that she had been dreaming again. "I'm here, George," she said as she unzipped the tent fly. "What's up?"

"What do you mean, 'what's up'? I heard you calling and thought something might be wrong."

"I was napping. Must have been dreaming."

"That must have been some dream." George laughed but then peered closely at her. "Are you okay, gal? You look a little funny."

"Sure. It was just a strange dream, that's all." But her words sounded hollow. Something strange was happening to her, but what,

Abby wasn't sure. But she was certain she wasn't ready to talk about it with George or anyone else.

"Whatever you say. I was wondering when you were planning on heading back to the big city."

"Sometime early tomorrow. I wanted to hike to Abrams Falls for the day, but I really need to go over some files for a trial next week, so I'm going to head back in the morning. Why?"

"Well, I told Jake I'd take him back to town this evening, but if I take him back in his car, I'll be stuck with no way back to Townsend."

"I guess I can follow you down and bring you back."

"I thought of that. But Jake really needs to stay off that foot, and I thought I'd try to get him to stay over one more night to make sure he behaves. We can take him back tomorrow whenever you're ready."

"But that still leaves you in town with no way back. And what about the store?"

"Since John took off today, he said he'd come in and work tomorrow."

"That takes care of the store, but how are you going to get back?"

George's deeply tanned face took on a reddish hue. "Uh, well, actually, I have this friend who'll bring me back."

Abby smiled at the older man's obvious discomfiture. "This 'friend' wouldn't just happen to be a lady, would it? Okay, George, have you been holding out on me?"

Caught, he straightened his shoulders and said brusquely, "Well, if you must know, it is a lady."

"Details, George, details! You're always so interested in my love life. Now spill the beans."

"All right, all right. You women sure are a nosy lot. Her name is Emily, and she was one of the Scout leaders of that group that scared that old 'coon so bad last spring."

"Not the silver-haired lady who was forever losing her glasses? She seemed a little ditzy to me."

"She's not 'ditzy.' She's a very bright lady, and I enjoy her company. Besides, I got her one of those string things for her glasses, and she doesn't lose them anymore."

Realizing she had hurt her old friend's feelings, Abby said, "I shouldn't have said that. I'm sure she is very nice. Sounds like you've been seeing quite a bit of her. And if she can keep up with you, she must be one sharp lady."

"So now that I've satisfied your curiosity, what do you think of my plan?"

"Sounds good to me. But how are you going to get Jake to stay put? I caught him hobbling around in the woods this afternoon when I went to take his glasses back."

"I could have done that. You needn't have wasted your afternoon."

"Oh, it was no trouble." Feeling the heat rise in her face, she hastily continued, "Besides, I wanted to check on his cast. Sometimes there is swelling, and I didn't want him to get into any trouble there alone."

"Uh-huh. You sure you're not interested in something besides his ankle? Like I said, he's a good-looking fella and—" Seeing Abby bristle, he quickly changed his tack. "So how was our patient anyway?"

"Im-patient. What is it with you men? I left him with a stack of books and strict orders to stay put. But if he's as hardheaded as you, he probably didn't."

"So why don't you come down for dinner and help me convince him to stay put? I can throw a couple of steaks on the grill, and you can tell Jake some gruesome tale about what happens to people with concussions and broken ankles if they don't behave."

Despite the teasing that she knew her acceptance would generate, Abby agreed. Aside from the fact that she found herself attracted to Jake, she didn't really want to spend the evening alone. The dream had unsettled her. If she packed up and went back to town tonight, George would know something was wrong. Perhaps if she stayed awake until exhaustion overtook her, the dreams would remain at bay.

"What can I bring?"

"Got enough fixin's for another batch of spoon bread? I've got a good bottle of wine unless you insist on that red beer you always drink."

"Wine sounds good. And yes, I can make more spoon bread. I can't believe you want more already."

"Can't get enough of that stuff, and mine never turns out right. I'll call Jake and have him turn on the oven when we get ready to leave."

Convincing Jake to stay didn't prove too difficult. When Abby and George found him dozing on the couch, he grudgingly admitted that his morning's ramblings had not been such a good idea after all. By midafternoon, he'd given up and taken one of the pain pills prescribed by the doctor; and from all appearances, he'd spent the remainder of the day where Abby had left him. While Abby made the spoon bread, Jake hobbled out to the porch to keep George company while he waited for the coals to heat. When she found them there a short while later, they were both in high spirits.

"George was just telling me about the bear-sized raccoon that visited the campground last spring."

"That was quite a night, all right. Did he tell you that he ended up with a girlfriend out of the whole deal?"

"Aren't those Scouts a little young for you, George?" Jake teased.

"All right, you two! Enough! Can't a man enjoy a little feminine companionship without a lot of grief from the likes of you? I've got half a notion not to feed either one of you."

"Oh, please, sir," said Abby in mock dismay. "Cross my heart, we'll behave."

"Just so you know who's boss. Now bring me those steaks, will you, gal?"

After the dishes were washed and stacked, they all went back out onto the porch to enjoy the cool evening air. George and Abby kept Jake laughing with tales of the various greenhorn campers they had encountered over the years, and he in turn told them about some of his more entertaining students. The talk and laughter eventually dwindled, and the three sat in contented silence until Abby caught herself nodding. When she looked over, she saw that Jake too was dozing, and George was snoring softly.

"Hate to break up a party," she said, "but I'm going to head back for camp."

"Huh? What?" George said with a start.

"Time for bed, old friend. We're all half-asleep, and I still have to drive back to camp. What time do you want to head for town in the morning?"

"Whenever you get around," Jake said. "I'm in no real hurry, so whatever is convenient. Sorry to put you out."

"No problem, son," said George.

"I have to get back and do some trial prep, and George here has a hot date." Abby kissed the old man's cheek before he could reply. "See you in the morning."

Chapter 10

IF ABBY DREAMED THAT NIGHT, they were fleeting dreams that left no lasting memory. She awoke to a crisp, clear dawn that promised a beautiful day. Her feelings of uneasiness vanished with the rain, and she decided to take one last ride before breaking camp. She arrived at the entrance to the loop road just as the ranger was opening the gate. There was no one else about, and she was pleased to see that she would have the road to herself. After stretching and a slow half-mile or so to warm up, she pedaled hard, enjoying the chill of the early morning air.

Slowing up on a particularly steep hill, she was treated to the sight of a mother skunk and her half-grown brood crossing the road on the way to the stream. The small platoon dressed in black-and-white paid her no mind as they followed dutifully along behind their mother. In the fields, countless deer browsed on the dew-laden grass. Squirrels chattered as they scurried around in the woods beside the road in search of food to fill their treetop coffers. The entire basin teemed with life today with all the creatures busily going about their preparations for the coming winter. This was the sort of day Abby relished—what she sought when she came here. The sound of the wind rushing past her ears and the burn in her thighs as she pedaled hard up another steep hill made her forget the strange sights of the previous days. She saw no trace of another human, real or imagined, and returned to camp both relaxed and exhilarated and almost sorry that she'd committed to leaving early. This would have been a perfect day for hiking. But then she remembered the case files waiting on her desk at home and set about the task of packing. Gear stowed and hair still damp from her shower, she headed out of the cove.

As she left the park and entered Townsend, she passed a group of teens with inner tubes on their shoulders. One last trip on the river, she thought with an involuntary shiver. The Little Pigeon River was cold even in the heat of summer. But as teenagers, Abby and Steven often joined the scores of other young people who floated the two-mile stretch between the park boundary and Townsend. Tube rental had become a cottage industry in the small town. In the summertime, trucks shuttled the tubers up to the jumping off point and then hastened back to town for another load of teens and tubes. This time of year, only the heartiest enthusiasts braved the chilly waters, and Abby noticed that several of the group she passed wore knee-length wet suits in deference to the season.

When she arrived at George's, she found the two men sitting on the porch, coffee mugs in hand. "Well, it's about time," said George as she got out of the car. "We were beginning to think we'd been stood up."

"Just had to get in one more ride before I left. Can you believe kids are still tubin' down at the Y?" she said, referring to the fork in the Little Pigeon River.

"Too cold for these old bones, but when I was a youngster, we couldn't wait to be the first ones down in the spring. That was *really* cold."

"I'll bet," said Jake. "Guess we're ready to go."

"Why don't you ride with Abby, and I'll follow in your car," said George.

"I guess that'll work if it's okay with Abby," he replied.

"Fine by me," she said. "Let me rearrange things. Wasn't counting on having a passenger."

"Don't go to any trouble. I can ride with George."

"Oh, it's no trouble," said George. "I'll help Abby throw some stuff into the back seat."

As George helped her rearrange the contents of her car, Abby said, "All right, old man, quit pushing. I'll admit Jake's a nice guy, but enough of your matchmaking already. If he's interested, he'll call."

"Sorry, gal." George's tone said he wasn't. "But I've known you both for a long time. Not sure which of you is the slowest out of the gate. You just need a nudge."

"More like a shove into oncoming traffic. Jake, your chariot awaits. By the way, where do you live?"

"Just head toward the university. I live just off Cumberland Avenue."

"I thought that was all pretty much taken up by students."

"Pretty much. But I found an old couple who was tired of renting to students. I have the whole top floor of an old house. The steps are going to be a bit inconvenient, but I'll manage. Give my landlady an excuse to mother me a bit more."

"Sounds like George. Since my folks moved back to Indiana, he's been my self-appointed guardian angel. Good thing he lives thirty miles away."

They passed the remainder of the trip in small talk. Absorbed in their conversation, Abby paid little heed to the directions he provided. When told her to stop, she looked at the house and gaped. "I can't believe it! You don't live here, do you?"

"Sure, I told you I have the whole top floor. It's really not bad."

"I know. I lived here when I was an undergrad."

"You're kidding me."

"Nope. Are the Santanas still alive? I thought they were ancient when I was in school."

"Alive and kicking. You're not by any chance that 'nice young girl who went on to medical school' that Mrs. S talks about, are you?"

"Guilty as charged." Abby laughed. "She always thought I should just marry a doctor. 'Medical school is not for nice girls like you,' she always said. At least my roommate didn't disappoint her."

"She hasn't changed much. Always asking when I'm going to find some young lady and settle down."

About that time, a tiny white-haired woman came out onto the front porch. Seeing Jake's crutches, she bustled down the walk to where the trio stood. "And what has happened to you, Professor?" she asked.

"I took a spill out in the woods," Jake replied. "Nothing serious, just a broken ankle."

"Come in, come in. Does it hurt? How did it happen? Tell your friends to come along too," she said as she took his arm and pulled him toward the porch.

"You haven't changed a bit, Mrs. S," said Abby.

The old woman stopped in her tracks and came back to gaze up into Abby's face. "Is that you, Abigail? Why, so it is! Joseph, come see who's here," she called to her husband.

Abby and George helped Jake to the house while Mrs. Santana hurried on ahead to find her husband and put the teakettle on. As they drank tea and ate the cake that their hostess brought out, Jake told the Santanas about his fall. "I guess I'd still be there sharing that old cabin with a snake if Abby hadn't found me," he finished.

"A good thing," Mrs. Santana said. "She's a doctor, you know. I always told her, 'Go to medical school and show those boys how it's done.' And now she's out in the woods rescuing lost professors."

"So how are the kids, Mrs. S?" Abby said, steering the conversation away from her career. "Where is little Joe these days?"

With little prompting, Mrs. Santana launched into an update of her various children and their jobs and families. When she rose to fill the teapot again, Abby also stood. "Don't bother. George and I have to be going. I have work to do, and he has a lady friend to meet."

"Back to the hospital then?" the older woman asked. "You doctors work too much. But let me wrap a piece of cake for you. Hospital food is just awful."

Mrs. Santana refused to let them leave until Abby promised to come back for a real visit. As they pulled away from the curb, George asked, "Why didn't you tell her you weren't a doctor?"

"Too complicated, George. In spite of what she says about showing up the guys, she wasn't keen on the idea of me being a doctor, and I'm sure wouldn't approve of my current profession. Especially if I told her I was dealing with criminal cases all day long," she said.

"Whatever you say, gal. You know how I feel about it." And uncharacteristically, he let the subject drop as he directed her to the Scout leader's home. There, they parted company with a hug and mutual promises to keep in touch. Abby then made her way home to immerse herself in work.

Chapter 11

WHEN THE PHONE RANG A few hours later, she decided to let the machine answer; but when she heard her mother's voice threatening to call the police, she picked up. "I'm here, Mom. No need to call the cavalry."

"Where have you been? We haven't heard from you in weeks, and I've been calling for days," said her mother.

"Is something wrong? Why didn't you leave a message?"

"You know how I hate those machines. I never can think of what to say when I hear the beep."

"How about, 'Hi, Abby, this is your mom. Call me.' It's really not that hard. And I wish you and Dad would break down and get one. Do you know how frustrating it is when I need to leave *you* a message?"

"So are you okay?" said her mother, ignoring the chiding.

"I'm fine. I've just been busy getting ready for a trial next week. And I took a couple of days off and went up to the cove. George says hi, by the way."

"I can't believe that old coot is still there." Her mother laughed.

"That 'old coot' is only a few years older than you and Dad. And he's just as spry as ever. In fact, he's got a new girlfriend."

"Some aging earth mother, no doubt. Or has he gone into his second childhood and taken up with some young chickie?"

"Sort of in between. She's about sixty, I'd guess, and a Scout leader. Remember me telling you about the raccoon in camp last year? Well, she was the leader of that troop. Apparently, they've been seeing quite a lot of each other."

"Well, good for old George. What sort of trial do you have coming up?"

"You don't want to know about it, Mom." Although her mother had resigned herself to the fact that Abby was an attorney, the thought of her daughter sitting across the room from murderers on a routine basis still bothered her. She didn't mind hearing about other sorts of cases, but her curiosity stopped with the word *homicide*. Over the years, the two women had developed a code—when Abby said her mother didn't want to hear about a case, her mother knew it was a murder trial and asked no further questions.

"So what have you and Dad been up to lately? Still playing lots of golf?"

"Not lately. We have a new hobby. Your aunt June brought over a box of their mother's old things. We found some fascinating old letters and pictures. She and your dad got to talking about the family, and it made me think that somebody ought to write things down so when you have children, you'll be able to tell them where they came from."

Abby ignored her mother's not-so-subtle hint and asked, "So what is your new hobby? Are you writing a book?"

"Not exactly. We're doing a family genealogy. We even bought a computer. Have you ever used the internet? It's really great."

"Uh, yes, I've heard of it. You mean Dad actually has decided to come into the twentieth century?" Abby asked in disbelief. For some strange reason, her father loathed many of the conveniences of the modern world—like answering machines and computers.

"You haven't felt the earth turn upside down, have you? But he's quite good at ferreting out information from the stacks at the library. We've traced the Mahoneys back to Ireland. Dad's a bit frustrated right now. He's traced his mother's line back to her great-grandfather but can't find anything about him before his marriage. It's as if he sprang full grown from the earth. Very strange."

"Have you found that we're related to royalty or anything juicy like that?"

"No, but one of your great-great-great-great-grandfathers on my side of the family fought in the Revolutionary War. He was captured by the Indians and carried off to Canada. Everyone gave him up for dead, but eventually he was set free and found his way back home about three years later. I even have his account of the capture."

"Wow, you guys really have been working. It's funny that you've started this project. I met a man up in the mountains this week, and he's doing genealogy too."

"Oh?" Stretched into three syllables, her simple *oh* fairly dripped with questions: Who is he? What does he do? And most importantly, is he married?

How does she do that? Abby wondered. "Don't get that tone in your voice, Mom. He's a friend of George's. It's just a coincidence, that's all. I've never met anyone doing genealogy, and in the space of a few days, I find out my own parents are doing it too."

The conversation then turned to news of their extended family, and when her mother rang off a few minutes later, Abby when back to work.

1862

Jacob woke with a start, the sound of a woman's scream still echoing in his ears. "Abigail," he shouted, throwing off the blanket.

"Simmer down, Cutter," said George Spencer from the other side of the dying campfire. "Just a bobcat on the prowl."

As the sound came again, Jacob knew his friend was right. "Damn, I hate those critters. Sound just like a woman screaming. Raises my hackles. Think I'd be used to it after all these months."

"Know what you mean. Seein's you're up, throw some wood on the fire. Don't want that old fellow wanderin' in here looking for a warm place to bed down."

"What if he's a she?" teased Jacob.

"Worse. Don't have a pretty wife waitin' for me at home, but I'm not that hard up even on a cold night."

Jacob laughed and tended to the fire. When he had a good blaze going, he settled back down on his blanket. The bobcat ceased its yowling, but he still couldn't go back to sleep. Every time he drifted off, he thought he heard Abigail calling to him. He tossed restlessly for a couple of hours and finally rose just before dawn. "Goin' down to check on Abigail, boys," he told George and the Tallent brothers, Jeb and Jeremy, who were camped nearby. "Somethin's wrong."

Jacob's grandmother had been a Cherokee medicine woman, and everyone agreed he'd inherited some of her special instincts. When they were young, George and the others teased him when he said he knew what was going to happen. But over the years, his hunches had proved correct more often than not. Wordlessly, the other three men also arose and started to break camp. If he was right this time, Jacob or someone else might need their help. A short while later, they were on the trail back down the mountain.

The four men arrived at the cabin just as the sun rose over the nearby peak. "Abigail, I'm home," Jacob called as they entered the clearing. Then he noticed there was no smoke coming from the chimney. "That's funny. She's usually up by now." When he opened the door, the overturned chairs, open cupboards, and unwashed dishes on the table told him he would not find his wife sleeping in the loft above. As he returned to the yard, he found the others just coming onto the porch.

"Cow and chickens are gone," said George.

"Someone's been in the corncrib too," said Jeb, the older of the Tallent brothers.

"Springhouse door is open, but it doesn't look like anythin's been taken," said Jeremy. "Heard your cow roaming around up behind. Reckon she needs to be milked. See if I can catch her."

None of the men spoke for a moment, but a single thought formed in each mind: bushwackers. "Abigail probably ran to your ma's when she saw them coming," said George. "They've never hurt any women. I'm sure she's all right," he finished weakly.

"Maybe, maybe not. George, I'm going to head to my pa's place," said Jacob. "Jeb, Jeremy, you'd best see to your own families."

"Right," said Jeb. "We'll check in at your pa's after. George is prob'ly right. Abigail's a sharp gal. Wouldn't do anythin' foolish." With that, the two brothers rode off.

"I'll come with you, Jacob. Nothing at my place for 'em to steal," said George.

Jacob smiled wryly at his friends' words. A confirmed bachelor, George had a small cabin halfway up Thunderhead Mountain. He lived off the land and worked at the sawmill from time to time for pocket money. Bushwackers were generally looking for food and guns. George's cabin held little food, and his gun was always on his saddle.

The two men rode in silence. Despite his friends' words to the contrary, Jacob knew in his heart that Abigail would not be at his father's house.

Chapter 12

THE TRIAL MADE NEXT FEW weeks hectic ones for Abby. The defendant was charged with the murder of two teenagers who had disappeared four years previously. As she prepared her closing arguments for the jury, her mind went back to the events leading up to this day.

The last time the Johnsons saw their daughter April, she was posed with her date before leaving for the prom. The photographs showed a fresh-faced blonde in a strapless sequined gown. Despite her grown-up attire, she appeared younger than her seventeen years. Tom Madison, the middle-aged detective sent to investigate, said she looked like a little girl playing dress-up in her mother's clothes. Beside her stood a young man who looked decidedly uncomfortable in the rented tuxedo he wore. Although he was clean and well groomed, something about him said that his normal attire ran to coveralls and that a close inspection of his nails would show a faint trace of grease.

At first, Madison and his partner, Rick Lewis, suspected the girl's date. Seated in the living room of their well-appointed home, the girl's parents told the detectives that they really didn't approve of the young man. "John's a nice-enough young man, but we really tried to discourage the relationship," said the mother in a tone that said he was simply not in their social class.

"Our daughter has always been strong-minded, and we were afraid if we demanded that she stop seeing him, it would only make matters worse," the father added.

"Besides, she's leaving for college in Boston in a few months, and we thought that the whole thing would end naturally," the mother continued.

When they went to the young man's home, Madison and Lewis learned that young man had also gone missing. The house stood in stark contrast to the home of the missing girl's. John Shelby's mother answered the detective's knock still in her bathrobe despite the mid-day hour. Amid the clutter of overflowing ashtrays and empty beer cans in the living room, she told the investigators that she had no idea where her son was. "Last time I saw him, he was all dressed up to take that girl to some dance." Coughing around the cigarette suspended from her lips, she said, "Spent his hard-earned money, he did, just to rent a tuxedo when he had a perfectly good suit hanging in the closet."

She took another deep drag on her cigarette, coughed again, and continued, "His boss down at the garage has been worrying me to death, calling to find out why he didn't show up for work. Told him the same thing."

She showed the officers to her son's room and then shuffled back to the kitchen. Immediately the officers heard the unmistakable *pop-whoosh* of a can of beer being opened.

Unlike the rest of the house, the boy's room was clean and tidy.

Madison let out a low whistle. "Are we in the same house?"

The bed was neatly made, and his clothes were hung in the closet with care. John's other belongings were stored neatly on shelves or in drawers. In one corner was a desk fashioned from a battered file cabinet and some concrete blocks with planks lain across the top. From the books there, it appeared that he was taking entry-level courses at a local junior college that offered night classes.

Lewis looked over the makeshift desk and then turned back to his partner. "Seems like this poor kid was trying to run away from home without leaving. 'Course, with Lady Astor out there for a mother, who can blame him?"

Madison nodded. "Mrs. Shelby, could you come in and see if anything is missing?"

The *flap-slap* of her slippers came down the short hallway. She stood in the doorway in a halo of smoke and glanced around. "Hard to tell. He doesn't even let me in here to clean."

Turning to the girl's classmates and friends, the detectives learned that April and John had gone to the prom as planned. Many stu-dents, including April's former boyfriend, remembered seeing them at the dance, but no one could say at what time they arrived or when they left. Other students told the pair that Bobby Davidson, the son of a prominent family, was devastated by the couple's breakup.

One boy, identified as one of Bobby's running mates, told them a reluctantly, "He told me April was just slumming and that she'd come back to him."

But April's best friend was more forthcoming. "Bobby was really mad. He said he'd *make* April come back to him. April just laughed, but it sorta creeped me out."

Bobby had appeared nervous but also a little defiant when the detectives first questioned him, but initially they chalked this up to the normal behavior of an overprivileged teen. However, bits and pieces of information gleaned from classmates and teachers gave the detectives enough suspicion to bring Bobby back in for questioning. Although fidgety and unable to maintain eye contact with the detectives with his parents' attorney by his side, he remained steadfast in his denial that he knew anything about the couple's disappearance.

"I saw them when they came in, but I had a date. She's a lot hotter than April, if you know what I mean." His attempt to seem worldly fell just short of the mark.

"Gee, Bobby, that's not what we hear," drawled Madison.

The boy's face may have paled a shade, but he didn't flinch. Lewis pressed harder.

"Yeah, we heard that you'd been making threats against April and John Shelby. By the way, have you seen John lately?"

Bobby didn't take the bait. "John's okay, but we really don't run in the same circles. Wouldn't really fit in at the country club and all that."

Even when they pressed, Madison and Lewis were unable to shake the young man's story. He insisted that he'd seen April and John arrive but lost them in the crowd and didn't see them for the rest of the evening. He and his date had been some of the last to leave the dance, and he hadn't seen the other couple. His date for the prom substantiated his alibi, and despite their suspicions, the detectives eliminated him as a suspect. Beyond that, and in spite of months of painstaking work, the detectives had been unable to turn up any leads or any real evidence of foul play. Finally, they told the girl's parents that it was most likely that the couple had simply run away. April's mother insisted that even if her daughter had gone off willingly with John, she would have to let them know she was safe. But with nothing more than a mother's instincts to go on, the detectives had to turn to other matters. The case ended up in the unsolved file.

Three years later, surveyors for a paper mill found a human skull as they walked through a stand of trees they were preparing to harvest. They immediately summoned the police, who discovered the remains of not one but two bodies buried in a shallow grave. Time, the elements, and animals had left little more than bones and a few strands of long wheat-colored hair. But a small scrap of sequined material clinging to one of the bones spoke volumes.

The detectives felt certain that these were the remains of April Johnson and John Shelby, but they would have to wait for the forensics report to confirm their suspicions. With no fingerprints or distinguishing features to go on, the forensics team would have to rely on dental records. And with only skeletal remains, determining the cause of death might be impossible. Although the bones had been scattered over several square yards of the forest floor, the skulls were intact, and there were no obvious sign of antemortem trauma. A search of the area turned up nothing more than a man's high school ring and one tiny gold and diamond earring. Until they could identify the "bodies" and how they had died, finding out who was responsible for their deaths would be impossible.

While the pathologists toiled away in the morgue, the detectives got a break. As it turned out, the land upon which the bodies were discovered belonged to Dr. Robert Davidson, the father of April's old boyfriend. Remembering their earlier suspicions, the detectives went to talk to Bobby Davidson. Now a junior at Vanderbilt, a flicker of surprise and something else crossed the young man's face when he opened the door of his off-campus apartment. He ushered them in and waited patiently for their questions.

"Bobby, we've found a couple of bodies on your daddy's land," said Madison.

The young man seemed almost disinterested in the whole affair. "Daddy's always had trespassers on that piece of land," he told them.

"Maybe a couple of those old bums just killed each other. Or maybe a bear got them. They do kill people, you know."

When the investigators told him they had also discovered a scrap of pink sequined material, the young man paled but said nothing. He agreed to allow the detectives to search his Jeep Cherokee. In spite of the lapse of time, they hoped to discover something linking the boy to the crime. Although they found several strands of blonde hair in the front and back seats of the vehicle, even if they belonged to April, her frequent presence in the car made them useless as evidence. The detectives found nothing else to link the car or Bobby to the crime.

Back at the lab, the news was more positive. "Dental records confirm that the female victim is April Johnson," reported the medical examiner. "But I don't have any records for the male vic. Amazingly, he had a full set of teeth and not one cavity."

"Great," said Lewis. "You mean there's no way to identify him?"

"I didn't say that. Those great teeth should yield enough DNA for testing if you can get me a something for comparison—a hair-brush or toothbrush would be good. It'll take a while, though."

"We'll get right on it. Can you tell us anything else, Doc?" asked Madison.

"The bones look to be of a male in his late teens or early twenties. Still working on cause of death."

The detectives returned to Mrs. Shelby's house. She opened the door in the same robe and cloud of smoke that greeted them three years previously.

"Yeah, that looks like Johnny's ring," she said, squinting at the ring in the small plastic evidence bag. "I thought you said they just run off. Have you found them?"

"Unfortunately, Mrs. Shelby, we've found some remains that we think are your son and Ms. Johnson," said Madison.

"Remains? You mean bodies?"

"Not exactly. I'm sorry to have to tell you this, but all we've found are this ring and, uh, er...," Lewis's voice trailed off.

"Oh." Tears filled her eyes and spilled down on to her dingy robe as she flopped heavily down onto the sofa in a belated show of maternal concern.

She managed only a disinterested wave of her hand when they asked if they could search John's room again. Fortunately, it appeared that after the detective's first visit, Mrs. Shelby had closed the door to her son's room and never reentered it. Whether because she was simply awaiting his return or because she failed to miss him in her alcoholic haze, the investigators were grateful for her continued lapse in housekeeping. There they found a comb with several strands of hair still clinging to its teeth. With the hair samples, the laboratory might be able to confirm the identity of the second body.

By the time they returned to the lab, the ME had more news. "Looks like your couple were stabbed to death." Holding up a long thin bone, he described several cut marks on both the arm bones and ribs. "Looks like he put up a fight. Somewhere in the struggle, he also sustained a skull fracture, just hairline though. Doubt that it killed him."

He went on to say that April's bones had similar marks indicating that she too had struggled with their attacker. The physician surmised that during the struggle, the man had received a blow to the head sufficient to render him unconscious, leaving the young woman to face their attacker alone. He could only speculate as to the weapon involved but suggested a knife with a sturdy blade such as those carried by hunters.

Madison and Lewis kept busy while waiting for DNA results. They reinterviewed the April's parents and as many of her classmates as they could find. Bobby Davidson remained their chief suspect, but they had little to support their theory other than instinct. Memories had grown fuzzy, and many of those attending the prom, including the suspect's date, were now at colleges out of state. They left messages and business cards with the parents but learned little from the students who had taken the time to return their calls. It seemed their investigation was about to stall again when once more their luck changed.

Melanie Reasoner, Bobby's prom date, called them when she came home between semesters. Not entirely to their surprise, the story she now told the detectives differed from her earlier statement. Although Bobby wanted to continue their romance after she went away to school, loneliness and the attentions of other young men led Melanie to break off the relationship. Apparently, Bobby still didn't handle rejection well, and Melanie described his pleas for her to reconsider. "He sent flowers and letters and called every day. At first I thought it was sorta sweet." But lately, she said, the tone of the calls and letters had been more threatening than pleading. "He hasn't exactly threatened me or anything," she told them. "But some things he's said make me wonder if he had anything to do with April's disappearance."

When the detectives asked her why, Melanie told them she hadn't been entirely truthful in her earlier statement. "Bobby was really mad when he saw them come into the dance," she said. "Called John a grease monkey and said that even dressed up, he still didn't fit in. He wouldn't dance and just kept slipping drinks from his flask. I made him take me home before he got too drunk to drive."

"What time was that?" asked Lewis

She frowned. "Must have been around nine-thirty. I remember I couldn't believe I was home from my prom before ten."

"And when was the dance over?" the other detective asked.

"It was supposed to end at midnight, but some of my friends said the band agreed to play one extra set, so I guess it was closer to one."

When asked why she hadn't mentioned this before, she continued, "About three o'clock, Bobby called to say he was sorry, and could he come over? He was all crying and saying how sorry he was. He was with me 'til 6:00 a.m."

The letters she gave the officers were long and rambling. His words alternated between telling her how much he loved her and warning her that it wasn't a good idea to cross him. Although there were no direct references to the victims, her story reinforced the detectives' suspicions. As they were leaving, Lewis asked, "Does Bobby ever go hunting?"

"Lordy, yes," the girl replied. "Deer, turkey, you name it, Bobby hunts it. He's got all sorts of guns and knives."

Abby had been peripherally aware of the case for some time. She read the initial reports of the couple's disappearance but dismissed it from her mind when the police were unable to prove the existence of a crime. But some months earlier, the case landed on her desk.

She knew Madison and Lewis well and trusted their instincts. But the case was mainly circumstantial. After six months, they still had nothing concrete to link the young man to the two deaths. Abby spent hours with them poring over the evidence they had compiled and discussing other possible avenues of investigation. "I don't suppose you guys have found a weapon or anything like that, have you?" she asked.

"Searched his car. Clean. Didn't have enough for a warrant for anything more when we first questioned him. Thought about asking for the weapon but somehow didn't think that'd work," said Madison with a grin.

"The docs say it was some sort of sturdy knife. His prom date said he owns all sorts of guns and knives. Didn't see anything in his apartment. My guess is that the knife is at the bottom of the Tennessee River by this time," said Lewis.

"What did he say when you asked him about the time he left the dance?" Abby asked.

"Real smooth about that," said Madison. "Said his girlfriend was mistaken. He was worried about his finals and just couldn't get into a party mood. Nothing to do with the other couple."

"So he says he went home and studied on prom night? Oh yeah, I believe that," said Abby with a wry grin. "Do we have any idea when the victims left the dance to at least establish some sort of window of opportunity?"

"No one seems to have noticed. Her friends didn't really know her date. Seems like they kept pretty much to themselves, dancing or sitting in a corner holding hands. A regular Romeo and Juliet," said Lewis. "Could have left at any time, and no one would have noticed."

"If we take the ex-girlfriend's word for it, the suspect left the dance between nine-thirty and ten. She didn't see him again until a little after three. Say ten and three, that leaves five hours unaccounted for."

"What about his parents? Do they back up the study story?" Abby asked.

Madison shook his head. "Out of town."

Abby sat back in her chair. "Could an eighteen-year-old stab two people and dispose of their bodies in five hours?"

"It's an hour and a half from town to where we found the bodies, so it's a stretch. But something about that boy just doesn't sit right with me," Madison replied.

"Unless he didn't dispose of the bodies right away," Lewis said. "The father had some medical meeting in Florida, and the missus went along to work on her tan. They didn't come home until Tuesday. That gives our boy a lot of time to clean up any messes."

"Did Dr. and Mrs. Davidson drive or fly to Florida?" Abby asked.

"Flew, I suppose," said Madison. "The wife didn't strike me as the type who would tolerate a drive to Miami."

"What sort of car do the parents drive?"

Madison slapped his forehead in disbelief. "Why didn't I think of that? My son, Tommy, always wanted to drive my car when he had a special date. Bet a girl would have a hard time climbing in and out of young Bobby's Jeep in a party dress."

"Who's on for warrants this week? Let me see if I can convince a judge to let us search the parent's car. Like you said, it's a stretch, but it's all we have. If we find anything there, we can probably get a warrant to search the house. I just hope these people don't get a new car every other year."

In the trunk of the Davidsons' car, under the spare tire, the forensics team found a tiny gold and diamond earring and more.

Chapter 13

ABBY WAS TIRED. THE JURY had been out for two and a half days. Despite Bobby Davidson's continued pleas of innocence, she was still confident of gaining a conviction; the weight of the circumstantial evidence was just too great. Even though the defense attorney had ably talked around much of the evidence found in the Davidsons' car and, later, their house, there was one thing he couldn't explain. In addition to the earring matching the one found with the body, the detectives also discovered a small St. Christopher's medal in the trunk of the Lincoln. John Shelby's mother had given it to her son on his first communion.

No, she thought, it wasn't the stress of the trial that was making her tired. It was the dream. When she learned of Steven's death, Abby's mother called her in the middle of the night to break the news. For months afterward, Abby relived that call in her dreams. The ringing of the telephone would wake her from a sound sleep, and she would hear her mother's sobs. And that was on the good nights. Many nights, she didn't sleep at all. If, for some reason, the phone actually rang in the middle of the night, Abby was nearly hysterical by the time she picked up the receiver. Gradually, as she worked through her grief, the dreams faded, and finally stopped. But at two that morning, the ringing phone had triggered the dream again. As she fumbled for the receiver in the dark, Abby felt the hot tears streaming down her face, and her sobs were audible when she answered. The startled caller mumbled, "Sorry, wrong number," and hung up.

After that, sleep was out of the question. At 4:00 a.m., she gave up and went out for a run. By six, she was in her office going over pending cases. It was now ten, and Abby's eyes burned. She leaned back in her chair and closed her eyes. Hearing a knock, she looked up to see Sandra, her secretary, peeking around the door. "Sorry, Abby, I just got a call from the courthouse."

"Is the jury back in?" Abby asked.

"You wish. Juror number eight's wife just went into premature labor, and the judge adjourned for the day," her secretary replied.

"Darn," said Abby. "I really wanted to get this thing over with today. Well, I'm doing no one any good here today. I'm going to take the afternoon off. Page me if you need me." As she left the parking lot, she glanced into the back seat to make sure that her hiking boots and jeans were there and pointed the car toward the mountains.

"George, where are you?" she called as she entered the store.

"Hey, gal. I'd about given you up for the season?" replied George as he emerged from the storeroom.

"I've been in trial since right after I last saw you. I only got away today on a fluke."

"So how you been, gal? Have you seen our patient lately?"

"Fine, aside from being too busy. No, I haven't seen Jake, have you?"

"Naw. Called a few weeks ago, said he was going to get the cast off soon, so I suspect he's back on two feet by now. Surprised you haven't heard from him."

"Me, why? I barely know the man."

"I sorta thought you two had hit it off. Seemed pretty friendly having tea with his landlady."

"He's a nice man, but things are too hectic in my life right now."

"You always say that, gal. 'Fraid you'll end up old and gray and alone like me."

"What about Emily? Has that cooled off?"

"No, it hasn't. And don't go changing the subject."

"Don't worry about me, old man. I'll settle down one of these days. Right now I need a bottle of water and some dried fruit if you have it."

Abby paid for her purchase and headed out. George went with her and held the door open. "Why don't you give Jake a call when you get back?" he asked.

"If he's interested, he'll call me," she said. Kissing her old friend lightly on the cheek, she continued, "Call me next time you're in coming to town. I'd like to get to know the other woman in your life."

As she started to move away, George took her by the arms and peered closely at her face. "Are you sure you're okay, Abby?"

"Sure, George, why do you ask?"

"You just don't seem to be yourself. Sorta like—," he stopped uncertainly.

"Like what?" she asked.

"Well, you've got the same look you had after Steven's plane went down. I haven't seen that look in your eyes in years, gal."

Abby blushed deeply. "Didn't sleep well last night, that's all. I'm fine. Really."

"Well, if you say so. Just remember I'm here if you need me."

"I know, George. Thanks. And I mean it about calling—I really want to meet Emily."

"I'll call you. Or better still, I may give Jake a call. Maybe we can make it a double date."

"You just never give up, do you, old man?" Abby laughed. "I'll see you later."

The newspapers had said that the fall colors were spectacular this year, but until now, Abby had had little time to think about it. As she started around the loop, she smiled with pleasure at the sight. Gazing out across to the far peaks, she saw a canvas splashed with color. Pausing to look at the trees in the near ground, Abby noticed that the individual trees stood like brightly painted ladies in their finest attire. To her left, a diminutive dogwood stood in a gown the color of cabernet, and nearby was an oak dressed in scarlet. Off to the left, a cluster of sweet gums stood like sisters clad in colors ranging from yellow to purple. But standing off to itself, at once a wallflower and the belle of the ball, was a red maple garbed in fiery red—a red so brilliant it almost hurt to look at it. In spite of the bumper-to-bumper traffic, Abby felt the tightness in her shoulder begin to ease. She was home again.

Traffic moved slowly, but she finally reached the Abrams Falls trailhead. There wasn't time to hike into the falls and back, but it was a good trail for walking even a short distance. Abby struck off up the trail with no goal other than to stretch her legs and enjoy the crisp, clean air. A mile or so in, the trail dipped down to within a few feet of the creek. There she found a tree that had conveniently fallen out into the water, creating a perfect place to sit with her toes dangling just above the water. Seated there in the sun, feasting on dried apples and raisins, Abby felt the last remnants of tension and weariness leave her body.

For the first time in weeks, she found herself thinking about something other than the trial. Her thoughts drifted idly for a while and then turned to Jake. She'd barely thought of him since she watched him hobble to the Santanas' front porch to wave goodbye. Now with George's words still ringing in her ears, she found herself wondering about the man she'd rescued. What did they have in common, she wondered, aside from a love of this place? No doubt he was intelligent, and from their short time together, he seemed to have a good sense of humor. But aside from that, she knew little. She couldn't remember the last time she'd been out on a real date and wasn't sure she really wanted to. Dating could be such a pain, she thought. After you went through all the awkwardness of getting to know someone, they turned out to be someone you really didn't want to know all that well. Like Tim. Their relationship had shown such promise until their ill-fated trip to the mountains. Sometimes it just didn't seem worth all the effort. *But then again*, she mused, *I already know that Jake likes the outdoors.*

Abby was startled out of her reverie by the faint sound of a voice. She hadn't heard anyone approaching on the trail above, and when she turned to see the speaker, there was no one there. Dusting off her pants, she headed back for the trail, intending to walk a bit farther before returning to her car. As she stepped onto the trail, she heard the voice again. "Abigail, where are you?"

It was the same voice she's heard the day she found Jake injured at the cabin. Looking around, however, she couldn't see the caller. *Not again*, she thought. *Well, I'm simply not going to play that game again.* Turning back down the trail, she saw the big man walking toward her. She stood there, uncertain whether to run or face the man. Before she could make up her mind, the phone on her desk rang.

Chapter 14

"WHA...HELLO," SAID ABBY GROGGILY. How long had she been asleep?

"Just got call from the courthouse," said her secretary.

"I know. Juror 8's wife just went into labor," Abby replied.

"What? No. The judge's clerk just called and said you'd better get over there," said Sandra. "What did you mean about juror 8?"

"Nothing. Call you when I find out what's up," Abby said as she picked up her briefcase and headed out the door.

She met Detectives Madison and Lewis as she was going up the steps to the courtroom.

"We heard the jury's reached a verdict in the Davidson case," said Lewis. "Is that so?"

"That's what I'm about to find out," said Abby. "All I know is that they told me to get over there."

"Surely they can't be considering letting him off?" Madison snorted. "We had the guy dead to rights."

"You know how it is with juries," said Abby. "We've made a good case, but it was all circumstantial. The boy still says he didn't do it."

"Yeah, that's what they all say," said Lewis.

The bailiff opened the door, and the jury filed back into the jury box. Abby peered at each face, seeking some hint as to their decision. Try as she might, she was unable to read the verdict in their eyes. The judge had not yet appeared, and as five minutes stretched into thirty, she heard rustling noises from various points in the courtroom. Behind her sat Mr. Johnson, with his arm tensed around his wife's shoulders. Her darkly circled eyes stared dully at the bench. Mrs. Shelby, who appeared each morning with more than a hint of alcohol on her breath, sat silently twisting a yellowed handkerchief.

Across the aisle, the Davidsons sat behind their son and carried on a whispered conversation with his attorney. Abby wondered if they were planning a celebration or an appeals strategy.

When the judge finally entered the chambers, and everyone rose at the bailiff's bidding. The entire courtroom turned as one and watched expectantly as the foreman rose to read the verdict.

"On the first count, murder in the second degree of April Johnson, we find the defendant, Robert Davidson, guilty. On the second count, murder in the second degree of John Shelby, we find the defendant guilty," he said.

Mrs. Davidson burst into loud and unladylike sobs. The Johnsons hugged each other and reached over to shake Abby's hand. Cora Shelby, who had watched the entire proceeding in stoic silence, stood and made her way to the aisle. She took a few steps toward the back of the courtroom then turned back to where Bobby Davidson's mother still stood sobbing and clinging to her son. "I don't know what you're carryin' on about. Your boy's only going to jail. Mine's in the ground." With that, she turned on her heel and marched out.

Madison and Lewis were waiting for her when Abby left the courthouse. "Congratulations, Counselor," said Lewis. "Can we buy you a beer?"

"Thanks. You gentlemen did a fine job on this case. I think I'll pass on the beer, though."

"What? No celebration?" asked Madison. "I've never known you not to toast a guilty verdict."

"Don't get me wrong, I'm pleased with the verdict," Abby replied. "But it's been a long few weeks, and I think I'll just head back to the office. Rain check?"

"Sure, any time," said Madison. "Again, good work."

Abby returned to her office not looking forward to the stack of paperwork awaiting her. Sandra handed her a stack of pink telephone message notes as she walked through the door. "Well?" she asked.

"Score one for the good guys," said Abby as she sorted through the messages.

"You sure don't sound very happy for a woman who just won a very difficult case," her secretary said.

"Oh, I'm happy about the verdict, but I just can't help but think of the three lives lost. Seems like a waste. By all reports, April and John were both good kids, and with his family connections, Bobby Davidson could have done anything he wanted. It's all such a shame."

"You okay, boss? I've never seen you this down after a win before," Sandra said, concern creasing her brow.

"Yeah, sure. Just tired. Didn't sleep well last night," Abby replied. "Think I'll answer these calls and call it a day."

At her desk, Abby started returning the calls. Two from public defenders who wanted to work out plea bargains, another from a judge's clerk to make a change in a trial setting, and one from her boss. As she hung up the phone after receiving congratulations from the district attorney, Sandra entered with another pink sheet in her hand.

"What now?" asked Abby. "I was ready to call it a day."

"I don't know," said Sandra. "Some guy named Jake Bartlett. Wouldn't tell me what he wanted, just asked that I have you call. Is there a new PD I don't know about?"

"No." Abby lips twitched with a smile she tried to conceal. "Actually, he's a college professor."

"Oh?" Sandra's raised eyebrows asked a dozen questions.

"A potential witness," Abby fibbed. Sandra, like George and her mother, was more interested in her social life than Abby would have preferred. Happily married with two grown children, her secretary thought it was high time that Abby settled down as well and took every opportunity to tell her just that.

"Oh," she replied in disappointment and closed the door.

"You're a difficult lady to track down," said Jake when he answered. "I've been meaning to call for weeks. Hate to admit it, but I couldn't remember your last name."

"Mrs. Santana could have told you," said Abby.

"Oh no. She worries way too much about my social life as it is. Wasn't about to give her that opportunity." He laughed. "Finally gave up and called George."

"Oh, goodie. So now *I* get the twenty-question routine from George."

"Already thought of that. Told him I had tracked down a professor to serve as an expert witness for you."

"And he actually bought it?"

"Must have. Didn't ask any more questions. Seemed disappointed, though."

"That's our George. So how are you? Still hobbling around on crutches?"

"Doing well," he said. "And I've graduated to a cane and a soft cast that I only have to wear when I'm up and about."

"Wonderful. How's your head? Any residual headaches?"

"Whoa, Doc, enough! Nothing worse than a woman who's a doctor *and* a lawyer."

"Sorry. Hazard of the trade."

"No problem. So how are *you*?"

"Fine, thanks. Just finished a big trial, so I'm trying to get my desk cleared off and see what's gone begging while I've been in court. The stacks are about a foot deep right now."

"Sounds like mine after finals. Always takes me most of the break to get things sorted out again. Too busy for dinner?"

"Never," Abby said with a chuckle. "I'm afraid I'm not one of those women who sometimes just forgets to eat. When?"

"It may be too late to ask, but are you free tonight? I know it's short notice, but I'm headed to North Carolina in the morning, and I'm not sure when I'll be back."

"What about your classes?"

"I don't have any formal classes this quarter, just overseeing a couple of thesis students. That's how I happened to be in the mountains the day I fell. After Christmas, I'll have a full schedule again so is my last chance for a while."

"Well, gee, I had planned an exciting evening with a TV dinner and a stack of briefs. I might just persuaded to forego the pleasure. What did you have in mind?"

"What about the Copper Cellar?"

"Gosh, I haven't been there in ages. Do they still have that wonderful crème brûlée?"

"I don't know, but we can sure find out if you're available."

"You've made me an offer I can't refuse. What time?"

They agreed on seven-thirty, and Abby gave Jake directions to her apartment. She hung up and went back to work with a smile on her face.

Standing in front of her mirror trying to "tame the mane," as she described doing her hair, she thought back on their conversation. *Perhaps I should have played at least a little hard to get*, she thought. But although she was a master at courtroom tactics and a pretty fair poker player, Abby had never been good at playing games with men. Either she liked them, or she didn't; and if the ones she did liked her back, that was great. If not, so be it. She didn't have the time or inclination to act coy or shy; it simply was not in her nature. "We'll just see what happens," she said to her reflection in the mirror. But deep down, she felt a twinge of something unfamiliar. Something she hadn't felt since she was sixteen and about to go out on her first real date.

Originally, the Copper Cellar was literally in a cellar. The upscale restaurant was one of the first of its kind along Cumberland Avenue, which bisects the University of Tennessee campus. Using a variety of copper pots and other items for decoration, the establishment gained in popularity with the students and others, specializing in steaks and grilled seafood. Eventually, a second Copper Cellar with its sister bistro, Cappuccino's, opened in the more-fashionable west end of town. As they pulled into the parking lot, Abby thought about an earlier visit to the Cellar.

It was her mother's fiftieth birthday, and her parents and three other couples were celebrating. As a surprise, Abby had driven home from medical school in Memphis and timed her arrival to coincide with dessert. Steven was overseas and unable to come home for the occasion. While still in junior high school, Abby had taken a black-and-white photograph of Steven kneeling in a mountain stream, cooling off after a long hike. The picture captured him with his head down and his hand barely grazing the surface of the water. It was a simple image, but it captured the essence of the boy-man. Knowing how much her mother missed her son, Abby had the photograph enlarged and framed. To her dismay, her mother burst into tears when she opened the package. Abby was startled by the strong emotion; her mother rarely cried. Regaining her composure, her mother reached into her purse and pulled out a tattered wallet-sized photograph taken from the same negative.

"Penny for your thoughts," said Jake.

"I was just thinking about the last time I came here for dinner. Seems like a million years ago," she replied and told him about the photograph.

"If it brings back bad memories, we can go somewhere else."

"Oh no. This is one of my favorite restaurants. And the memories aren't bad."

"You still miss him, don't you?" The words came as a statement, not a question.

"Only every day. Now feed me, sir. I'm starved."

"Yes, ma'am," he said with a deep bow. "Right this way."

Looking over the top of his menu a short while later, Jake said, "I thought you were starved. You haven't even opened the menu."

Abby laughed. "Don't need to. I always get the same thing here, and it's always fabulous."

"So what do you recommend?"

"The nine-ounce filet, rare, baked sweet potato, and salad with the house dressing."

"Rare?"

"Yep. Rare. I want to be able to rescue it with a couple of Band-Aids. My dad is a great outdoor chef, and he never cooks a piece of meat longer than five minutes on a side. He says any more, and it loses its flavor."

When the waiter arrived, Jake gave him Abby's order and then said, "I'll have the same, but I like my steak cooked a little. Make mine medium rare. And bring us a bottle of Rosemount Shiraz."

Noting the look on Abby's face as the waiter retreated, Jake said, "Sorry, I didn't even ask. Is that wine okay? I can change the order," he said, raising his hand to call the waiter back.

Grabbing his hand, she replied, "No, it's perfect. It's just that most people I know have never heard of that wine. I'm not exactly a wine connoisseur—I either like it, or I don't—but that's the first bottle with a cork that I ever bought. I still love it."

"Me too. A couple of friends of mine dragged me to a wine-tasting last year, and it featured wines from Australia. Been stuck on this one ever since. Guess I should be more adventuresome, but hey, if it ain't broke…"

Abby and Jake spent the next hour in that sort of getting-to-know-you conversation that Abby usually detested. But this time, she felt no first-date self-consciousness, and they chatted more like old friends than two people who barely knew each other. Jake spoke of growing up in North Carolina. He was the second of five children. When his father died in 1969, he and his older brother, Lucas, had become the men of the family at nine and eleven.

"Nineteen sixty-nine. Vietnam?"

"No. Heart attack. He was a civilian firefighter at Fort Bragg. Mom always worried that he'd be killed in fighting a fire. We never thought about him getting sick. He was always so healthy. He left for work one morning, smiling and happy, and at noon they called from the base. He was already gone by the time Mom got to the hospital."

"How awful."

"Yeah, it was a rough time. But at least he didn't suffer. After that, we moved to Asheville to be closer to Mom's family. Must have been hard raising all of us on her own."

"She never remarried?"

"Not until a few years ago. At their high school reunion, she ran into a fellow she had dated before Dad. Dan's a good guy. It's good to see her happy. She never complained about being alone, but there's a light in her eyes these days that I haven't seen in a long time."

"She sounds like a special lady."

"She is. But enough about me. What about you? Have you always lived here?"

"Seems like it, but no. We moved here from Indiana when I was six. I can't imagine growing up in a big family. Steven was four years older, but we were always close. I was a tomboy tagalong sometimes.

Must have been a pain. Fortunately, Steven was away at college by the time I started dating. Dad was scary enough. If Steven had been there, I would never have had a date."

"I know what you mean. Luke and I were pretty hard on the girls when they had dates. It was pretty well known that none of the boys had better mess with the Bartlett girls. It's a wonder they managed to find husbands."

"I know what you mean. One summer evening. I came home from a date to discover Steven and three of his friends lined up in the rocking chairs on the front porch waiting for me. Needless to say, with those four as an audience, I didn't get so much as a good-night peck on the cheek."

"So how did you get to be an assistant district attorney? That's a far cry from being a doctor."

Abby told him about the illness that changed her plans and the saga that brought her to her current position. "It's really different, but the medical training comes in handy more frequently than you might imagine. Especially the time I spent working in the coroner's office. And I get to meet the most intriguing people," she finished with a wry smile.

"Oh, I'll just bet you do. Thugs and dopers. I bet that really makes your mom happy."

"Well, she's pretty cool about it most of the time. She worries about me, though, but I guess all moms are that way."

"Do you enjoy what you're doing?"

"For the most part, although I have to admit that lately…" She paused.

"'Lately what?"

"Oh, I don't know. It's just harder now than it was when I started. Seems like I see the same faces over and over again. And then there are the ones like the trial I finished today."

"You didn't prosecute the Davidson case, did you?"

"'Fraid so. What do you know about the case?"

"Well, only what I've read in the papers. By all accounts, he was a nice kid."

"Sure…if you don't mind the fact that he butchered two other kids."

"But from what I've read, he's still maintaining his innocence. And there were no witnesses. How can you be so sure he really did it?"

"Because it's my job to be sure!" Abby snapped.

Surprised by her tone, Jake said, "Sorry. I wasn't questioning your abilities. It's just that I can't imagine doing what you do. What's more, I can't imagine you doing it. You don't seem like the Perry Mason type to me."

"Perry Mason was a defense attorney," she said, embarrassed at her tone.

"Okay, the Jack McCoy type," Jake replied, referring to the assistant district attorney on the TV crime drama *Law & Order*.

Smiling, she said, "I didn't mean to snap. This trial has been a hard one. I have no doubt that he did it, but it's all just such a waste of young lives. Dealing with dope dealers and the like is easier somehow."

"I know I don't know you all that well, but it's easier imagining you fixing up kids in the emergency room than sending them to jail."

"You've been talking to George, haven't you?"

"No, I haven't." And then, grinning sheepishly, he continued, "Well, yes, I have, but I think he's right. It's easier to picture you as a female Marcus Welby than a hard-bitten prosecutor."

"You watch way too much television." Abby laughed. "Like I keep telling George, I'm happy enough with what I'm doing. Besides, it's too late to turn back now."

"It's never too late. Besides, you're already a doctor. You have a great bedside…uh, er, rock-side manner. I'll bet you'd be great in a family practice or something. How hard could it be to go back and pick up where you left off?"

"Plenty. Look, can we just drop this? Let's have some coffee, and you can tell me about this trip you're taking."

Waving his white napkin like a flag of truce, he said, "Okay, you win. This round, anyway. Do you want some crème brûlée with your coffee?"

Over coffee, Jake told her about the line of research he hoped to pursue while in Asheville. "I think I told you about the locket, didn't I?" Abby nodded, and he continued, "Well, Aunt Sarah lived in this wonderful old house outside of Asheville. When she died, she left it to my grandfather, who was her only living nephew by that time.

His grandfather was almost seventy by the time his aunt passed on, so he rented the place out. When he died, the house passed to Jake's mother, who was still dealing with her husband's death, and the house remained as a rental property.

Jake continued, "Last year, my sister Sarah talked Mom and Dan into letting her turn it into a bed and breakfast. While she was cleaning out the attic, she ran across several old chests full of letters and other family stuff. She's been saving it for me until I had time to go through it."

"Do you have any idea how far back this stuff dates?"

"Not really, but Aunt Sarah was born in 1867, so there is at least a chance that some of it belonged to her parents. I'm hoping it will shed some light on the locket and maybe lead me back to Cades Cove."

"Sounds interesting," Abby said. "You know it's funny, my mom and dad have just started digging into our own family tree. I didn't think anything could get them off the golf course, but they really seem to be enjoying it."

"Where in Indiana did you say they lived?"

"Just outside of Fort Wayne. Why?"

"Well then, they're probably using the Allen County Library. It's supposed to be one of the better collections in the country."

"That's what Mom said. I guess they've uncovered quite a lot of information. Dad's even discovered a bit of a mystery man way back somewhere on his mother's side. Sort of like your grandmother, I guess."

"I guess we all have mysteries if we dig deep enough," Jake said as the waiter discreetly laid their check on the table. Glancing around to find that they were the only patrons remaining, he continued, "I had no idea it was that late. Looks as if they'd like us to leave."

"I had a good time," said Abby when they reached her door.

"Good enough to try it again when I get back?" asked Jake.

"I think that can be arranged. When are you coming back?"

"I'm not sure exactly. Depends. I don't know whether Mom and Dan are doing the Thanksgiving thing this year or not. What about you? Will you go up to see your folks over the holiday weekend?"

"No, it's their turn to come down here. We trade off Christmas and Thanksgiving, and it's my turn to cook the turkey. Always an exciting proposition," Abby said with a grin. "I'm not the world's greatest cook."

"Would you mind if I called you while I'm gone?"

"That would be nice."

"I guess I'd better be going," Jake said without moving.

He stood there looking down at Abby for a long moment until she finally said, "If you're wondering, this would be a good time to kiss me. And if you're not, it's getting chilly out here, and I'm going inside."

He replied by taking her into his arms. When he finally released her, he smiled down and said, "Now scoot inside and lock the door. I want you safe and sound when I get back."

"Yes, sir," she said. "Drive carefully and happy hunting."

As she locked the door, she noticed the lingering taste of his lips on hers and smiled. She fell asleep as soon as her head hit the pillow and awoke with the same smile on her face.

1862

Abigail awoke to find that she had been thrown across the back of a mule. Her head throbbed, and her ribs bounced painfully off the mule's spine with every step it took. When she moved, she also realized that her hands and feet were bound. The weasel-faced man had her mule's lead, and although she couldn't see her other two captors, she could hear their voices.

"Don't know why I let you talk me into bringin' her 'long, Luke," said the leader of the group. "I oughta just chuck her off a cliff. Killin' never bother'd you afore."

"But we ain't never killed no woman b'fore, Josh," replied the younger man. "Shoulda just left her there."

"Yeah, and she'd a sent the menfolk after us. Least mebbe this way it'll be awhile 'fore anybody misses her," Josh said. "At least she can cook an' such, but you're gonna to take care of her if there's trouble."

Abigail shuddered at the thought of the other uses the big man might find for her. And then thinking of the baby, she told herself that she would just have to find a way to survive. Jacob and the others would come looking for her, and in the meantime, she would be careful not to cause any trouble.

When they paused to water the animals, the Weasel came back to check on her. She flinched when he touched her arm, and he called over his shoulder, "Reckon she's still 'live, Josh. Whut we gonna do with her now?"

"I'll take care of her, Matt," said Luke. "Here, go water my horse."

"I don't take orders from no boy. I believe I'll just take care of her myself," said the Matt. He licked his lips and rubbed his hands together.

"I said I'd take care of her. Now step aside," said the younger man.

"Let her be, Matt. Tend to the horses like Luke says," said Josh.

Luke untied her feet and pulled Abigail off the back of the mule. As he did, he said, "Now promise me you won't try to run off, or I'll have to tie your feet again."

"I promise," Abigail said. "Could you untie my hands too?"

"Josh'll skin me if I do that," he said, but he readjusted and loosened the ropes binding her hands. "Better?"

"Yes, thank you. Could I maybe have some water too?" she asked.

Handing her the canteen, he said, "My name is Luke. What's yours?"

"Abigail Cutter," she replied. "Where are you taking me? And why?"

"Well, Josh figured you'd raise a ruckus if we left you behind. We're headed back home to North Carolina."

"Best git movin' again," called Josh. "Git her back on the mule and see to it she b'haves."

"Can I trust you not to run off if I let you sit up and ride?" Luke asked.

"I wouldn't even know where to run." But as she stood, she managed to snag the skirt of her dress on a branch, leaving a scrap of cloth for any who might seek her. "Where are we going in North Carolina?" she asked.

"We live on Wolf Mountain. That's in Jackson County. Don't suppose you've ever heard of it," Luke answered.

"No, my folks came from up in Virginia. Is it very far?"

"Far enough. Not sure exactly how far. We been all over these parts," he replied.

Abigail had no idea where Wolf Mountain was. For that matter, she had no idea where they were right then. Until shortly before she met Jacob, she had never been out of Virginia. Her mind went back to the summer when she'd first met him.

A letter arrived one day from her uncle. Her aunt had taken ill down in Maryville, and he needed help tending their three young children. The next day, Abigail found herself on a train headed south with instructions to stay as long as her aunt requested. A few weeks after she arrived, the doctor told her uncle that getting out of the city would be good for his wife's health, and he bundled her, Abigail, and the children into a wagon and took them over the mountain into Cades Cove to stay with his mother.

One day, her aunt sent her into the settlement with her uncle's younger sister, Melinda. As they passed the blacksmith's shop, Abigail was nearly bowled over by a laughing young man who was leaving.

He grinned down at her as he snatched the cap from his head. "Ma'am." He nodded and blushed and ran off.

"Who was that?" she asked of her companion.

"Oh, that's just one of the Cutter boys. Never can remember which is which."

Something about him instantly appealed to Abigail. He had none of the arrogant swagger of the young men and boys who frequented her father's store back home. She'd certainly never seen any of them blush.

That Sunday at church, she saw him again along with his large family. There was to be dinner on the grounds that day, and after what seemed like hours of shy glances, he finally came over and introduced himself. "Jacob Cutter, ma'am. Pleased to meet you."

Abigail was instantly smitten, and her feelings for the shy young man grew as the summer waned. By the time her aunt's health returned and before she could be bundled off back to Virginia, she and Jacob stole away to meet the preacher at the Primitive Baptist Church. There, with only Melinda and Jacob's friend George, they were married.

Her father was furious and at first threatened to have the marriage annulled. Although they were not wealthy, they were well educated and lived in a fair-sized town where her life would have been if not luxurious, at least comfortable. Abigail's father thought she could do much better than the quiet young man from the mountains. He didn't want to see his only daughter live the hardscrabble life of a farmer's wife. But when he saw how determined she was and with much encouragement from Abigail's mother, he relented.

After they were married, Abigail and Jacob had had little cause to leave the cove. They grew corn and a few vegetables, had a cow for milk, and she kept a few chickens. They had the corn ground into meal at Mr. Shields's mill, and sometimes Abigail would trade corn for wheat flour. If they needed other things, they rode over to Snider's store over in Tuckaleechee Cove.

And now she was totally lost and in the company of strangers with Lord knew what sort of intentions. But she knew that Jacob would find her no matter where they took her, and she was determined to help in whatever way she could.

The three men pushed hard, intent on putting as much distance as possible between themselves and anyone who might be following them. Each time they stopped to rest or water the horses, Abigail managed to leave some sign of their passage. A scrap of petticoat here, a pile of small stones hiding a button or a hairpin there—any small thing that her husband might recognize and that her captors would not notice. It was a pitiful trail, but she prayed it would be enough.

Chapter 15

Before she knew it, Abby was planning her Thanksgiving dinner. Jake called from North Carolina every two to three days. He told her about the boxes of things he had found in Aunt Sarah's attic. It was a treasure trove of family history—letters, land records, and the greatest find of all, diaries. Abby was just beginning to look forward to his late-evening calls to report his progress when he suddenly stopped calling. At first she was disconcerted, and then relieved. *Relationships are just too complicated,* she told herself. *I don't need to get entangled right now.* But there remained a little part of her that was sorely disappointed. No one had touched her on that many levels for a long time. Not only was Jake charming and intelligent, his kiss had awakened long-dormant feelings that Abby wasn't quite sure she was ready to deal with.

As she sat poring through recipe books, the phone rang, "Hey, gal, how you doin'?" came George's familiar voice.

"Fine, thanks. You?"

"Fine as frog's hair now that most of the tourists have left for the season and I can get some work done around the house. I'm trying to get enough wood cut to last me through the winter. Emily wants to know what she can bring for Thanksgiving dinner."

"That's sweet, but she doesn't have to bother. I'm doing the turkey, dressing, and mashed potatoes, and Sandra's bringing a cranberry salad, green beans, and bread. Surely that will be enough to fill us all up."

"What, no spoon bread?"

"Of course, I'd forgotten that. We'll all be asleep before the basketball game is over."

"How about dessert?"

"Pie for sure. Mom and I have made pumpkin pies for Thanksgiving since before I could reach the counter."

"Emily makes a mean apple cake with fresh apples and just a touch of rum. How about if we bring one of those?"

"Ooh, that sounds yummy. But honestly, George, she doesn't have to bother if she doesn't want to. I thought she might enjoy not having to cook."

"When she first found out that the kids couldn't make it home, she was relieved at the prospect of a leisurely holiday, but she's just like an old plow horse and can't stand to be out of the harness."

Abby could hear a muffled but indignant comment from Emily in the background. "You'd better take care, old man, or you won't make it 'til Thanksgiving. Tell Emily the cake sounds delicious and thanks."

"When are your folks getting in?"

"Tuesday evening, late. A couple of my trials got canceled, so I have the whole week off. All I have to do is get the apartment cleaned and shop."

"Well, I'd better let you go. By the way, have you heard from Jake?"

"Not lately," Abby said carefully, lest her voice betray any hint of disappointment.

"That rascal. I thought he'd be back by now," said George. "He stopped by on his way to North Carolina. I sorta got the impression that you two had pretty well hit it off.

"It was just one date, George. Nothing more. You have an overactive imagination. Guess he decided to stay there for Thanksgiving."

"I just can't believe he hasn't called, that's all."

"No big deal. See you guys around noon on Thursday?"

"Looking forward to it, gal. See you then."

Hanging up the phone, Abby found herself wondering what Jake had said to George. Shaking her head, she went back to her recipe books wondering what had possessed her to invite a houseful of people for dinner when she had only cooked a turkey once before in her life.

A cold rain was falling Tuesday evening when Abby went to pick up her parents at the airport. Wednesday dawned clear but cold, and by evening it had become quite cloudy again. By Thanksgiving morning, they awoke to a wintry scene. "Oh dear," said her mother, looking out the window after breakfast. "I thought we left this stuff back in Indiana. I hope your guests will be able to make it."

"Now, Maddie, quit worrying," chided her husband. "There's only a couple of inches. That's nothing."

"It's nothing in Indiana, Dad, but it doesn't take much to make a mess of things here, or have you forgotten?"

"No, I haven't forgotten. Of course, the roads usually weren't nearly as bad as what you and your brother did to the driveway," he said, referring to the family's first winter in Knoxville.

"That was Steven's fault, not mine," Abby said in mock innocence.

"Now, as I recall, young lady, it was you who did the asking," said her mother.

It was mid-January, and Abby and Steven were longing for snow. Not only had they endured a brown or, at best, green Christmas, they hadn't missed a single day of school due to snow. When their new schoolmates told them that they always got out of school for snow, they had been skeptical. The schools rarely closed for snow in Northern Indiana, and Steven always hoped the big snows would come on Friday, so they would have the entire weekend to sled. Now here they were with a house on a hill and a driveway just made for sledding, and they hadn't seen so much as a single flake.

Finally one Wednesday morning, they got their wish. They awoke to snow flurries, and by 10:00 a.m., the schools began closing. There was barely an inch of snow on the ground, and Abby and Steven couldn't believe that they were being sent home. By midafternoon, there was finally enough snow on the driveway to drag out their sleds. But it didn't take long for their sleds to wear ruts in the shallow snow, leaving ice-covered patches of blacktop. As they trudged back up the hill, Abby slipped on one of the icy spots and fell.

"Wow," said Steven as he helped his younger sister to her feet. "That's really slick. I wish the rest of the driveway was like that. We could really fly."

"I wish we'd get more snow," said Abby. "Snow is better. I don't like the ice, I can't walk on it."

Looking at the sun peeping through the clouds, Steven said, "Afraid that's not going to happen. But I bet if we put some water on the driveway, it would freeze over. We could make it like a toboggan run."

Abby was less enthused, but Steven talked her into asking their mother if it would be okay for them to make a toboggan run on the driveway. Madeline Edwards was at her sewing machine when Abby appeared by her side. "Mommy, Steven wants to know if we can make a 'boggan on the driveway," six-year-old Abby said, not entirely certain what a toboggan was. Steven had assured her that it was really fast and fun and that he would make sure she didn't fall.

"A what dear?" her mother asked distractedly, not looking up from her sewing.

"The snow is going away, but Steven says we can make a 'boggan run if we pour some water down the driveway. Can we, Mommy?"

Intent on the sleeve she was stitching into the dress she was making, Abby's mother didn't respond. "Is it okay? Steven says he won't let me fall."

Fitting the dress carefully under the pressure foot of the machine, Madeline moved her head up and down with the motion of the needle. Taking this as a nod of assent, Abby said, "Thanks, Mommy. Come out and watch us later."

Carrying buckets from the kitchen sink, the two children soon turned the driveway into an icy track. When it was finished, Steven stretched out on the sled and told Abby to climb on his back and hold on tight. As they raced down the hill at top speed, Abby felt as if she was flying. Again and again, they tore down the hill. This was the best sledding either child had ever seen. Their mother called them into the house as it began to get dark.

They were sitting in the kitchen drinking hot chocolate amid piles of dripping clothes and boots when their father came in. "I want to know who's responsible for that skating rink we used to call a driveway," he thundered. "My car is now in the Johnsons' front yard."

"What are you talking about, Steve?" Madeline asked her husband.

"The drive is completely covered with ice. Halfway up, the car turned around sideways and slid all the way back down the hill."

"It's our 'boggan run, Daddy. Did you like it?" said Abby brightly. "Me and Steven did it. The sled goes really fast." Finally sensing her father's irritation, she said, "Mommy said we could."

"What were you thinking, Maddie?" he said, turning to Abby's mother.

"What do you mean, I said you could?" she asked Abby. "I don't remember you asking me any such thing."

"Sure, I did," Abby said. "You were sewing my new dress, and I asked if we could put water on the driveway to make a 'boggan run, and you shook your head yes."

Turning back to her husband, Madeline said, "I'm sorry, Steve. You know how I get when I'm sewing. The needle just sort of mesmerizes me, and I guess I was following it with my head."

Steven had been silent throughout the entire discussion and was just about to slip out of the kitchen when his father said, "Just a minute, young man. Since you were the ringleader in this little escapade, you can help me salt the driveway so I can get the car into the garage."

"Tattletale," he said to Abby as he went out the door to destroy their playground.

They all laughed at the shared memory, and Abby said, "I guess we all learned not to ask Mom anything when she's sewing." She peered out the window at the downy flakes that were rapidly covering the street. "I'm not worried about Sandra and Mark getting here. They live here in town. I just hope George can get out of Townsend."

"We'd better get those pies going so we can get the turkey in the oven," said her mother. "Don't worry about George. He's not about to miss a meal."

The two women set about their tasks, and the apartment was soon filled with the sweet, spicy smell of baking pies and the aroma of the roasting turkey. By the time they cleaned up the kitchen, it was nearly noon. Abby went to her room to shower and change. "Unless they ran into trouble on the road, George and Emily should be here anytime. Dad, can you do the honors with drinks 'til I get dressed? There's a plate of veggies and dip in the fridge."

The sound of laughter greeted her when she returned to the living room a short time later. George was regaling her parents with a tale about some hapless camper. "Where's Emily?" Abby asked, kissing the old man on top of his head.

"Her daughter out in Seattle went into labor about four this morning. The baby's not due for another month or so and Sheryl needed Emily to take care of her other kids. I put her on a plane a little while ago."

"Steve and I were really looking forward to meeting her," said Madeline.

"Tell the truth now, Mom. She said she wouldn't believe you'd found another woman who would put up with you until she saw her with her own eyes," Abby said.

"Well, your mom's not too far from right. After Jenny died, I didn't figure there'd ever be another woman in my life," George said. "Em was really disappointed too. But you know how it is with grandmothers."

"I don't, but I can imagine," said Madeline with a pointed look at her daughter. "I keep hoping Abby will get busy and make us grandparents while we're still young enough to enjoy them."

"All right, you two. Enough! I'll get around to it one of these days," said Abby, getting up at the sound of the doorbell.

Abby's secretary, Sandra, and her husband, Mark, arrived laden with dishes and covered with melting snow. "Man, it's really coming down out there," said Mark.

Abby made introductions all around and went off to the kitchen with Sandra to see what dishes needed to be kept warm. When they returned to the living room, George was gazing out the window. "Looks like the roads are starting to get bad," he said, his brow furrowed.

"Don't worry, George. If it gets too bad, you can stay here," Abby said as the old man returned to his chair.

The men were soon involved in a debate over the merits of the UT Volunteers and the Vanderbilt Commodores basketball teams in the annual Thanksgiving game while the women retired to the kitchen to put the finishing touches on the meal. While she was setting the table, Abby glanced up and noticed George at the window again. It wasn't like George to let a little snow bother him, and she wondered what was troubling her old friend. I'll take him aside later and find out, she thought. Right now, though, I have to get the turkey out of the oven.

As the group gathered around the table a short while later, there was a knock at the door. "You expecting more company, gal?" George asked, grinning broadly.

His grin made her suspicious. "What are you up to, old man?"

When she opened the door, there stood Jake, a huge bouquet of flowers in one hand and a bottle of wine in the other. Without a word, he swept her into his arms and kissed her soundly.

"Wha...what are you doing here?" she stammered when he finally released her, blushing and flustered. "And why haven't you called?" This, in spite of her previous resolve not to let him know she cared.

"What sort of greeting is that for a fellow who's braved snow in the mountain passes just to get to see you? They were about to close the road at Newfound Gap when I got there. I had to beg the ranger to let me through."

"Hello, Jake," said George. "Glad you made it, son. I was beginning to worry."

"You knew he was coming," said Abby. "And you didn't tell me?"

"Jake was afraid you'd be mad 'cause he hadn't called. I figured if we surprised you in front of people you wouldn't throw anything at him."

Remembering Sandra, Mark, and her parents, Abby blushed again. She made introductions all around and then escaped to the kitchen to fetch another plate and silverware. Jake followed her to the kitchen.

"I'm sorry I didn't call. I meant to. I just got so involved in my work that the days just got away from me. I'll leave if you want me to."

"If I had any sense at all, I'd send you packing," Abby replied. "But after that display you just put on, I'm not about to let you leave me to face that crowd alone. You will, however, pay for your sins."

Grabbing her up in his arms again, he said, "Just name your price," he said as he kissed her.

Dinner was a lively affair. Jake's trip from Asheville had been quite eventful, and he kept them all laughing with tales of his minor mishaps on the road. Abby was amazed at how easily he seemed to fit in. He showed none of the awkwardness of a stranger who finds himself amid a group of people who are already well acquainted. She was particularly surprised at her father's response. Despite her age, her father still acted like she was sixteen when it came to the men in her life. He was always cordial but cool when Abby introduced a new man. She was always afraid that at any moment, he might grab the unsuspecting suitor by his collar and ask, "And just what are your intentions, young man?" But she needn't have worried. The two men discussed everything from sports to literature, and by the time the meal was over, they acted as if they'd known each other for years. Her mother smiled knowingly every time she caught her daughter's eye, and Abby knew she would have to face the third degree before the evening was over.

When the meal was over, the men retired to the living room to watch the pregame show while the women cleared the table. Sandra and Madeline pounced as soon as they had Abby alone in the kitchen, demanding to know everything there was to know about Jake.

"Honestly, you two. I barely know the man. We've only had one date."

"That hello kiss didn't look like he barely knew you," teased Sandra. "Come on now, tell us."

"I met him in Cades Cove when I took a few days off in September. He fell and broke his ankle, and I just happened to find him and helped get him to the hospital. Honest, that's all there is to tell. He called me a few weeks ago, and we went out to dinner."

"And?" said her mother.

"And nothing, Mom," said Abby. "He's been in North Carolina ever since, and he called a few times. That's it."

Abby could tell from their expressions that neither woman was convinced, but to her immense relief, they finally let the subject drop. Jake's arrival had taken her completely off guard. She hadn't really had time enough to sort out her thoughts, much less being ready to share them with her mother and Sandra. When they joined the men in the living room, Jake was telling them about his discoveries.

"The letters were great," he said. "But the real find was the diaries. Aunt Sarah apparently started keeping a diary when she was just a girl. She was born in 1867 and lived to be nearly a hundred. She literally saw the United States go from the horse and buggy to the space age."

"What a treasure," said Abby's father. "Did Abby tell you about our foray into genealogy? We're really just getting started, but it is fascinating."

"Steve's right," said Abby's mother. "I did find an account of one of my ancestor's capture by Indians back in the Revolutionary War, but it's not in his own hand like your diaries. Something you can actually touch that came from that far back in time."

"Maddie's research is coming along better than mine right now. A cousin on my father's side has researched that line back hundreds of years, so I decided to concentrate on my maternal ancestors. Ran into a dead end pretty early. The records go back to my great-great-grandfather and then nothing. Seems like his life started when he got married, and we can't find anything before that."

"When was that?" asked Jake.

"Oh, I don't remember exactly, but sometime shortly after the Civil War. Why?"

"Have you researched the Civil War rosters to see if maybe he was in the war? Sometimes men mustered out somewhere far from home and for one reason or another just never went back. But the war rosters should tell you where he mustered in, and that might send you off to an entirely different state."

"I hadn't thought about that," said Steve. "As I recall, he would have been about the right age to have been a soldier. Thanks for the tip. I'll try that when we get back."

"Who will try that?" asked Madeline.

Grinning sheepishly, Steve said, "I guess you will, sweetie. That sounds like an internet thing to me."

"And we know how computer literate *you* are, Dad," teased Abby.

"That's just one too many new tricks for this old dog," he replied. "Besides, Maddie's getting to be quite good at—what is it you call it—surfing. I'd rather go to the library."

"Sounds like you two make quite a team," said Jake. "I have a bit of a puzzle myself. My great-great-grandmother is supposed to have been from Cades Cove, but I haven't been able to find the link. She also kept a diary of sorts, but not in a book, and over the years, the pages have been shuffled quite a bit. One page will be dated 1901, and the next page in the pile will be dated 1880. I finally decided to try to put them in order before I do any more reading."

"Well, I wish you luck," said Steve. "It certainly is an addictive pastime."

"I know," Jake replied. "I have a full schedule of classes next semester, so I want to get as far as I can before I have to start teaching again."

"Time for the game," said Abby. "Family tree climbing will have to take a back seat to the Vols for a little while."

For the next few hours, there was little conversation other than a mix of cheers and jeers aimed at the television. The game was a nail-biter with the University of Tennessee's Volunteers winning in the last few seconds of the game. When the game was over, they realized that the snowstorm had intensified, and the evening ended with a flurry of coats and gloves and trips out to the cars to scrape windows. At Jake's insistence, George agreed to stay with him for the night rather than risk getting stranded on the unplowed roads leading to his cabin. As George said his last goodbyes to her parents, Abby walked outside with Jake.

"Are you still mad at me for not calling?" he asked.

"Well, it's not very flattering to think that I was replaced by a bunch of old papers."

Jake pulled her into his arms. "If I promise it won't happen again, can I see you again?"

"Are you sure you want to promise? I'm apt to get distracted in the midst of a case myself, so I guess I can cut you a little slack just this once. Yes, I'd like to see you again."

1862

"Looks like they went this way," said George as they came to a fork in the trail. "Here's another little scrap of lace. Are you sure this is off something of Abigail's?"

"It looks like it. I can't afford to buy her such, but her mother sends her petticoats from Virginia. She sets great store in them. I'll bet she's mad as a hornet about tearing it up."

As the two men turned their horses to follow the faint trail, George shouted, "Look out, Cutter!"

The small man crept into the clearing like the weasel he so resembled. The first man he'd shot was sprawled on the ground, bleeding profusely from the hole in his shoulder. Not long for this world, *Matt thought as he went through the man's pockets. Moving to the other man, Matt noted the head wound with satisfaction.* My aim's improving, *he thought. A cold rain was beginning to fall as he left them there to die.*

*****

Abigail was dozing uneasily by the fire when she heard Matt ride back into their camp. He was leading a horse, a horse she recognized as George's. She should have known he'd be with Jacob; the two men had been friends since childhood and George stood up with them when they married. Feigning sleep, Abigail listened intently to what her captors had to say.

"Was anyone tailin' us?" Josh asked.

"Yep, there was two of them—a big fella on a bay horse and a smaller man. The bay ran off, but I managed to catch the other. She's a fine little mare, ought to fetch a good price. You were right. She's been leaving a trail for them, tearing up her petticoat, looks like," Matt said, pulling a handful of lacy scraps from his pocket.

"Did you take care of them?"

"Won't be needin' them horses, that's for sure."

Abigail bit her lip to keep from crying out. Jacob was dead. She feared the men who held her captive, but knowing that her husband would be looking for her had given her the strength—the will—to sur-

vive. What was she going to do without him? What about their baby? How could she ever hope to escape now?

*****

The cold rain was still falling when Jacob awoke several hours later. It was full dark, and his head pounded with every beat of his heart. Gingerly, he touched a place above his right ear and felt the sticky blood. Feeling farther, he realized that the bullet had only grazed the side of his head, but there was a fair-sized knot below the bullet's path where he'd struck his head when he fell off his horse. He tried to stand, but a wave of nausea forced him back to his knees. "George, you alive?" he called.

A low moan came from nearby. On hands and knees, Jacob followed the sound of his friend's voice and found him leaning against a tree. George was conscious, but the front of his shirt was covered in blood from a wound just below his collarbone. He'd managed to pack the wound with moss to stop the bleeding, but he didn't look good.

"How you farin'?" asked Jacob.

"Not too good," his friend mumbled.

"Got to get you back to Doc Hobart. Think you can ride?"

"My horse ran off. Think I heard yours around here somewhere."

Jacob gave a shrill whistle that was answered by a low nicker from his horse. The two men staggered to their feet. With some effort, Jacob helped George mount the big bay horse and struggled up behind him.

As they turned back toward the cove, George said, "Sorry, Cutter. I didn't see him 'til it was too late."

"Did you get a good look at him?" Jacob asked.

"Just a glimpse of gray through the trees. One of them must have doubled back to see if anyone was following. We walked right into an ambush."

"Well, Abigail must still be alive, or they wouldn't have bothered. I'll head back out in the morning."

But it would be several weeks before Jacob would be well enough to look for Abigail. By the time they reached the settlement, both men were thoroughly soaked, and Jacob was shaking uncontrollably. He managed to get George to Dr. Hobart's door and then collapsed. When he finally recovered from pneumonia and the effects of the gunshot wound, all traces of the trail were gone.

Jacob searched for Abigail throughout the remainder of summer and into the fall, but it was no use. Past the point where he'd been shot, there was no sign of Abigail or her captors. When the first snow came, Jacob made a decision.

"H'lo, Cutter," George said, looking up from the knife and sharpening stone in his hands. "Get down. How about a drink?"

After his friend retrieved the jug from its shelf in the cabin, the two sat in silence for a while.

Jacob took a long pull on the jug. "Just came to say goodbye. I'm heading out."

"Where to?" George asked, even though he knew. Jacob had been talking about joining the war for several weeks.

"Kentucky, to enlist. Gonna kill some Rebs."

"Won't bring her back, Jacob. 'Sides, you know them that took Abigail were just low-down bushwackers. Probably deserters."

"I know, but there's nothing for me here anymore."

"Your mind's made up?"

"Reckon so."

George took a deep swig of the corn liquor and put the cork back in the jug. "Well, let me get my belongings."

When they came to the crest of Thunderhead Mountain, George paused to gaze at the cove below, but Jacob never looked back.

A few months later, George was killed in the Battle of Stones River, near Murfreesboro. Jacob got leave to carry his friend's body home for burial but didn't tarry. He returned to his unit in time for the disastrous Battle of Rogersville where two-thirds of the regiment was captured. When the captain's horse was shot, pinning his leg beneath the animal, Jacob dropped his musket and ran to his aid. As he helped the injured officer limp to safety, a Confederate Minié ball found its mark. While he lay on the ground with the sounds of the battle around him, Jacob heard a soft voice. He couldn't see her in the chaos and smoke, but knowing she was there, he smiled.

"Abigail," he whispered, and then all was dark.

Chapter 16

THE WEEKS BETWEEN THANKSGIVING AND Christmas flew by. Abby agreed to plea bargains in several cases with less-than-stellar evidence. This gave her an unexpected opportunity to use the vacation days that she thought she would lose at year's end. Ostensibly, her years of service with the District Attorney's office entitled Abby to nearly four weeks of vacation a year, but it was rare for her to be able to manage more than a few days away, much less two whole weeks. She was really looking forward to the time off and a long visit with her parents and extended family in Indiana.

Her relationship with Jake had progressed with little conscious effort on either's part. At first, Jake called each evening, and the two shared the events of their respective days. Then it was dinner two or three times a week. Unlike Abby, Jake was a gourmet cook, and he enjoyed surprising her with new and exotic recipes. When it was Abby's turn to cook, they survived on whatever she managed to scrape together from her meager pantry or Chinese carryout. The two spent hours talking about everything and nothing; sharing tales of their growing-up years and hopes and dreams for the future. Unlike her past relationships, especially those with other attorneys, Abby felt no need to compete with Jake. The two were easy in each other's company, more like old friends than recent acquaintances.

She had a wealth of knowledge and experience that he appreciated, and he was a natural-born teacher, pleased to share his knowledge with an apt pupil. Their differences complemented each other. Abby learned that while Jake loved to cook, he hated to clean up afterward. On the other hand, she could not relax until the dishwasher was loaded and turned on, so while Jake got ready for his next day's classes, Abby tidied the kitchen. Jake was interested in current events but seldom had the time to read the paper. A creature of habit, Abby at least scanned the newspaper from front to back each morning before going to work. In the evening, she would bring him up to date on world events over dinner.

And then one morning, she awoke in Jake's bed. It was not something that either planned; it just happened. One evening, as Abby started for the closet to retrieve her coat, Jake simply took her by the hand a led her to the bedroom. When she awoke the next morning, it was with a stretch and a smile reminiscent of Scarlett O'Hara the morning after Rhett carried her up the stairs. From the first, Jake's kisses stirred something within her. They seemed to share a chemistry that she neither could nor felt the need to describe. It was simply there, and when they finally came together, their lovemaking was as natural as the rest of their relationship. There was none of the first-time fumbling that both had experienced in the past, none of the morning-after awkwardness.

"Mornin'," Jake said as he entered the room clad in a well-worn bathrobe and carrying a breakfast tray. "Sleep well?"

"Well, but not long," Abby replied. "And you can wipe that self-satisfied grin off your face right this minute!"

"Oh, sure, like you're not wearing a Mona Lisa smile on your own face this morning. Coffee?"

"Later," she replied, tugging on the cord to his bathrobe. Sometime later, Abby sat bolt upright in bed when she heard a door slam downstairs. "Oh no! The Santanas. I forgot all about them. Mrs. S never misses a thing. She's going to know I spent the night."

"So? We're both consenting adults. Anyway, she's crazy about you. Every time I see her, she's full of questions and stories about when you lived here. I think she knows you've done this before."

Abby blushed to the roots of her hair, then laughed. "I guess you're right. It just feels like the time my grandmother caught my boyfriend and I smooching on her front porch when I was fourteen."

After that and as their schedules allowed, they spent more and more time together. When Abby began making plans for the holidays, it was with mixed feelings. She was anxious to see her family but now reluctant to leave Jake. "I'm going to miss you. I wish you could come to Indiana with me," she said over dinner the night before she left.

"Me too. But my sister, Mary Alice, is expecting me. This is their first Christmas in the new house, and she's so excited about having the whole clan in for dinner. Besides, after I ran out on Mom's Thanksgiving plans, I need to mend some fences."

"And how long were you planning on staying in North Carolina?"

"Oh, I don't know. I hadn't really thought about it. Why?"

"Are you driving or flying?"

"Since I'm going clear to Hatteras, I thought I'd splurge and fly. Again, why?"

"I don't suppose you'd be interested in making a little side trip, would you?"

"That all depends. What did you have in mind?"

"Well, my cousin Amanda always has this big New Year's Eve do, and I thought maybe you might like to come up for that. We could drive back to Tennessee together."

"Oh, now I get it. You just want someone to share the driving," Jake teased. "And here I thought it was just because you couldn't bear to be away from me for two whole weeks."

He ducked as a sofa pillow sailed past his head.

"Actually, I was hoping to be able to spend part of the holidays with you. Sure your folks won't mind?"

"Mind? No, they won't mind, but now that I think of it, are you sure you want to face the entire clan?"

"I can handle it if you can." Jake smiled but then turned serious. "Speaking of which, do we need to talk?"

"Don't you know the words 'we need to talk' are the worst four words you can say to a woman?" Abby replied. "I don't know. Do we?"

"Well, at the risk of scaring you off, I think it's only fair to warn you, Ms. Abigail Cutter Edwards, that I've fallen in love with you. I know it hasn't been that long, but that's how I feel." He paused, peering intently into her eyes as she processed his words. When she didn't respond for some moments, Jake blurted out an apology.

"I'm sorry. I didn't mean to spring it on you like this. If I'm moving too fast, just say so, and I'll back off."

Abby stared at Jake for a few more seconds. She felt her lips began to twitch, and before she could stop herself, a short laugh escaped. Hurt flashed across Jake's face.

"I'm sorry—"

"So you don't share my feelings," he said, now pacing back and forth.

"No, it's not that. It's just—"

"It's okay, I understand."

"Would you let me finish? You should see yourself," she said. "You've got that deer-in-the-headlights look on your face. And no, it doesn't mean that I don't share your feelings. You just caught me off guard, that's all."

"So how *do* you feel about me?" he demanded.

Crossing to stand in front of him, Abby reached up and cupped his face in her hands and said simply, "I love you too, of course."

Chapter 17

TEN DAYS LATER, ABBY MET Jake at the airport in Fort Wayne. "God, I missed you," he murmured against her hair when she greeted him at the gate.

"Good. I was afraid when you got away and had time to think about it, you'd regret our last conversation."

"Not a chance. You?"

"No regrets. Butterflies, maybe, but no regrets."

"Butterflies, I can handle," he said as he kissed her.

When his bags were stowed in the trunk, they headed out into the countryside. Gazing out across the snow-covered remnants of the past summer's corn crop, Jake said, "Sure is flat."

"Now that's an original statement."

"Sorry. I guess you've heard that before. I've always heard about how flat it is in the Midwest. Can't believe how far you can see."

"Yeah, it's nothing like Tennessee. When we first moved away, I couldn't wait to get back here to where you could see all the way across three farms. The mountains and ridges seemed to close in around me. Now I can't imagine coming back."

As they turned onto the interstate, Jake continued, "I thought your folks lived in town. It looks like we're headed out into the country."

"They do, and we are. I guess I forgot to tell you, we're going to stay at my aunt June's. She's lives up north a bit on what was the original family homestead. We've spent the holidays there for as long as I can remember. Mom and Dad are already there."

"Speaking of which, what have you told them?"

"All there is to tell—that I've invited my friend Jake to spend a few days with us."

"*Friend?* Funny, I thought we'd moved a bit beyond friendship?"

"Well, unless you're ready to face Mom picking out china patterns and Dad's 'just what are your intentions, young man?' speech.'"

"Oh. Okay, pal, friends it is," he said as they turned off the highway, and the rambling old farmhouse came into view. "Wow, this place is great. When was it built?"

"Don't know for sure, but a long time ago. It's passed through to the eldest daughter in the family since sometime in the 1800s. Sort of an odd succession, but there you have it. Well, are you ready to meet the clan?"

Taking a deep breath and blowing it out with a mock shudder, Jake replied, "Ready as I'll ever be, *friend*."

Later that evening over dinner, Jake repeated his question about the age of the house, prompting Abby's cousin Amanda to launch into a spiel worthy of a docent. "The original deed to the land dates back to 1845, and as near as we've been able to discover, the house, or at least the oldest part of the house, was built around 1850. Your rooms are in the original part of the house. Of course, it's gone through a number of additions and renovations over the years. It makes for some odd twists and turns, but it's a solid old place."

"Abby tells me it always passes to the eldest daughter. Why not the eldest son?"

"Well, our great-great-great-great-grandfather, or GG4 as I call him, was a little eccentric. His oldest son apparently disgraced the family in some way. There are veiled references to a 'blot on the family name' in some old letters. Anyway, he left the house to his daughter Louisa, saying that he wanted the house to continue to pass to the oldest daughter. Guess he just didn't trust the sons to do justice to the family name."

"So is Louisa the woman married to your mystery man?" Jake asked, turning to Abby's father.

"That would be GG3," Amanda interjected.

"That's right," said Steve. "You've got quite a memory. And by the way, thanks for the tip about the Civil War rosters. I think I've found him. I'm waiting on some documents to confirm it, but it appears that he was from Tennessee. I have no idea exactly how he ended up here though."

"You *have* been busy. Glad the tip paid off. I'm still trying to sort out all the letters and journal pages I found. I've been a bit distracted of late—ouch!" he said as Abby kicked him under the table.

"It stands to reason," added June. "I found a letter written by his granddaughter, another Louisa, to her husband during World War I. Apparently, he was wounded, thought he wouldn't be able to run the farm when he returned. Anyway, she tells him about her grandfather who lost his arm and still managed to make a go of the place."

"Once I can confirm that I have the right man," Steve continued. "I'll start trying to figure out the rest of the Tennessee connection. Funny how things seem to go full circle."

"Enough history for one night," said June. "I think I created a monster when I gave Steve and Maddie that old box of letters. Who's up for a game of euchre?"

"I'm game," said Jake. "Abby's told me about your famous marathon euchre games. Sounds like fun, but you'll have to teach me."

"Yep," said Steve. "For some reason, they don't seem to have heard of it south of the Mason-Dixon. None of our friends had heard of euchre or pinochle, so Maddie and I had to learn bridge."

The next several hours were filled with card-playing and laughter as Jake tried to learn the intricacies of the unfamiliar card game. Before long, his head was swimming with right and left bowers and counting trumps. Finally, he threw up his hands and tried to give Abby his seat at the table. Instead, she took a seat beside him and helped guide his play. By the time the game broke up, Jake and his partner Steve managed to win a round against Madeline and June with only minimal direction from Abby. It was late when Abby and Jake headed upstairs to their rooms.

"Suppose I could come over for a visit after the rest of the household goes to sleep?" he asked.

"*Friends*, remember. Besides," she continued, opening the door to give him a view of the single twin-sized bed in the room, "I think Aunt June already suspects something. When she showed me to my room, she asked very pointedly if the bed would be big enough for me. Now off with you, sir!" she ordered. "And hey, in case I haven't mentioned it lately, I love you."

"Love you too, friend. Sweet dreams."

But Abby's dreams were not sweet. They were darned strange, she thought to herself the next morning. Sometime near dawn, she awoke to the sound of someone knocking on the front door. Wondering briefly who could be calling at that hour, she turned over and snuggled back down under the covers. When the knocking persisted, Abby flung the covers off in aggravation and went downstairs to the front door. When she opened it, there was no one there. As she started to close the door, Abby saw a man in a uniform walking toward the house. The uniform and something in his stride struck a chord in her memory. Steven's come home! Then she realized the man was wearing a tattered Union uniform. As the man drew nearer, she realized that it was the same man she had seen in the cove. The same man who was searching for the illusive Abigail. He looked older somehow and thinner, but it was the same man. Just as she noticed that one sleeve of the man's uniform hung empty, a gentle tap on her bedroom door aroused Abby from her dream.

"Good morning, sunshine," said Jake. "Are you decent? I brought you some coffee."

"Come on in," she mumbled as she sat up in bed and tried to clear the troubling images from her head. "You're up awfully early. What time is it anyway?"

"A little before six. I couldn't sleep, so I went down and made coffee. Hope your aunt doesn't mind."

"A little before six, my Aunt Fannie!" Abby exclaimed when she looked at the clock on the other side of her bed. "It's five after five. What in the world got you out of bed at this ungodly hour? It was nearly two when we went to bed."

Perched on the foot of her bed, Jake hesitated before answering, "I just couldn't sleep, that's all. Maybe it was all the traveling, or that last piece of mincemeat pie."

"This from the man who can eat a pizza with anchovies and then sleep like a baby. Come on, now. What really got you out of bed before dawn?"

"Well…does your dad or uncle or anybody sleepwalk?"

"Not that I know of. Why?"

"I must have just been dreaming then. It's nothing," he said. Changing the subject, he continued, "So what are we going to do today?"

"Not so fast there, pal. Something or someone got you out of bed in the middle of the night, and you don't seem to want to go back to bed. Now tell me what's going on," Abby demanded.

"All right. Promise you won't laugh or have me committed?" When she nodded, he continued, "You know how you can be sound asleep, and something brings you instantly awake?"

Another nod.

"Well, there I am, sawing logs like ninety, and all of a sudden I get this feeling that I'm not alone. When I opened my eyes, there was this man standing at the foot of my bed just staring at me." Jake hesitated again. "This is where it gets weird," he said. "Here's this old guy just staring at me, and there's just enough light that I can see that he's got this little smile on his face. When I moved to get up, he just vanished."

"Did he say anything?" Abby asked, a bit more sharply than she had intended.

"Why? What do you mean?"

"Just what I said. Did he speak to you?"

"Well, not to me exactly, and this is really weird too. It sounded like, 'Abigail, Abigail, you finally found me.' Now how strange is that? That's when I decided your dad must be sleepwalking, and I figured he just got to my room by mistake."

"What did the man look like? What was he wearing?"

"Now that you ask, I don't know exactly. He must have looked something like your dad since that's who I mistook him for. Why all the questions? What's going on here?"

"In a minute. One more question. Did he have one or two arms?"

"Two, I think. No, wait a minute. I'm not sure. He was holding on to the footboard with just one. I guess the other could have been missing, or maybe I just didn't see it. I wasn't at my best, given the circumstances. Now what gives?"

"It's a long story," said Abby. "And *you* maybe calling the men with the butterfly nets for *me* when I tell you. But I think maybe you had a visit from GG3—Dad's mystery man."

"You mean a ghost?" Jake sputtered. "Is this house haunted? Amanda didn't say anything about ghosts in all of her tales about the house."

"I know," Abby replied. "But there's more. And here, as you so aptly put it, is where it gets *really* weird."

She quickly told him all about the man she had seen in the cove and how he kept calling her name. "At first I thought it was Steven. He used to call me Abigail just to get my goat. But it was more than just that. He's about the same size, and he even walks like Steven. The day you broke your ankle, I was chasing him. I guess, in a way, he led me to you. He vanished just as I entered the clearing around the cabin. I was standing there trying to figure out where he'd disappeared to when I heard you calling."

"Do you really think it's the same guy?"

"I don't know. I'm still trying to get my mind to grasp the fact that I may have been chasing a ghost. I guess chasing the ghost of a long-dead grandfather is better than chasing the ghost of a recently dead brother, though. It was really beginning to bother me. I thought I'd dealt with my grief. When GG3 or whoever it is showed up, I thought maybe it was time to head for the neighborhood headshrinker."

"Well, now I guess you can take some consolation in the fact that if you're crazy, I'm crazy too," said Jake. "But hey, something just occurred to me. If it's the same guy, we've got a well-traveled ghost on our hands. I always thought ghosts sort of did their haunting all in one place."

"Don't look at me," said Abby. "I'm no expert on the paranormal. But if Dad's research pans out and GG3 really was from Tennessee, that might explain seeing him in both places."

"Yeah, well the next time he goes looking for Abigail in the middle of the night, I hope he manages to find the right door. He's your ghost, not mine."

"Oops, I hear someone stirring downstairs. Better get out of here before Aunt June gets any more ideas."

As she headed for the shower, Abby pondered the ghostly presence. Had they really both seen a ghost, or had they both been dreaming? *Oh well, at least I'm in good company,* she thought as she shampooed her hair. It was comforting to know that maybe she wasn't losing her mind after all.

The remainder of their visit was filled with visits to Abby's childhood haunts and calls on and from a variety of relatives and friends. Neither had any more nighttime visits from the ghostly stranger, and by unspoken agreement, they didn't discuss him with the rest of the family. On New Year's Eve morning, June turned the house over to Amanda for the party and left with Madeline and Steve for more sedate festivities in town. "There's plenty of places to sleep is this house," she cautioned on her way out the door. "Don't let anyone drive if they're not up to it. And you two behave yourselves," she added to Abby and Jake with a wink.

As promised, Amanda's party was big. The house was filled with an assortment of friends and relatives, many of whom Abby hadn't seen in years. She was pleased to see that Jake seemed at ease in the midst of the raucous group of strangers. Shortly before midnight, he and one of Abby's cousins donned party hats, and using drinking straws as batons, the two led the group in a warbling rendition of "Auld Lang Syne." By 3:00 a.m., most of the guests had departed or headed for the rooms Amanda assigned. Shortly after she retired, Abby heard a tap at her door and opened it to find Jake standing in the hallway clutching a pillow. "Someone's sleeping in my bed. Can I bunk with you?"

"It'll be a tight squeeze, but come on in, Goldilocks. But remember, Aunt June said we have to behave," she said sternly.

"But while the cat's away..." He grinned as he closed the door.

When they finally awoke around noon, they found Abby's parents and aunt sitting at the dining-room table poring over a stack of papers.

"Well, it's about time you two crawled out," said Steve. "Look here. The documents I was waiting for came in the mail while we were gone. They confirm the identity of my great-great-grandfather. Any you're not going to believe this, Abby, but he was from Blount County."

Chapter 18

THE DOCUMENTS IN STEVE'S HAND told a spare history of their ancestor. Jacob Cutter mustered into the Second Tennessee Infantry Regiment in the fall of 1862. The regiment saw action near Murfreesboro at the Battle of Stones River and, after being converted to a mounted infantry, pursued Confederate raider John Hunt Morgan through Kentucky, Indiana, and Ohio. In November of 1863, Jacob and more than half of the regiment were captured at the Battle of Rogersville.

"The regimental records indicate that Sergeant Jacob Cutter lost an arm and was taken with the officers to Libby Prison in Richmond, Virginia," said Steve.

"Given the state of battlefield medicine at that time, it's a wonder he survived," Abby noted.

"Wait," her father said. "It gets worse. He was sent to Andersonville in 1864 and spent the remainder of the war there. From what I've read, nearly a third of the prisoners at Andersonville died."

"GG3 must have been one tough old bird," said Amanda from the doorway. "I can't believe you finally found some record of him. But I thought Andersonville was in Georgia. How the heck he end up here?"

"I'm still not sure about that," replied Steve. "The records show that from Andersonville, he was sent to Camp Chase, Ohio. That's over around Columbus, isn't it, June?" His sister nodded, and he continued, "Your mom pulled some stuff off the internet about Camp Chase. It was a Union prison camp, and late in the war, the North and South exchanged some ten thousand sick and wounded prisoners. I guess that's how he got out of Andersonville."

"Something must have drawn him to Indiana instead of back South," said Jake. "Isn't there anything in the old family records about him?"

"Not that we've found so far," said Madeline. "But Steve's like a terrier after a rat when it comes to a secret. We'll figure it out eventually."

"Abby, maybe you can help," said her father.

"Oh, I don't know, Dad," she replied. "This is all very interesting, but I wouldn't know where to start."

"I think I know where your dad is headed with this," said Jake. "If your GG3 was from Blount County, maybe we can find out something about the rest of his family. If he wrote home somewhere along the line, maybe we can find out why he never went back to Tennessee. I can help you look, Abby."

"Well, if you don't mind—legal research I can do, but I'm afraid this family-tree stuff is all Greek to me."

"No problem. Once you get started, it's really not too difficult," said Jake. Turning back to Steve, he asked, "Do you know where in Blount County he came from?"

"No, sorry. The records only give the county of residence."

"We'll start with Maryville. There just aren't that many towns in the county. If there are Cutters around, we'll find them."

"I'm sorry to interrupt all this family stuff," said Amanda, "but the Bowl games are about to start. Can we dig up GG3 later?"

The next morning, Abby and Jake headed home after a prolonged leave-taking. Aunt June insisted on cooking a huge country breakfast and packing enough "lunch" to feed a small army. "You never know when you'll be hungry. This way, you won't have to stop as often," she said when Abby exclaimed that there was way too much food for the two of them.

Abby pondered the story of her great-great-great-grandfather as the flat countryside of Indiana turned into the bluegrass hills of Kentucky. What would make a man reared in the mountains want to become a farmer in Indiana? Especially a man the war had left with only one arm. There had to be easier ways to make a living. Jake too seemed lost in thoughts of his own, and the two drove along in companionable silence for several hours.

"Penny for your thoughts," Jake said after a while.

"I'm not sure they're worth that much," said Abby. "I've been mulling over the story of GG3. I guess I've just lived in Tennessee too long, but I still can't figure out why he didn't come home after the war. I wonder what he did before the war. Surely, if he left a sweetheart or wife behind, he would have wanted to get back home. And even if there wasn't a woman, what about the rest of his family?"

"War does strange things to men. It's hard telling. With a little luck, maybe we can find his family. That may prove the key to the whole thing."

"Maybe, but it seems like a long shot to me. And while we're talking about long shots, something else has occurred to me. You don't supposed the *JC* on your grandmother's locket could be Jacob Cutter, do you?"

"Oh, come on now. Finding GG3's family is going to be enough of a challenge. You don't really expect to solve two mysteries at once, do you?"

"I guess it is too much to ask for," Abby replied.

"Seems pretty far-fetched to me. But if I've learned anything about genealogy, it's that people are related in all sorts of bizarre ways, and you never know who your distant cousin will turn out to be."

"Kissin' cousins at that." Abby laughed. "I know I promised Dad to do some digging, but I'm going to be pretty busy when I get back. I hope he doesn't mind waiting until the courts give me a little break."

"I know what you mean. I'd almost managed to forget that I have a full schedule this semester. We'll just have to fit it in when we have time. I'm going to try to get the rest of the letters and journals I have sorted out this week before I have to put it aside and earn my keep."

Chapter 19

As she predicted, Abby found a stack of new cases awaiting her attention when she returned to her office. Fortunately, most of them were pretty run-of-the-mill breaking and entering and other petty crimes, and she was relieved not to have to face any new homicides so early in the new year. Perhaps the worst of the lot involved a gang of inventive thieves who managed to rip off a dozen or so Salvation Army bell ringers before being captured.

Their plan was simple: dressed in Santa garb, a gang member would appear at a busy donation site and claim that he had been sent from to headquarters to relieve the weary ringer. Instead of returning the bucket of money to the Salvation Army at the end of the shift, he met up with his cronies to divide the loot. By selecting posts near the upscale department stores and boutiques, the gang managed to net several thousand dollars. The plan was to hit multiple sites all on the same day and then move to another town. However, one of the gang members decided to go back for a second try and was captured by an undercover officer. Proving the adage about no honor among thieves, he quickly made a deal, and the police managed to round up all but one of his cronies before they left town.

As Abby related the case to Jake over dinner, he shook his head in disbelief. "Man, how low can you get?"

"I know," said Abby. "I guess it could have been worse. They could have dressed up as Santa and robbed the kiddies."

"How do you deal with these guys, Doc? Doesn't it ever get to you?"

"Most of the time, no. The only ones that really bother me are the Bobby Davidsons and the repeaters."

"Bobby, I understand. What a waste. But what do you mean repeaters?"

"Repeat offenders. Sometimes I find myself prosecuting someone who should still be in jail for a previous crime. When I see too many of them in a row, I get to wondering what I'm doing."

"So why do it, Ab? You don't have to, you know. I mean it's not as if you don't have any other options."

"Okay, who have you been talking to—George or my mother?"

"Both, actually, but that has nothing to do with it. I know I haven't known you all that long, but are you really happy doing what you do?"

"Happy enough. Believe it or not, I'm very good at what I do."

"In my experience, you're good at nearly everything you do," Jake said with a wicked grin.

"By that *nearly* everything, I take it you don't appreciate my gourmet cooking," she replied, looking across table littered with Chinese takeout containers. "Somebody's got to do it, and besides, I've been out of medicine too long."

"How do you know? Have you ever looked into it? You've got your license, and you've put in lots of hours at that clinic, for cryin' out loud. Surely they wouldn't make you start all over again."

"I'm happy enough with my life. Why should I give it up?"

"Right. And I suppose the lure of working with hardened criminals and the big bucks that you make are just too much to give up," he said, looking around her tidy but far-from-luxurious apartment

"Look, can we just not talk about this? I like what I do. Can't you just accept that?"

But her words had a hollow ring, even in her own ears. Jake let the subject drop, but Abby suspected that it would not be the last time they had this conversation. How had he managed to read her so quickly?

On Sunday, they decided to drive up to the cove. Life was about to get hectic again for both of them. Jake was due back in the office on Monday, and in addition to the new files on her desk, Abby had a number of trials scheduled for January. There was no snow in town, but a quick call to George told them to wear their boots and heavy coats if they planned to do any hiking. The roads were open, but still icy, he warned. "I just put a big pot of stew on. Stop by and join me for supper on your way back," he said as they rang off.

A crystalline world of ice and snow greeted them when they entered the cove. A brief ice storm had preceded the snow. Instead of a landscape made soft by a blanket of snow, they found one that appeared larger than life. Each limb, branch, and twig was coated with a quarter-inch layer of ice that worked as a magnifying glass and to make them appear larger than they were. The bright sun beaming down on them made the trees sparkle as if encrusted with diamonds instead of ice. Although the loop road was closed, it was well tracked, and it was obvious that the park rangers had been making routine rounds. Although they saw no signs of life as they walked, the patch-work designs of the game trails across the open fields made it obvious that many of the cove's inhabitants remained active in spite of the harsh weather. The deep and distinct paths left by foraging deer and the shallower tracks of rabbits told Abby and Jake that they were not alone. Here and there, they saw signs that mice and other tiny critters had ventured out in search of food as well. In one spot, tufts of hair and a few drops of blood told the story of a hunter becoming the prey. Looking for food in the snow was a risky endeavor for mice and rabbits. Barred owls and red-tailed hawks were always on the lookout for a tasty morsel.

For the most part, they walked without talking, simply delight-ing in the beauty of the day. As they strolled along, Abby realized that it had been a long time since she had enjoyed hiking with anyone this much. Most people felt the need to fill the silence with idle chatter rather than merely savoring the moment. When they were children, Steven's competitive spirit kept him from being a good hiking com-panion. While Abby always wanted to investigate each leaf and rock along the trail, her older brother was more interested in seeing how fast he could reach the summit. But as he grew older, he learned to appreciate walking for its own sake, and their hikes became times for sharing rather than rivalry. Since his death, most of her hikes had been solitary affairs, and she was inordinately pleased that Jake seemed content just to share the experience.

She sighed a deep sigh, and Jake said, "That sounds serious. What's on your mind?"

"Just taking it all in," she replied.

"I know what you mean," he said, and as they lapsed back into a comfortable silence, she smiled to herself.

True to his word, George had a hearty supper of beef stew and corn bread waiting when they arrived at his cabin several hours later. As they warmed themselves in front of the fireplace, George asked, "Well, how did he do, Abby?"

"Fine," she replied with a wink.

"Am I missing something here?" Jake asked.

"Abby here is pretty picky about who she hikes with. She threw the last man she went hiking with in the creek because he couldn't keep his mouth shut," George said. "Seein's how you look no less for the wear, I'd say you passed, muster."

"Now, George"—she laughed—"you know perfectly well he managed to fall in the creek all on his own. I had nothing to do with. I must admit, though, the thought did cross my mind a time or two that day."

"I didn't realize it was a test," Jake said.

"I wouldn't exactly call it a test," said Abby. "But for what it's worth, you passed with flying colors. I guess I'll just have to keep you."

Pulling her close for a quick kiss, he replied, "That's good because I was just thinking the same thing."

George turned toward the kitchen with a knowing smile.

1862

    It came as a surprise to Abigail that she awoke at all the following morning. The conversation she overheard in the middle of the night hit her more forcefully than any physical blow her captors could have delivered. When she finally fell into a troubled sleep around dawn, she was quite certain that the sun would not rise again. Jacob was dead, and all hope of rescue was gone. But as the sun filtered down on her through the trees, she felt the baby stir and realized that even if Jacob was lost to her, there remained a part of him living within her. She silently promised him that no harm would come to his baby and arose to face another day.

    Secure in the knowledge that no one would be following them, Josh slowed their pace. They turned first north then again south and seemed to be heading no place in particular. Leaving Luke to guard Abigail, Josh and Matt raided several remote farms, returning with more horses and foodstuffs. In addition to grain and other staples, their last incursion netted a stash of corn liquor. When they made camp the following evening, Josh broke out the jug, and he and Matt were soon well into their cups.

    Abigail awoke to the feel of rough hands. "Come on, gal," Josh said as he pulled her to her feet. "Time you and me got better acquainted. You're a right purty little thang. Been wonderin' what you might look like under all them clothes."

    Abigail clutched her blanket as a meager shield. Thus far, the men had been content to use her simply as servant to cook and carry water for them. Aside from making sure that her feet and hands were tightly bound before they retired to their bedrolls, they ignored her. Luke alone was kind to her, seeming almost apologetic in his manner and surreptitiously helping her with her chores whenever possible. She looked around the camp for a means of escape. Her gaze fell on Matt, who returned it with the look of a scavenger waiting his turn at the kill. Luke stood to one side, looking pained but uncertain. Turning to him, she found her voice, "Please help me. Don't let them do this to me."

    "Come on, Josh, have another drink and leave her be," said Luke. "We're already in enough trouble if the law catches up to us."

"Whut law? They ain't caught us yit, so I ain't skeered." Then peering at the younger man, Josh asked, "What you been up to while we was gone, little brother? You ain't taken a shine to this gal, have you?" As he shoved Abigail away from the firelight, he added, "Mebbe when I git done with her—"

As Luke grabbed the larger man's arm, he didn't see Matt coming up behind him. He heard Abigail's scream, and then everything went black. When he came to sometime later, he saw Matt reenter, retying the length of rope he used as a belt.

"Yore turn, boy." Josh laughed. Fingering the scratches on the side of his face, he added, "Be keerful. Fights like a cougar, that one."

"Yeah," said Matt. "But she's quiet now. Wimmen's like horses. Gotta show 'em who's boss."

Luke found Abigail some distance from the camp. From the looks of her, Josh and Matt had not taken her easily. As he came near, she struggled to cover herself with the tattered remnants of her dress. "Please, not you too," she whispered as he removed his coat.

"Shh, quiet," he said as he placed it around her shoulders. "I'm not going to hurt you, I promise. I didn't mean for any of this to happen. We were just supposed to steal some horses and supplies."

She whimpered as he moved to touch her.

"Hush now. Let me take a look at you."

Wetting a piece of her dress with water from his canteen, he cleaned the blood from the side of her mouth. Then he soaked the cloth with the cool water again and placed it carefully on the darkening bruise under her left eye. Abigail sat mute as he tended to her, afraid to trust him in spite of the gentleness of his touch.

"What's going to happen to me now?" she finally asked.

"Are you hurt anywhere else?" he asked. "Do you think you can ride?"

"What do you mean?"

"I mean that I'm going to get you out of here if I can. Josh and Matt will drink themselves to sleep in a little while, and if you're able, I think I know a place where we'll be safe 'til I can figure out what to do."

Abigail didn't know whether to trust him or not, but she was pretty certain of her fate if she remained with the other two men. Luke was offering her some form of escape even if she was not sure of his motives. "I'll try. Where are we going?"

"You let me worry about that. We'll leave as soon as the others are asleep. For now, though, we've got to go back, or they'll get suspicious. Trust me?"

"You're my only hope," Abigail replied.

When they reentered the clearing, Josh noted Luke's coat wrapped around Abigail's shoulders. "Well, now, ain't you the gen'leman?" he sneered. "Ain't coverin' nothin' we ain't seen. Com'ere, gal, and have a drink. Bet yore thirsty."

"Leave her be, Josh," Luke said.

Something in his tone brought the older man up short. He started to his feet, but his whiskey-soaked limbs would not respond. "Deal with you in the mornin'," he muttered. "Tie her up good 'fore you go to sleep."

When Josh and Matt drifted off into a drunken slumber, Luke made ready for their escape. He moved two horses away from camp and packed their saddlebags with food and water for the journey. Returning to the remaining horses, he untied their reins and left them to wander at will. Shortly after moonrise, Luke roused Abigail from her uneasy sleep. His hand over her mouth kept her from crying out in fear.

"It's Luke," he whispered. "I've got the horses ready. Still think you can ride?"

Abigail nodded, and he helped her to her feet. As she started to her feet, her body was wrenched in a spasm of pain. Clutching her abdomen, she gasped. "The baby." And sank to her knees.

Luke caught her as she fell unconscious into his arms. He hesitated; he hadn't planned on this. It was a hard ride to reach their destination, and he wasn't even sure he'd be able to find the place again. But looking at the two sleeping forms on the ground, Luke knew there was no other choice. His knowledge of women and babies was minimal, but he knew that reaching the medicine woman was her only chance. He could only hope that his memory was true. Lifting Abigail's limp body, he carried her to where their horses were tethered. As he stood there pondering how to get her on the horse, Abigail came to.

"What happened?" she asked.

"You fainted. Are you sure you can ride? What about the baby?"

"The baby's not supposed to come until Christmas. I think I can manage if you'll help me up."

Luke was skeptical but helped her into the saddle, and they rode off. When the pale light of dawn replaced the moon's light, Luke stopped to rest the horses and check on Abigail. She climbed unsteadily down from her horse and promptly fainted again. Luke knelt and touched her cheek. She was burning up. He doused her face with water from the canteen, but she didn't stir. With any luck, the liquor they had consumed would make Josh and Matt sleep beyond sunrise, but Luke knew they needed to put more miles between them.

Leaving Abigail where she lay, Luke quickly cut some sturdy saplings and set about cutting off their branches. He then used ropes and blankets to fashion a makeshift bed between the poles. When he was finished, he tied the travois to Abigail's horse. As he laid her gently on the blankets, he realized she was bleeding. She stirred briefly and mumbled a single word, Jacob, *before lapsing back into unconsciousness. Riding as quickly as the travois would allow, Luke prayed that they would make it to the settlement in time. When they stopped to rest the horses, he tried to rouse Abigail and get her to swallow some water. She spoke a few times, but her words made no sense and didn't seem to be directed at Luke. The sun was dropping low over the mountains when they entered the small settlement the following evening. A dozen copper-colored faces stared back at the young white man and even whiter woman lying on the travois. A tall white-haired man clad in the traditional dress of a Cherokee elder came out of his cabin and stared in disbelief.*

"Grandfather…E-do-di," Luke said. "I've come home."

Abigail awoke as she was being handed down into the arms of two Indian women. Weak with pain and fever, she thought she was dreaming and simply closed her eyes again. They carried her to the lodge of the medicine woman and left her to the old woman's keeping.

"Will she live, Grandmother?" Luke asked.

"You know that's not for me to say, young one. Now go and get some food and let me tend to your woman. How far gone is she?"

"I don't know. This is not my woman."

Shaking her head in disapproval, the old woman turned back to her patient and left Luke to face his grandfather.

"What have you done?" the old man asked as Luke sat next to him as the evening gave way to night. "Why have you come back to us after all these years?"

Under his grandfather's steady gaze, Luke felt his face flush with shame.

In the early 1830s, Luke's Cherokee grandfather, Koo-le-cheh, owned a small but prosperous farm in Northern Georgia. His land adjoined that of a white farmer by the name of Bartlett. Their children played together and attended the same one-room school nearby. After the removal of the Choctaws, Chickasaws, Creeks, and Seminoles from their ancestral lands, the United States government turned its attention to the Cherokees.

"Koo-le-cheh and some others are not going with the government agents," James Bartlett told his father.

"Too bad. I had hoped the government would tire of this effort before it reached our Cherokee neighbors."

"I'm going with them, Father. Mary and I want to be married, and Koo-le-cheh has granted me permission."

"Are you sure about this, son? If you're caught, the army will treat you as one of them. You'll be sent to the Territories too, or worse, put in prison."

"I know. But my mind is made up. We leave for North Carolina tomorrow."

The settlement was remote, and any whites that knew of the Cherokees' presence apparently didn't mind and left them in peace. James and Mary remained with her family for a number of years. The land was poor, but they managed to eke out a living. Shortly before the birth of their first child and wanting a better life for this child and those to come after, they acquired a small piece of land on Wolf Mountain.

The land, while somewhat better than that around the settlement, was still poor, and life was hard. After Josh, there were three other babies, but they were all stillborn. When her son was nearly ten, Mary found she was pregnant again and prayed that this time she would carry the child to term. Luke was a healthy baby, but his delivery was difficult.

"I'm not well, James," Mary told her husband. "You have too much to do with the farm to tend to me and the baby. Let me go back to the settlement for a while."

"What about Josh?"

"Josh will be fine here with you. He already helps me with some of the chores, so he'll be a help to you."

James had little time to tend to a newborn, so he agreed.

Koo-le-cheh was pleased at the sight of his daughter and her infant son, but his joy was short-lived. Mary was sicker than even she realized, and she died when Luke was six weeks old. Koo-le-cheh sent word of Mary's death to James, fully expecting his son-in-law to return to collect his infant son. But the messenger returned with a letter back, asking if his Luke could remain in the settlement for the time being.

"The time being" of James's letter turned to months and then to years with no further word to indicate that he remembered his son. But Luke thrived among his mother's people, and although Koo-le-cheh told him about his white father, the boy had little time to think about his absentee parent. He was a happy child and an apt student, who learned to speak both Cherokee and English at his grandfather's knee. Koo-le-cheh also taught him to hunt and fish, as well as how to coax vegetables out of the rocky soil of their mountain village. The years went by, and Luke gradually forgot that he had family outside the settlement.

When James suddenly reappeared to take him back to the farm, ten-year-old Luke was puzzled and hurt.

"Why do I have to leave, E-do-di [Grandfather]?"

"This is your father. Remember I told you how he brought you and your mother to us when you were just a baby?"

"But he is a white man. How can he be my father?"

"Many years ago, people from our village lived far away where the Cherokee and the white men lived as friends. Your father's people were our neighbors, and your mother and father decided to come here to live instead of being moved to the Indian Territory."

"It will be all right, son. You have a new mother and baby sister waiting back on the farm," James said.

Luke went hesitantly with the strange man. "I'll be back soon, grandfather," he promised as he turned to go.

That was eleven years ago. Since then, Luke had only been back to visit one time, and that was the summer after his return to his father's home. When he returned in the autumn tanned to a copper brown from a summer spent in the sun, the boys at school called him a filthy redskin and teased him about his Indian blood. Luke suffered a number of blackened eyes and bloody noses that year, but he gave as many as he received. By the end of the year, he'd made an uneasy peace with his tormentors. When his father told him he must remain on the farm the following summer, Luke was relieved not to have to choose between his two families.

"It's been a long time, Grandfather. Can I tell you in English?" Luke asked.

The old man frowned but nodded. Luke told him of the white man's war and how he had come to return to the settlement with another man's pregnant wife.

Chapter 20

IT HAD BEEN A BAD week. By Wednesday, Abby was beginning to believe that every petty criminal in the county had resolved to pick more pockets, sell more dope, or mug more old ladies in the new year. By Friday, she was convinced of it. The good news was that in spite of their resolve, the criminals didn't seem to be improving at their chosen vocation. More and more of them were being arrested on a daily basis. The bad news, at least from Abby's perspective, was that the pile of files on her desk was growing alarmingly. Barely a month into the year, and there was already a backlog of cases. To make matters worse, a lot of them were repeaters.

She hadn't seen Jake in nearly two weeks. The first few 5:30 p.m. calls to cancel their dinner date had been accepted with little grumbling, but after a week, he began to get testy.

"Working late again?" he said in lieu of hello.

"Sorry, I really thought I was going to get away on time tonight."

"Gee, where have I heard that line before?"

"Sorry, but I warned you going in that it could get like this."

"I know, it's just that—"

"What, you wish that I was a doctor? What makes you think that would make my hours any better?"

"I wasn't going to say that," he said. "But the thought had crossed my mind," he muttered under his breath.

"Well, I'm not a doctor. I'm a prosecuting attorney, and lousy hours go with the territory. If you can't live with that, maybe we'd better just call it quits right now."

Abigail heard his sharp intake of breath and then, "Look, Ab, I'm sorry. I guess I was just feeling a little neglected and sorry for myself. I know you're tired, and I didn't mean to bug you."

"Apology accepted. I'm sorry too. We've got another batch of repeaters on top of everything else, and that always makes me cranky."

"Poor baby. Do you think you might get that pile on your desk whittled down by next Tuesday?"

"No promises, but I'll try. What did you have in mind?"

'You let me worry about that. Just make sure you're home by six o'clock sharp."

"Yes, sir. I'll do my best, sir."

"See that you do. Now get back to work so you get home at a decent hour. Call me when you get in so I know the gypsies didn't carry you off."

"You're worse than my mother." She laughed. "I'll call you later, and hey, in case I haven't told you today, I love you."

Determined not to ruin whatever surprise Jake was cooking up, Abby took home a briefcase full of papers over the weekend; and by Tuesday, the stack of new cases on her desk was beginning to dwindle. By five o'clock sharp, she had her briefcase in hand and was on her way out the door.

"I'm going home to a long bubble bath and a date with my fella," she told Sandra on her way out the door.

"In that order?" Sandra teased.

"Now that you mention it...," Abby replied. She paused as Sandra reached for the ringing telephone.

"District Attorney's office. May I help you? No, I'm sorry, Ms. Edwards has already left for the day." Waving Abby out the door, she continued, "Would you like to leave a message?"

Looking at her watch, Abby sighed and said, "It's okay. I'll take it."

"Abby, this is Tom Madison. Glad I caught you. We've got a homicide. Can I come over and show you what we've got? I'd like to get some warrants this evening if possible."

Making a face at Sandra, she said, "Sure, Tom. See you in a few minutes." But as she slammed the phone back in its cradle, she said, "Damn. If I don't get home on time, Jake will never forgive me. Find out who's on warrants this week for me, will you?"

Madison arrived a few minutes later, and they went into Abby's office. Instead of coming in with the usual courthouse gossip, the detective got straight to the point. "We think Jess Adler is back in town," he said, tossing a file of crime-scene photos down on her desk.

"Adler? I can't place the name, but it sounds familiar. What case was it?"

"That's right. I guess it was before your time. I forget sometimes what a young squirt you are," he said. His teasing manner quickly faded as he continued, "The victim was a thirteen-year-old girl by the name of Michaels."

"Not Kerry Michaels?" Abby asked.

"Yeah, that's right. I thought this was before your time. Maybe I've got my years mixed up."

"No, you're right. I assisted with her autopsy when I was with the coroner's office. It was my first torture case, really ugly. She's one of the reasons I became a prosecutor. But I thought he'd been committed to the state hospital for life?"

"Yeah, he was up until a few months ago, but can you believe it, they let him out? He convinced the doctors he was 'no longer a threat to himself or others.' Probably met some sweet young resident and convinced her to sign off on his discharge orders. Anyway, he's been living in a halfway house run by the state."

"But what makes you so sure he's responsible for this one?" Abby said as she opened the file. "Never mind, I see what you mean," she continued as she flipped through the photographs. The ligature marks and neat rows of cigarette burns were identical to those Abby had seen on Kerry Michaels, and that haunted her for months thereafter. "So what do we have for the judge?"

"The girl disappeared on the way home from school. The school is about three blocks from the halfway house."

"That's not much to go on. Do you have anything to tie the girl's disappearance to Adler?"

"Not exactly, but her body was dumped on an empty lot within a half a mile of where we found the Michaels girl. And then of course, there's these," he said, pointing to the photographs. "Adler's old man used to run a store in that neighborhood, so Jess grew up there and knows the area like the back of his hand. The store and most of the surrounding buildings are empty now. The neighborhood kids report seeing lights in the old store the last few nights, but we haven't turned anything up yet. The CSU boys are still there."

But Abby remained skeptical. "I see your point," she said. "But it's still all circumstantial. Have you talked to the people that run the halfway house? What about Adler? Have you spoken to him yet? Come in," she said at the sound of a knock.

Madison's partner, Rick Lewis, entered, looking every bit as grim as the older man.

"CSU's done," he said as he took a seat and ran his hand through his mop of sandy hair.

"And?" Abby and the older detective said in unison.

"Not much. It looks like someone's been in the old store, but we couldn't find any anything. If he did her there, he was awfully tidy about it. The ME says that she wasn't killed where she was found, but it's rained the past two nights, and he's not too hopeful about finding any fiber evidence."

"So back to my questions," said Abby. "What exactly do we know?"

For the next hour or so, they reviewed everything they knew about Jess Adler. In the end, Abby wasn't convinced they had enough to get a warrant to search his room at the halfway house. The people who ran the place reported that Adler was a model resident. He returned promptly each afternoon when his shift at the bakery was over and participated in the group therapy sessions that they held each evening. The detectives planned to be waiting for him when he returned the following afternoon.

"Okay, then," said Madison. "We'll give you a call tomorrow. Sorry we kept you so late."

"Oh no! What time is it?" Abby asked. "I was supposed to be somewhere at six o'clock, and I completely forgot. I'll talk to you guys tomorrow. Right now I have to make a call." She looked at her watch—seven-thirty. Jake would be furious. Abby dialed her home phone number, but there was no answer. Next she tried Jake's apartment; again, with no response. Shaking her head, she picked up her briefcase and headed home.

"Jake, are you here?" she called as she entered her apartment. His car wasn't in its usual spot, so she wasn't surprised when he wasn't there. The table had been set for dinner, and the disconsolate remains of two red candles drooped over the rims of their holders. Abby followed the lingering aroma of garlic and tomatoes in the air and found what had probably been an excellent dinner in her trash can. She kicked off her shoes and wandered into the bedroom. There she found a dozen heart-shaped balloons floating above her bed. Valentine's Day. It had been so long since she had a reason to remember the holiday; the date hadn't even registered until now. On the nightstand by the bed, she found a tiny black velvet box. It was empty. The note beneath it said simply, "I guess you just aren't ready for this."

Abby plopped down on the sofa. *I've done it now*, she thought. She dialed Jake's number again. Still no answer. Retrieving her shoes from the living-room floor, she grabbed her purse and headed out the door. The shades were closed in the upstairs apartment, but the lights were on. Jake didn't respond to her first knock, but when she knocked a second time and rattled the doorknob, he finally opened the door but didn't invite her in.

Shivering in the cold February dark, Abby said, "You're mad, and you have every right to be. I screwed up. I am so sorry. Can we talk about it?"

"You're right. Ever hear of a little device called a telephone? It's the latest in technology and really easy to use."

"I know, and I'm sorry. A homicide case came in just as I was leaving. Look, it's cold out here. Can I come in so we can talk?"

"Not tonight. It's late, and I'm tired. I don't want to say anything I might regret." With that, Abby found herself alone on the porch.

Chapter 21

ABBY STOOD THERE A MOMENT, not knowing whether to stay and fight or just leave it be for a while. In the end, she turned around and drove home. Jake's anger was evident by the pile of dishes he left in her sink, and she filled it with water and started cleaning the kitchen while thoughts swirled in her mind. On the one hand, she felt righteously indignant. She had a responsibility to the people of Knox County. She had never shirked that duty and wasn't about to start now. Jake knew what she did for a living, and sometimes her time was not her own—he should have been more understanding. The kitchen cleaned and her mind still in turmoil, she tackled all the other chores that she truly detested. By midnight, the grout in her bathroom was white as snow, and her closets had been completely rearranged and decluttered. Abby's sense of indignity began to fade with her energy, and as she readied herself for bed, another part of her brain heard a little voice telling her that maybe she had forgotten their date on purpose. Maybe, it said, you're trying to make him run.

She dismissed that thought from her mind as she turned down the covers and turned out the light. Two hours later, she was still staring at the ceiling, and the little voice was getting louder and louder. *How absurd*, she thought. *I love Jake. I would never do anything to hurt him. He just doesn't understand.* In exasperation, she threw off the covers, grabbed a pillow, and headed for the living room. She pulled an old John Wayne movie off the shelf, popped it into the DVD player, and settled down on the couch. Watching old Westerns always calmed her. Her conscious mind focused on the simple plot while her subconscious worked away in the background on whatever was troubling her. Sometimes by the end of the movie, she knew what she was going to do about the problem without knowing quite how she arrived at her conclusion. She drifted off to sleep as the Duke found himself falling in love with a beautiful Quaker girl.

"Coming. Just a minute," Abby called as she snatched the afghan around her and headed for the door. *Jake! Finally he's come to his senses*, she thought as she swung open the door. There stood Steven.

"Wha…what are you doing here?" she asked. "You're dead."

"Of course, I'm dead," he replied. "And you will be too if you don't close that door. Besides," he continued, "I might ask you the same thing. What are *you* doing here?"

"I live here."

"That's not what I mean, and you know it."

"What, Steven? I hate it when you get that attitude and act like I'm six again."

"You shouldn't be here, Doc. Or should I say, *Counselor*? And by the way, why is that? I thought we agreed that you were going back to finish your residency."

"I found something else, that's all."

"I know why you started, Doc, but why are you still doing it? You're not happy."

"Yes, I am. And besides, I'm good at what I do."

"I know you are, but happy? I don't think so. When was the last time you got the same kick out of convicting some petty thug that you got out of making a difficult diagnosis?" Steven held up his hand as she started to protest. "And don't try to tell me that working in that crappy little clinic once a month fulfills that need. A few sutures here and there and giving a bunch of flu vaccine just isn't the same."

"You're comparing apples to oranges, Steven. I like being a prosecutor. It's just different, that's all."

"Doesn't wash. I seem to recall a midnight phone call the first time you pushed on somebody's belly and realized that there was a liver in there and that you knew what it was. I've never heard anyone so excited about a liver. You had a fire back then that I just don't see in your eyes anymore. And again, you shouldn't be here."

"Now what do you mean?"

"Jake. You love him, don't you? So why are you pushing him away?"

141

"I do love him, and I'm not pushing him away. He just doesn't understand."

"Don't give me that—I saw you. You started to pick up the phone and call him and then didn't. You did it on purpose."

"You sure have a lot of nerve. What about Cheryl Ann? You can't tell me you didn't love her, so why didn't you marry her when you had the chance?"

"Yeah, well, so I was too involved in being a jet jockey that I didn't see what I was throwing away until it was too late. I just don't want to see you make the same mistake. You were doing so good there for a while, but now you're just trying to provoke him into a fight. Jake loves you. Let him. Quit throwing up barriers."

"But—"

"No buts, just do it. And as to your career, you have a gift, Doc. Don't waste it. Don't be afraid to take a chance just because it might not be the most sensible thing. Do what feels right in your heart. Don't worry about the details. They'll take care of themselves."

"It's not as simple as all that. And what makes you so smart? You couldn't even keep from getting shot down."

"Jeez, one little mistake. And it *is* that simple. Just do it. I've got to go, and you've got fences to mend. By the way, GG3 says thanks for finding Abigail."

"But I haven't found Abigail. Steven, what are you talking about?"

"Ask Jake."

"Jake? What's Jake got to do with it? What do you mean?"

"That's for you and Jake to figure out."

Abby awoke with a start. The room was empty, and the DVD player was making its end-of-program noises. "Steven?" she called, still not quite sure it had all been a dream. Usually, her dreams of Steven were reflections of childhood memories, not conversations in the present. As she sat there pondering the dreamed conversation, she heard a knock. *Oh no, not again*, she thought. *Well, I'm just not answering it this time.*

A second knock, a little louder this time. "Abby? Are you there? It's Jake. Can we talk?"

She answered the door with some hesitation, and when she saw Jake standing there she was still not certain whether to believe her eyes. As he reached to take her into his embrace, she pinched him hard on the arm.

"Ow! What the...? Abby, what's the matter with you? I come all the way over here in the middle of the night, and all you can do is pinch me."

"I'm sorry, Jake. I just had to be sure I wasn't still dreaming."

"I thought you were supposed to pinch *yourself* to make sure you weren't dreaming—not someone else."

"I know, I know. But I just had the strangest conversation with my brother, and I just had to make sure that you were really you."

"What are you talking about?"

"Never mind about that right now. What are you doing here?"

"Can I come in? It's really cold out here."

Abby started to tell him it served him right for leaving her in the cold earlier, but she held her tongue. Moving into the living room, she stirred the embers in the fireplace and added a log. When she had a fire going, she joined Jake on the couch.

"I came to apologize. I was pretty rough on you tonight. I had this romantic Valentine's dinner planned, and being stood up really ticked me off."

"It was mean leaving me there on the porch, but I suppose I deserved it. I really am sorry. It's been crazy at work that I didn't even remember what day it was until I saw the balloons. I know I should have called."

"Why didn't you?"

"I don't know exactly. I got a call from a couple of detectives just as I was leaving—right on time actually—and then time got away from me. At least that was my excuse when I came to see you. But now I'm not so sure. Steven says I did it on purpose."

Jake looked at her quizzically, and she continued, "I couldn't sleep and came out here to watch a movie. I fell asleep and dreamed about Steven. At least I hope it was a dream. I'm not ready for Steven as a ghost. Anyway, he has this theory that I'm afraid to let you get too close. That I'm afraid you'll mess up my well-ordered little world and make me think about things that I'd really rather leave alone."

"Was he right? Did you do it on purpose?"

"I honestly don't know. Maybe I did. I'm confused about so many things right now. My job, my future, you name it."

"Am I one of those things?"

"Actually, no. The only thing I'm really sure about right now is that I love you. And no offense, but that scares the hell out of me."

"If you can only be sure of one thing, that one gets my vote. I was afraid you'd changed your mind. You've been so distant these past few weeks."

"I'm not used to feeling conflicted about things. When I decided to go to law school, I went at it full bore and without a backward glance. Maybe part of it was Steven's death. He was so insistent that I finish my residency. Maybe I was trying to get back at him for dying by doing something else. How twisted is that?"

"Oh, I don't know. Grief can make you do some really strange things."

Abby was silent for a few moments, and then with a shake of her head she went on, "Maybe I'm just burned out and looking for someone to blame it on. Or it's just a case of the grass being greener. Working at the clinic is fine, but how do I know I'd be any good at it full-time?"

"You don't know, but if you're not happy now, maybe it's time to consider a change."

"You make it all sound so simple. What if they want me to start all over? I'm not sure I'm ready for that. Besides, I can be a major pain in the butt when I'm distracted, as you may have noticed. And I get really distracted when I'm studying."

"A pain? You? I can't believe it. Anyway, I can handle it. I deal with students all day, remember? You need to do whatever makes you happy. If going back to medicine is it, just do it. We'll muddle through somehow."

"I like the sound of that."

"What?"

"*We.* I think maybe I could get used to that."

Drawing her into his arms, Jake just smiled. They talked on for a while about inconsequential things, and as they snuggled there on the sofa, Abby felt more at peace than she had in months. Dawn was beginning to tint the winter sky a pale pink when they finally retired to the bedroom. As she was drifting off, Abby thought about Steven's cryptic comment about GG3 and Abigail, but the memory was quickly lost in the mists of sleep.

1862

Head down and eyes on the ground, Luke told the old man about growing into manhood in his father's world. Gaining acceptance had not been easy. Even Josh, who had somehow inherited his father's blue eyes and fair complexion, joined the other boys who tormented him. The only time he dared to remind his older brother of their shared Cherokee blood, he received a sound thrashing. At eighteen, still seeking the acceptance of his brother and the other young men his own age, Luke joined the local militia organized to fight the Yankees. He watched in dismay as the group degenerated into little more than a roving band of thieves. Although some of the arms and ammunition they took finally made its way to the Confederate Army, much of their plunder was cached away in the barns and storehouses of the leaders. Luke feared reprisal from Josh more than he did the militia, so he continued to ride with them.

He finished his story with the raid on Cades Cove and his escape with Abigail while Josh and Matt lay in a drunken stupor. The old man was silent for a time. There was no sound except for the snap and pop of the logs on the hearth. Finally he spoke, "They will follow you."

Luke pondered the statement. Or was it a question? He couldn't tell from his grandfather's tone. "No, Grandfather. I don't believe they will. Josh isn't much of a tracker and besides…," he faltered. "Besides, I reckon they were pretty much finished with her."

"And what will you do with the woman now?"

"Stay here until she's well enough to ride. Matt killed her husband, but she told me her people live somewhere in Virginia. I'll take her back to them, I guess."

The two men looked up as the medicine woman entered the cabin.

"How is she, Grandmother?" Luke asked.

The old woman was really his grandfather's sister, but Luke had always called her by the term of respect used for any female elder.

The old woman gazed at him in stony silence for a time before she replied, "The woman will live, I think. Her spirit is strong. But the baby…" She shook her head. "What did you do to her?"

"Not me, Grandmother. My brother. But I should have done something to stop them. I didn't know about the baby until…after. Can I see her?"

"She sleeps. It may be many days before she wakes. I will tell you when."

Fever wracked her body, and it was nearly two weeks before Abigail awoke. For days she wandered through some crazy place between darkness and light, a jumbled world of past and present, reality and dreams. One minute, she would be sitting on the front porch of their cabin with Jacob and their baby; and in the next instant, her mind was filled with the rough hands and foul breath of a big man who tore her clothes and pinned her to the ground. Somewhere in between, she was aware of an old woman who seemed to be caring for her, forcing her to drink warm broth and a vile-tasting brew. At first Abigail thought it was the granny woman who tended the sick and delivered babies back in the cove, but this woman spoke in a strange tongue and wore odd clothing. Occasionally it occurred to her to ask the woman who she was, but then the fear and pain would surface, and she was content to let the darkness overtake her again.

One day she simply woke up. The sun was shining through the open door. Without knowing quite how she got there, Abigail found herself watching the slow progress of a spider as it worked its web in the corner of the doorframe. An old woman dozed in a chair by the hearth where a large iron pot bubbled and hissed. As she struggled to sit up, the woman woke and came to her bedside. Laying a cool hand on Abigail's forehead, the old woman smiled and muttered something unintelligible. Abigail's puzzled expression made her smile again, but when she spoke again, Abigail understood her words. "Good. You are awake. No fever."

Crossing to the doorway, she called out to someone and was joined by two men. The older man had long white hair and wore strange clothing like the woman. He came to her bed, touched her head, smiled, and nodded. A young man who looked vaguely familiar hung back with a hangdog expression.

"Where am I?" Abigail asked.

"In the village of my grandfather," Luke replied.

"But who are you? How did I get here?"

Luke shot a worried glance at the medicine woman. "Time for talk later. Now you need food."

Shooing the two men out of the cabin, she prepared a meal of rich venison stew and bread for Abigail. "Eat," she said. "The meat will help you gain strength. Then you will rest again. We will talk later."

Abigail wanted to argue. Her mind was filled with a million questions, but suddenly she was very hungry. The stew was delicious, and the bread was still warm from the oven. When she had finished every morsel, the old woman returned with a cup of strange-tasting tea. "Drink this and then sleep."

"Please, who are you?"

"My English name is Charlotte. Luke is the grandson of my brother. He brought you here after…"

"After what?

"Your questions can wait. Sleep now. You are safe here."

What does she mean by that? *Abigail wondered. But it was just too much trouble to ask. The pattern of waking, eating, and sleeping was repeated several times over the next two days. Each time she tried to ask questions, "later" was all that she got in return. On the third day, Charlotte helped her bathe and dress and make her way to the front porch, where the young man joined her.*

"Feeling better?" he asked.

"Better," she replied, "but still confused. Where am I, and who are you?"

"I'm Luke," he said. "Luke Bartlett. Don't you remember me?"

Abigail looked at him. Somewhere in her mind, there was a spark of recognition. Then she remembered. "You're one of the men who came to my cabin, aren't you?"

Luke could no longer look her in the eye. "That's right. I am so sorry for everything that happened. I never meant for anyone to get hurt. Your husband, the baby…I'm sorry."

"What are you talking about?" she asked. "I'm not married."

Luke stared at her in confusion. The old woman who had been sitting silently next to Abigail during this conversation stood and said, "Enough talk for today." With that, she bustled the protesting Abigail back into the cabin and tucked her into bed and gave her another cup of the herbal brew.

"What is wrong with her, Grandmother?" he asked when Charlotte returned outside.

"Sometimes the mind fills with clouds when the memories bring too much grief. Her heart is full of pain. If it is as you say, that her husband is dead, as well as her child, the clouds will protect her until she is strong enough to accept their loss."

"But how long will it be before she remembers?"

"I cannot tell you that, young one. What you and your brother have done is a bad thing. It may be many moons before the mists that cloud the woman's mind are lifted."

"I know it was wrong, Grandmother. But I never meant for any of it to happen."

The old woman shrugged and muttered something under her breath. "Leave now. The woman will sleep for now. You may speak with her tomorrow."

* * * * *

Abigail's body grew stronger with each passing day, but her memory remained cloudy. She understood that she had met Luke in a distant place, but other than that, she seemed to have no memory of the events that brought them to his grandfather's village. But Abigail seemed in no hurry to return to her home. In fact, except for acknowledging that Luke had been there, she seemed to have no memory of her life in the cove. She made no mention of Jacob or the baby and appeared content to spend her days helping the old medicine woman sort through the herbs that she used in her craft or dozing before the fire. When Luke asked the old woman about this behavior, Charlotte simply shook her head and told him to be patient.

But as the days grew shorter and frost began painting lacy patterns on the morning windows, Luke found patience difficult. By now he had little fear that his brother would try to find them, but Luke knew that the winter snows would make returning Abigail to the cove or to her father's home in Virginia impossible in the coming weeks. If they waited much longer, it would be spring before they would be able to leave their mountain hideaway. It wasn't so much that he wanted to rid himself of the pretty young woman; in truth, he grew fonder of her each day. But as his affection grew, so did his fear of her reaction when her memory *returned. He was certain that her warm gaze would turn chilly when she remembered the loss of her husband and child and realized his part in the whole affair. No, he thought, better to get her back to her own people as soon as possible.*

For her part, Abigail was happy. She was not certain who these people were or how she had come to be among them, but they were kind to her and made no demands. For a while, she simply watched from the porch as Charlotte went off into the forest looking for the plants she used in her potions and poultices.

"What is this root?" Abigail asked one evening as she watched the old woman sorting through the roots and leaves that she had gathered. She sniffed it and continued, "Hmmm, it smells good. Where have I smelled this before?"

"We call it kanstatsi. You probably know it as sassafras, but some call it ague tree. In the spring, it is a good tonic to cleanse the body. It is also good to ease the pains a woman suffers after giving birth."

"I wonder if the old granny woman back in the cove knows about this. She was always gathering roots and berries." Abigail paused and looked off into the distance. The thought of the granny woman triggered a fleeting memory that left her with a feeling of deep sadness. She shrugged and went back to the table, but Charlotte noted the change in her demeanor and nodded almost imperceptibly. Good, she is beginning to remember, *she thought.*

A month later, Abigail awoke in the middle of the night and screamed out a single word—Jacob.

Chapter 22

ABBY SMILED AS SHE AWOKE to the sound of Jake's off-key singing coming from the shower. As she lay there in the half-light of a cloudy winter's morning, she thought about the previous evening. She'd told Jake that wanting him in her life was the only thing that she was sure about, and the morning light only reinforced that feeling. *Now all I have to do is figure out what I want to do with my life*, she thought. *Simple. Yeah, right.*

"That's an awfully serious expression for so early in the morning," Jake said, stepping out of the bathroom.

"Just trying to sort things out," she replied. "But the sight of you standing there in nothing but a towel makes rational thought a bit difficult."

Reaching for the knot tied around his waist, Jake grinned. "I can always lose the towel if it is a distraction."

Abby tossed the covers back and moved quickly to his side. Planting a quick kiss on his cheek, she said, "Down, boy! I'm already way late for work. Can I have a rain check?"

"Well, if you really want one," Jake said as the towel dropped to the floor.

"On second thought…," she said as her nightgown followed Jake's towel.

Later, as they both headed back for the shower, Jake asked, "What's on tap for you today?"

"A couple of motion hearings and a pile of paperwork. And then there's that new case that came in yesterday. I think I'm going to pass it to another attorney. It's going to take a lot of time, and I need to spend more time on other things right now. What about you?"

"Nothing outside of my classes. I may try to get some work done on the letters if I don't have any student conferences scheduled this afternoon. I'm anxious to get them sorted out so I can tell who's who through the years."

As they parted at the door, Jake said, "This new case. It's pretty important to you, isn't it?"

"Yes, but you're more important."

"That's good to know, but you do what's right for you, and we'll work it out."

"I know I can be stubborn and a pain in the backside some-times, but I really do love you," Abby said as she stood on tiptoe to kiss him.

As it turned out, the matter of Jess Adler came to an abrupt and violent resolution a few weeks later. The detectives had been forced to back off their investigation of the ex-convict when they were unable to find anything conclusive to tie him to the murder. But one night in late March, they responded to a call and found Adler dead, his intended victim standing nearby, badly battered and covered in blood, but alive.

Madison had been correct when he speculated that the physician who signed Adler's discharge papers was young and attractive. At least he supposed she would be pretty when the bruises she received in her struggle with the would-be killer faded. Fortunately, this time, Adler picked the wrong target. Although she was young and petite, this lady was no victim.

"When I decided to go to work at the state hospital, my dad insisted that I take some self-defense courses," she told the detectives. "He said if I was going to be dealing with crazy people, I needed to be able to take care of myself. I did it just to make Dad happy, not because I ever thought I'd need it," she finished with a shudder as they carried Adler's still form past her.

"Your dad's a smart man," said Madison. "Do you feel up to answering some questions?"

She nodded, took a deep breath, and started, "I'm not sure how he got in. I thought I'd locked the door. I was in the kitchen, and he grabbed me from behind. When I realized who he was, I tried to talk to him…to reason with him…but he kept hitting me. No matter how hard I fought back or tried to get away, he was always one step ahead of me." She paused, and tears spilled down her cheeks.

"Take your time, ma'am," Lewis said as he handed her a cup of tea.

"Thanks, I'm okay." Her fingers moved to the bruise that was rapidly forming on her cheek, and she continued, "When he gave me this, I went down and just stayed. He must have thought I was unconscious because he left me alone for a minute. I could hear him rummaging around in the pantry. That's when I remembered the knife in the sink." The young woman began shivering uncontrollably.

"I think we get the picture," said Madison. "Let's get you to the hospital and get you checked out. If we need you to answer more questions, it can wait 'til later."

As she hung up the phone after Madison's call, Abby sighed a deep sigh and closed her file on Jess Adler. In spite of her promise to Jake to give the case to another attorney, she'd never quite been able to turn loose of the file. She wasn't sure she would have been able to let go of it even if they had been able to dig up any evidence against him; there was just too much history there. Feeling as if a huge weight had suddenly been taken off her shoulders, Abby picked up the phone. "Hey, handsome, how about Cappuccino's for dinner?" she asked when Jake answered, "My treat."

An hour later, they were ensconced in their favorite table with a bottle of wine. As he filled their glasses, Jake asked, "So what are we celebrating?"

"Not exactly a celebrating," Abby replied and paused, not quite certain how to continue. "I guess I have a confession to make."

Jake grasped the table and clutched his chest in mock despair. "Is this a 'we need to talk' sort of confession?" he said with a grin.

"Smart-aleck! You can be as bad as my brother sometimes. Remember that case I said I was going to give up—the new murder case?"

"I remember. Does this mean you're not going to be able to go away with me for spring break?"

"Well, yes and no. I fully intended to turn it over to someone else, but I just couldn't do it. Jess Adler was pure evil. He killed two teenage girls. I wanted to make sure he was put away for good."

"What do you mean *was*? What happened to him?"

"His latest victim got the better of him. He's in the morgue. Case closed."

"Well, if that's the case, what's to prevent you from going to North Carolina with me?"

"I need a little time alone. I was thinking about going up to the cove for a few days. I know I promised to help you with your research, but do you mind?"

"I'll miss you, but what's up?"

"We're fine, if that's what you're worried about. I need to decide whether I want to stick with law or try to go back to complete a residency. This is big stuff, and I just think better when I'm in the mountains…alone."

Jake was silent, and fearing she'd hurt his feelings, Abby quickly continued, "It's just that you're a distraction. A very pleasant distraction. I need to make this decision for myself, by myself. I know it will impact you too, but I need to start by making the right decision for me."

"I guess I can accept that. I've been trying to keep my mouth shut on the subject, but you know my opinion. So when are you going?"

"The same week we'd planned on. I already have the vacation scheduled."

"I guess I can manage. Mom will be disappointed too. She was looking forward to meeting you."

"I know. I was looking forward to meeting your family, but I really need this time."

"No problem. Maybe we can go back over for the Fourth of July. We usually have a big family gathering around that time. Then you can meet the whole clan at once. Are you brave enough for that?"

"Well, you managed pretty well with the Edwards clan at Christmas, so I guess I can handle it. And by the way, are my services as a research assistant *all* you'll miss?" she teased.

"Why, whatever do you mean, Ms. Edwards?"

Chapter 23

GEORGE WAS DOZING ON HIS stool behind the counter when Abby entered the store a few weeks later. "Wake up, old man. Someone's liable to carry off the merchandise."

"I'm not asleep, gal. I'm just resting my eyes."

"Yeah, I know. That's what my dad always says when we catch him snoring in front of the TV. Got a spot for me for a few days?"

"Sure enough. Your regular site is open if you want it." George's gaze moved past her to the screen door.

"Jake's gone to North Carolina to do some more family-tree climbing if that's what you're looking for."

"I thought you were going with him to meet the folks and all that."

"We had a little change of plans."

"Is there a problem?"

"No, you old fussbudget. Jake and I are fine. I just needed some time on my own." Seeing the expression on his face, she continued, "I wish you could see your face. Honest, George, everything is fine. I just have to work some things out, and I can't do it with Jake around."

"Everything all right at work?"

"I swear you are nosier than any three old ladies. If you really must know, I'm trying to decide whether to go back to school or not." Raising her hand to stop the remarks she knew were coming, she added, "And I already know your thoughts on the matter, thank you very much, so please just let me work this thing out for myself."

"All right, I can take a hint. But I just want what's best for you, gal."

"I know you do, and so does Jake, but this has to be my decision."

"Enough said. So how long are you staying?" he asked as she moved toward the door.

"I'm not sure, at least three days. I have the whole week off, but I'm just going to play it by ear."

Once she had her tent set up and gear stowed away, Abby took her bike down off its rack on top of the car and headed into the cove. Today her plan was simple—she would ride a bit, maybe walk along one or two of the trails, and generally just try to clear her mind. There would be time enough for serious thoughts over the next week. She set a pace more suited to exercise than nature watching, and she soon felt her face flush and her calves burn. The winter stiffness was leaving her limbs, and despite the ache, it felt good.

The sun was climbing past midday when Abby stopped at a turnout to rest. There were a number of these turnouts around the Loop Road where drivers could pull off and enjoy the view without blocking traffic. Just off the pavement, there was a massive old tree with great spreading branches. At its base was a place where the trunk formed a perfect cradle for a weary back. Easing down into the notch, she settled down to eat the peanut butter and jelly sandwich she had stashed in her pack. Beneath the branches of this ancient tree was one of her favorite spots to sit and read or think. Despite its proximity to the road, the girth of the trunk hid her from passersby; and since most visitors to the cove didn't venture out into the fields, she'd spent many a solitary hour in its comfortable shade. The tree overlooked one of the many large fields in the cove framed by woods and the misty blue mountains that gave the Smokies their name. The mountains on the far side of the cove were just beginning to don their springtime garb of pale green. Here and there, the verdant expanse of trees was broken by the dogwoods and redbuds that created splashes of white and pink like hats carelessly tossed on a grassy bed.

Long about sundown, the field spread before her would be filled with grazing deer, but now the field was empty, and Abby had no company save a noisy squirrel in the branches above her head. After finishing her sandwich, Abby leaned back against the tree and closed her eyes. She hadn't meant to doze, but when she awoke abruptly some time later, it was with that prickly, hair-standing-up-on-your-neck feeling that she was being watched. The squirrel had gone silent and Abby sat there listening intently half-expecting to hear the now familiar voice calling for Abigail. But she heard nothing. The field before her now held ten to fifteen does browsing quietly and giving no sign of anything amiss.

Thinking that perhaps she as she napped she had missed the sound of an approaching car or hiker, she looked around, but there was no on there. Seeing nothing out of the ordinary, she leaned back and tried to relax. *Nope*, she thought, *there is someone or something out there watching me.* Unable to shake the uneasy feeling, Abby was just about to get back on her bicycle and ride on when out of the woods to her right stepped a large buck. She froze, barely daring to breathe. He was a stately fellow, but something about him looked odd. Then it dawned on her—he had no antlers. By summer's end, this majestic animal would have a rack that any self-respecting hunter would covet, but now he simply had small velvet-covered prongs. He slowly turned to face her, and for one brief instant, their gazes locked across the short expanse of grass. Then as suddenly as he appeared, he was gone. She wasn't even aware of his movement as he simply faded back into the trees.

* * * * *

The following morning after a breakfast of spoon bread and coffee, Abby set off for the Abrams Falls trailhead. It was two and a half miles back into the falls, but it was an easy hike, just right to work out the stiffness caused by yesterday's ride. She encountered a number of other hikers on the trail. Most, like Abby, were headed in, but a few early birds had already completed the trek.

About a mile or so up the trail, Abby heard the pounding of running feet coming up behind her and moved to one side as two teenaged boys thundered past her. She was about to step back onto the trail when a boy of perhaps nine or ten ran by shouting, "Sean. Kevin. Wait up."

"Last one there's a weenie," came the reply from up the trail.

"Some things never change."

Abby turned to see a somewhat breathless and red-faced woman coming up the trail with a little girl of four or five in tow.

"Did a trio of human tornadoes blow through here recently?" she asked.

"Yes, but one of them is losing steam," Abby replied.

"Poor Sam. How far behind them was he?"

"Not far. They were barely out of sight when he came by. Spring break?"

"Only for children. I think it's a plot to drive mothers insane. Either that or a grandmother's curse for what my sisters and I did as children. After being cooped up in school all winter, they tend to go a little crazy."

"I know. My brother and I used to drive my mother to distraction, especially when we got to be the age of your older boys. Steven insisted on making every hike a race to the top. And let me guess, I'll bet your little girl is more interested in the wildflowers and rocks than making time."

"How did you know that?"

"I was the same way, still am for that matter." Turning to the little girl, she said, "My name is Abby. What's yours?"

"Katie."

"Katie, have you ever seen a pair of Dutchman's-breeches?"

"What's that?"

"They're little white flowers that grow around here, and they look just like a row of little boys' pants hung on the clothesline."

"Really?" Katie's blue eyes widened.

"Really. But you have to look closely for them. Sometimes you can find them right along the edge of the trail."

"We'll look for them when we get up to the waterfall, Katie, but right now we'd better go find your big brothers."

"But I want to look for the little white pants, Mommy."

"I know, sweetie, but Mommy needs to make sure the boys aren't getting into trouble. I promise we'll look for the flowers as soon as we catch up with them."

"Would it be okay for Katie to walk along with me while you catch up with the boys?"

"Oh, I wouldn't want to impose."

"No imposition. I enjoy nurturing little nature lovers. I'll take good care of her."

"Can I please stay with Abby, Mommy? I'll be good."

"No, Katie, I don't think so. We don't really know this lady."

"Oh, I'm sorry," said Abby, pulling out her badge and identification card. "I promise I'm not a kidnapper or anything. I'm an attorney for the county down in Knoxville. Look, here's my ID."

"Are you a policeman?" Katie asked, wide-eyed again.

"Not exactly, but I help them put bad people in jail."

Hearing more shouts from up the trail, the woman asked, "Thanks. You can't be too careful these days. I'm Marilyn Sanders. Are you sure you don't mind?"

"Sure. I'd welcome the company. We'll have a nice stroll while you chase after the boys."

"I really appreciate it. They're good boys, but they sure have a knack for trouble. Katie, you behave for Miss Abby," she admonished and hurried up the trail.

Abby and Katie followed along at a slower pace. The trail ahead was overhung with the evergreen leaves of mountain laurel and rhododendron. Pointing to the leaves overhead, Abby asked, "Do you know what these are, Katie?"

"No, what?"

"Well, these with the long narrow leaves are rhododendron, and the ones with the shorter leaves are mountain laurel."

"Laurel and ro...rotor...rotordendron?"

"That's close enough. In a couple of months, these bushes will be covered in pink and purple flowers. See how they hang down on both sides of the trail? The first time my daddy brought me up to see them when I was a little girl, I thought it looked just like something from Snow White. It's like walking through a tunnel lined in flowers."

"Where are the flowers now?"

Not quite certain how to explain botany to a five-year-old, Abby hesitated. "Let me see now. Do you have special clothes that you don't wear every day?"

"Uh-huh."

"Well, the laurel and rhododendron are sort of like that. They only wear their flowers part of the time."

"Is it like my Easter hat? Mommy only lets me wear it on Sundays."

"That's right. And doesn't that make it more special?"

"Uh-huh, but sometimes I wish I could wear it all the time."

"I know what you mean, but I bet you'd get tired of staying dressed up all the time."

"I guess so." Tugging on Abby's hand, she continued, "Can we go find the little pants flowers now?"

"We sure can. You watch on your side, and I'll watch on mine, and let's see who can find them first." And hand in hand, they set off up the trail.

A short distance up the trail, Abby spotted a cluster of the white-and-yellow blossoms and pointed them out to Katie.

"But they don't look like the pants my brothers wear," the child said.

"I guess they don't. But a long time ago, before people had snaps and zippers, men held their pants up with rope instead of belts. See how the yellow part sort of looks like a bow?"

"Oh, I see. They sorta look like pants. Are there any other flowers out today, or are they all like the rotordendron?"

"Lots of flowers are just like the bears and wake up early in the spring. Let's see what we can find. But keep to your side of the trail. It drops off over here. I promised your mom I'd take care of you."

Katie proved to be quite adept at spying small patches of blossoms amid the remnants of last season's fallen leaves. She fairly danced up the trail and waited impatiently for Abby to identify her discoveries. "Ooooh, these smell good. What are they, Abby?"

Gazing down at the fragrant pale-pink petals and pulling out her wildflower guide, Abby replied, "I'm not sure, but I think that's a trailing arbutus. I've never seen one before." Flipping through the pages, she continued, "That right, a trailing arbutus. It says here that the ladies who used to live down in the cove would use the flowers for perfume."

"Can I pick some to take to Mommy? They smell sooooo good."

"I know they do, Katie, but we can't pick the flowers. They're very rare, and they're protected by law."

"What does that mean?"

"There aren't very many of these flowers around, and government wants everyone to be able to enjoy them, not just a few people. So they passed a law that says if you pick them, the rangers can arrest you."

"Really? Would we have to go to jail?"

"Well, probably not to jail, but we'd have to pay a fine, and they wouldn't be very happy with us."

"But I want Mommy to see the arbuts."

"How about if we take a picture for her? Then you can both enjoy them all year long."

That solution satisfied the child, and as Abby paused to snap some pictures, she was off again in search of other blooms. Some, such as wild strawberries, violets, and even a trillium, unusual in this area, Abby was familiar with. But others, like spiky purple pinxter flower that resembles honeysuckle and the bright fuchsia-colored gay wings, she had to look up in the guide. Katie demanded a picture of each, and Abby was glad she had a large memory card in her camera.

They eventually reached the falls to find Marilyn spreading their picnic lunch on a blanket in the sun while the boys played on the rocks. "They couldn't wait to get their feet in the water." She laughed. "But that lasted all of about ten seconds. I tried to tell them it was too cold, but you know how boys are."

"I know. This water is never very warm, but this time of year, it's really cold. My brother and I always had a contest to see who could keep their feet in the longest. It was always short."

"Sounds like you and your brother hiked up here a lot."

"We did. All over the park actually, but Cades Cove has always been my favorite."

"Do you still get to hike with him?"

"No, Steven was killed in the Gulf War."

"Oh, I'm so sorry."

"No need to apologize. You had no way of knowing. It's funny, but even after all these years, I sometimes still expect to find him at the end of the trail waiting for me."

"In a way, he is. I'm not overly religious and don't exactly believe in ghosts, but I believe that the spirits of our loved ones always stay with us. It's only natural that you would feel his presence in this place that you both love."

"I never really thought about it that way. I do know that if it had been the other way around, Steven would still come up here. There's just something about these old hills that gets in your blood."

"My children seem to be headed the way of you and your brother. They just love it here. Did Katie behave herself?"

"She was great. I think you have a budding botanist on your hands. She found more wildflowers today than I've seen in years. I had to resort to my guide to answer all her questions."

"That's my Katie. Seems like for every question you answer, she finds three more. I hope she wasn't too much of a bother."

"Not at all. I don't get to spend much time with kids in my line of work, and I really enjoyed it."

"Will you join us for lunch? We have plenty. Katie, go call your brothers."

After lunch, the older boys went to explore the area downstream from the falls, leaving Sam with his mother and Katie. When the remains of the meal were packed up, Katie took her mother by the hand and said, "Come on, Mommy, I want to show you the flowers Miss Abby and I found."

"That sounds like fun. C'mon, Sam, let's go see what you little sister has found."

"Aw, Mom, I don't want to go look at flowers. Can't I go with Sean and Kevin instead?"

"No, I don't think so. They're climbing around on the rocks, and it's too dangerous for you. You'll have to go with us for now."

"Darn, I wish I was older. I don't want to hang around with a little girl."

"C'mon, Sammy, the flowers are really pretty, and I'll show you some that look like pants."

The boy grudgingly went with his mother and sister, and Abby settled on a large outcropping of rock to enjoy the sunshine and solitude. A large brook trout swam lazily about in the pool beneath her seat. Rummaging in her pack, Abby found the sandwich left uneaten when she accepted the invitation to join the Sanders' picnic. Tearing the crust off the bread, she began dropping small pieces into the water below. At first, the trout seemed to ignore it, perhaps a veteran of the park's catch-and-release program. But with a sudden flash of red and yellow, he shot to the surface and snatched the bread from the surface and then disappeared. Apparently, this fellow had been sent to check things out because the pool was soon filled with hungry trout eagerly waiting for the next morsel to hit the water. When the bread was gone, she rolled up her pack, tucked it under her head, and soon fell asleep.

1865

The captain didn't tell me his family was wealthy, *Jacob thought as he trudged up the lane to the farmhouse. Although modest in size, it was far grander than even the richest houses in the cove. As he neared the front door, he was suddenly aware of his appearance. He ran his fingers through his hair and beard in an attempt to make himself more presentable and looked down at his clothing. His uniform was threadbare in places and painstakingly patched in others with bits of cloth scavenged from blankets or the uniforms of comrades far past caring. As an ever-present reminder of a place called Rogersville, his left sleeve hung empty. But in losing his arm that day, he'd saved the captain's life and, in a sense, his own.*

Jacob hesitated a moment when he reached the front door. He gazed down at his uniform again, considered going around to the back door, then straightened his shoulders and raised his hand to knock. Before his hand reached the door, a young woman threw it open. She called out over her shoulder, "I know, Mother, but I really need some things in town. I'll take the carriage and be back in plenty of time."

Her laughing eyes became serious as she turned and saw Jacob standing there with his hand raised. Another one, *she thought. A steady stream of scruffy men in blue had stopped for handouts after the war. She took a step back. "May I help you?" Then, "Jacob?" She called into the house again, "Mother, it's Jacob." Turning back to him, she said, "You are Jacob, aren't you? Thomas wrote and said he was bringing you home, but where is he?"*

Jacob dropped his gaze. "I'm sorry, ma'am..." He faltered, uncertain how to break the news that instead of coming home, Thomas had boarded a train headed for the West.

"Not dead? He can't be dead. We just got a letter saying he was well and on his way home. What happened?"

"No, ma'am, he's not dead. It's just that...uh...he decided not to come back to the farm."

Arriving at his daughter's side, Ezra Shepard demanded, "What do you mean he's not coming back!"

"*Where are your manners, Ezra? Let the poor man come in and sit down before you start the inquisition,*" *said his wife, Rebekah. She pulled him inside and led him to the parlor.* "*Are you hungry? From the looks of you, those Johnny Rebs haven't been feeding you too well.*"

"*I want to know where my son is!*"

"*Tell me, Jacob, is our son alive and well?*"

"*Yes, ma'am, fit as a fiddle when I left him.*"

"*There now, Ezra. Thomas is fine. Jacob can tell us all about it after he's had something to eat. Louisa, heat up the stew while I show Jacob the washroom. I'm sure he'd like to clean up after his journey.*"

Leaving her husband to sputter in frustration, Rebekah led Jacob to the back of the house. While he was bathing, she called to him, "*I've put some of Thomas's clothes on the bed for you. They should fit well enough until we have time to get you to town.*"

Jacob took his time washing up. It had been many years since he had the luxury of a bath with water unused by others. He barely recognized the pale and gaunt reflection in the mirror as he shaved—another reminder of Andersonville. When he left the cove, his beard was dark brown. When had it become so gray? The clothes Amanda provided were well-made but hung loosely on his thin frame. Time to face the music, *he thought and went into the kitchen.*

Chapter 24

"SAM, WHERE ARE YOU?" MARILYN came back into the clearing, dragging Katie behind her. "Abby, have you seen Sam?"

"Not since you left, but I did doze off. How long has he been gone?"

"I'm not exactly sure. Katie was showing me some flowers, and when I turned around, he was just gone. I thought he might have gone looking for Sean and Kevin. Have they been back?"

"I haven't seen a soul since you left. Why don't you stay here, and I'll go see if I can find them. Sam's probably with them and having a big laugh because he managed to give you the slip."

"He won't be laughing when I get a hold of him." But her expression belied her words.

Abby headed off in the direction the boys had taken. They had followed the creek instead of getting back on the trail, so she followed the stream, stopping periodically to call out. Several hundred yards downstream, Sean replied, "Over here."

"It's me, Abby. Is Sam with you?"

"No, he's supposed to be with Mom," said Kevin.

"I know, but he's wandered off. Your mom and Katie are back at the falls. Go help them look, and I'll check out the trail between here and the falls.

As Sean and Kevin headed back upstream, Abby scrambled up the steep bank to the trail above. The trail meandered along the ridgeline high above the stream, and if Sam had taken it, he may not have seen his brothers below. Abby felt a knot growing in her stomach. These mountains could be deceptively tranquil, and more than one child had been lost when he or she wandered off. Laurel and rhododendron thickets formed an almost impenetrable barrier down the sides of the ridges. It a hiker was knocked unconscious in a fall, he might not be found until it was too late.

Forcing these dire thoughts from her mind, Abby started up the trail. She had gone only a dozen or so yards on the trail when she heard her name. Turning to look behind her, she saw a familiar form standing there. He waved and said, "Here I am, Abigail. Come this way."

"Not now," Abby said more to herself than to the apparition. "I don't have time to go chasing a ghost or whatever you are." Resolutely, she turned to go the other direction. But now the man now stood in front of her, pointing back the way she had come. She started toward him, determined to go around or through him. Calmly, he said, "You're going the wrong direction, Abigail."

Despite herself, she stopped. "I'm not Abigail. At least not the Abigail you think I am. Anyway, how do you know where I'm going?"

"The boy didn't come this way," he said and disappeared.

Shaken, Abby just stood there. Common sense told her the boy had come this way looking for his older brothers. And how did the man—she couldn't bring herself to call him ghost—know what or who she was seeking? It made no sense. Then she remembered how she found Jake when she first answered the man's call. Could he really know? "I must be crazy," she muttered to herself and headed back toward the falls.

Marilyn looked up expectantly when Abby entered the clearing, but her face fell when she realized she was alone. "Sean and Kevin said you told them come back this way."

Abby nodded. "If you don't mind, I'm going to send Sean back to the trailhead to send for help."

Marilyn's lips quivered.

"Just a precaution. He can get someone on the loop to notify the rangers at the mill. And who knows, Sam may have decided to go back to the car on his own." Abby hoped she sounded more calm and reassuring than she felt.

Katie listened to this conversation in growing alarm. Tearfully, she asked, "Is Sammy lost, Mommy?"

"No, honey. I think Sammy is just playing hide-and-seek with us. Miss Abby will find him."

"Can I go look too?"

"No, Katie," Abby replied. "I'm 'it' this time. You stay with your mommy 'til Sammy and I get back."

Abby headed back to the trail. When she reached the crest, she met the boys. One look at their pale faces told her they hadn't found their little brother and that they were now well and truly scared.

Sean turned wordlessly and hurried off at her instruction.

"What about me?"

Reaching in her pack, she pulled out her cell phone to Kevin. "Remember where the path leading down to the falls breaks off from the main trail?" He nodded, and she continued, "Just beyond there's a side trail that goes up to the top of the ridge. If you get a signal, just hit dial. A man named George will answer. Tell him where we are and that Abby said to send the rangers."

"Do you think we'll find him? I've heard stories about kids..."

This was one of those times when honesty was not the best policy. "Sean's probably found him already, somewhere down the trail just ambling along."

He trotted off, and Abby turned back toward the trailhead, wondering if she was doing the right thing. It still made more sense that Sam had gone looking for them in the other direction. Was she risking a child's life by heeding the words of a ghost? In answer to her unspoken question, he was there on the trail several yards in front of her. He beckoned and moved away from her. Abby followed.

The man moved quickly, and Abby struggled to keep up with his long strides. The trail at this point was steep and rocky, little more than a yard-wide path cut into the side of a mountain. To her left, it rose up at an angle that didn't allow her to see the top. On her right, it dropped off sharply into a rhododendron thicket. It was impossible to see the ground just a few feet off the trail. She sent a small prayer heavenward. You could lose an elephant in those thickets. *Please don't let him be down there*. Placing her faith in the man on the trail, she hurried on. The man remained just in sight, but no matter how quickly Abby moved, she was unable to close the distance between them. As she started up the second of the three ridges between the falls and the trailhead, she realized that the man had stopped. He stood there looking down at the creek below.

When she reached that spot, he was gone. Abby looked over the edge and saw only a sea of green undergrowth and twisted limbs. "Sam, are you there?" No reply.

She turned to move down the trail but found herself face-to-face—face-to-shoulder, actually—with the man. He was standing in the middle of the trail and again looking down toward the creek. The laurel was thinner here, but the ground was still steep. Several small trees and one large one lay on the ground, probably the victims of a distant winter storm. There was nothing to indicate that a small boy had passed this way. The man stood steadfast.

"Okay, I followed you here. Where is he?" she said, not really expecting a reply. She got none. "Help me!" she shouted.

"Help *me*," came a hoarse reply.

And there he was, about ten feet off the trail, half-sitting, half-lying against a large log.

"Sam! Are you okay?" She dropped her pack and scrambled down to him.

"My arm hurts really bad."

When she reached the boy, Abby saw why. Even without her medical training, it would have been obvious that Sam's arm was badly broken. The bones between his elbow and wrist were both fractured, and the broken ends threatened to pierce the skin. She began to assess him for other injuries and look for symptoms of shock. Aside from the fracture, his injuries appeared minor with the exception of an angry red mark on the boy's throat. The jagged scratch showed signs of swelling, and its proximity to his windpipe was worrisome.

As she gently palpated his neck, Abby asked, "What happened here?"

"I was following the bear and fell. Then I took a nap."

"What bear?" Alarmed, Abby scanned the surrounding brush. If the bear was still around, they could both be in danger.

"He's gone now. The man in the green suit chased him away."

Abby peered into the boy's eyes and felt around on his head. There was no sign of trauma, but as he spoke, she noted a wheezy rattle sound.

"Did the man go for help?" she asked, hoping that help was already on its way.

"No, he just chased the bear and then stayed to keep me company."

Abby looked around. There was no sign of a bear or the man in green. "Sammy, we have to do something about that arm so we can get you out of here. I'm going after my pack. I'll be right back."

She scrambled back up the hill, her mind racing. The arm was bad, but nothing she couldn't take care of, but his neck was another matter. The raspy rattle probably meant damage to his larynx. If it was fractured, the swelling would eventually obstruct his airway. Creating an artificial airway meant cutting into his neck. She'd done it before—once, and in a hospital. How long had it been since the injury? No way to know. She glanced at her watch. About thirty minutes had passed since Marilyn and Katie came back to the falls. Obstruction of the airway could take as much as an hour but could occur in much less. He was already showing signs of confusion and respiratory distress. How much did he weigh? Could she carry him back to the trailhead? Maybe, but at maybe 80 pounds to her 120, probably not. Did she risk going back in search of Kevin or Marilyn? Definitely not. So what was the plan? Stabilize his arm and try to get him back up to the trail while he could still help her. If there was time, she'd try to get him as far down the trail as possible. After that… She didn't want to think about that.

Did she have everything she might need? Since Jake's accident, her first aid kit was better stocked than that of the average hiker, but she was hardly equipped to perform surgery. A Swiss Army knife, antiseptic pads, and bandages weren't much, she thought, but it might have to do. *What can I use to keep the airway open? A nice piece of sterile tubing would be nice*, she thought, digging deep into her pack. "A-ha," she said as her fingers found a sports bottle with a sturdy plastic straw. She made her way back down to the injured child, pausing to pick up a couple of sturdy sticks to use for a splint.

Back at Sam's side, Abby watched him for a few moments to see if he was showing any signs of agitation, a sure sign of increasing air hunger from the swelling in his neck. His face was pale and damp to the touch. Although his breathing was a little noisier, he still seemed to be moving air. She needed time to immobilize the arm and get him back to the trail. Forcing down her own rising apprehension, she said, "Okay, Sammy, I have a plan. Can you help me?"

"I'll try."

"I need to fix your arm so it won't move."

"I want my mom. She's a nurse." He shrank away from her touch.

"Would you believe I'm a doctor?"

"No way."

"Yes way. Besides, I have my Girl Scout first aid badge too."

That seemed more acceptable. "Kevin got his too."

"I promise I'll be as careful as I can, and I'll tell you what I'm doing before I do it, okay?"

He slowly nodded.

"Did Kevin ever practice on you?"

Another nod.

"I'm going to use these sticks to make a splint. Did Kevin do that?"

"No, a board."

"That would be better, but we'll have to make do. This is going to hurt, but I need you to be still. Can you do that for me?"

His eyes widened in fear, and if possible, he turned a shade paler, but he nodded again. He cried out when she lifted his arm, "Make that old bear stop pulling on my arm!"

"Shoo, bear! Go away!" she said as she fashioned a crude splint of sticks and an elastic bandage she'd added to her kit after Jake's accident. "There. Better?"

He nodded drowsily and wheezed. "Better. I'm sleepy."

"I know, sweetie, but we need to find your mommy."

"Abby? Sam?"

Abby stood up and saw Kevin trotting down the trail toward them. "Down here," she called.

"I got through! George said to tell you the cavalry's coming," Kevin said as he clambered down the slope. "Hey, squirt, you had us worried," he said, tousling Sam's hair. His smile faded as he noted his brother's pale face and bandaged arm. "How ya doin'?"

"Abby's a Girl Scout." Sam wheezed.

"What's wrong with his voice?"

Abby pulled Kevin a few steps away. "Looks like when he fell, he hit his neck."

"But he'll be okay, won't he?"

"We need to get him out of here…I don't know how much time we have."

"What do you mean?"

"I just think we should probably get him to a hospital," Abby sidestepped his question.

"Is he going to die?"

"Not if I can help it. If it gets too bad, I'm going to need your help."

"What about Mom? Should I go back for her?"

"No time for that. Sean should be headed back up, and he can go after her."

"What do you want me to do?"

"Help me carry him. The rangers will be coming up from the trailhead. We need their radios."

Between them, they half-walked, half-carried the injured boy up the steep bank to the trail. By the time they reached level ground, Sam was struggling for air, and Abby didn't like his color.

Kevin looked at her in alarm. "What's happening?"

"When he hit his neck, he injured his windpipe, and now it's swelling and making it hard to breathe. If he quits breathing, I'm going to have to make an airway."

The frightened teen turned even paler. "How…?"

"I'll explain later. Maybe it won't come to that."

But they managed to get only a few feet farther down the trail when Sam's body sagged in their arms.

"He's quit breathing! Help me get him down. We don't have much time!"

Chapter 25

"We don't have much time, Doctor."

Abby started at the sound of the nurse's words. It was her first night on call in the emergency room. Her scalpel was poised over the papery skin of an elderly woman, the victim of a vicious mugging and near strangling. "The attending is tied up in Trauma 1. You have to do this," came the nurse's voice again, more anxious this time."

But what if I miss? Abby's brain screamed in reply. *I've never done this on a live person before.*

"Now, Doctor, you have to do this now."

You have to do it. This time, it was her own brain speaking. *Do it. I have to do it.* She closed her eyes and took a deep breath to steady herself. When she opened her eyes, she saw the smooth neck of the ten-year-old under her hands.

Abby pulled her first aid kit and the water bottle out of her pack. "Okay, here's the deal. I'm going to have to make a cut in Sam's neck and use this straw to make an airway."

"You're going to do *what*?" Kevin's voice cracked.

Handing him the straw and her knife, she continued, "We don't have much time. Cut a piece of the straw about four inches long and then wipe it down with an alcohol pad out of my kit."

Abby took iodine and alcohol pads out of the kit and prepped Sam's neck; then retrieving her knife from Kevin, she wiped it down as well. "Be ready to hand me the straw as soon as I make the incision. Then hand me some gauze squares and tape. Understand?"

Kevin gulped and nodded.

"Don't worry, there won't be a lot of blood. Ready?"

Another nod.

Abby's outward calm belied her inner turmoil. As she ran her fingers over the child's neck to find the depression that marked the incision point, she heard Dr. Tucker's slow Southern drawl describing the procedure. "In cases of sudden obstruction, the airways are most commonly opened by one of two procedures. The laryngotomy, or cricothyrotomy as it is sometimes called, is the anatomically simpler approach, and the best choice in an emergency." The memory of his voice had a calming effect on Abby's frazzled nerves, and when she looked down at her hands, they were steady. She reran Dr. Tucker's lecture in her head where he'd gone on to explain that this was the procedure of choice because in making the small vertical incision, one was less likely to sever the adjacent arteries.

It might be simple to you, Dr. Tucker, Abby thought. *But here on the side of a mountain with only a frightened fourteen-year-old to assist me,* simple *isn't a term that springs to mind. I need more time. I need to be sure I'm going to hit the right spot.*

"What are you waiting for?" Kevin sounded small and far away.

She looked down at her hand and the knife that Steven had given her when she was a Girl Scout. *You're out of time, Doc,* she heard him whisper. *You're this kid's only hope. Now do it!*

A sudden calm overtook her. Abby took one last deep breath and made the incision. She saw the skin part and briefly felt resistance as the blade found and penetrated the tough membrane it was seeking. Kevin was ready with the straw when she put out her hand. Inserting it into the incision, she heard a welcome whoosh of air and watched as the boy's chest began to rise and fall. "Thank God," she whispered and looked up at Kevin. "He's getting air again. Hand me the gauze and tape so I can stabilize the straw."

Kevin's hands were shaking.

Abby smiled at him. "I think Sam's going to be okay. See how the pink is coming back to his cheeks? That's a good sign. You make a pretty good assistant."

"How…how did you know what to do? I thought you were a lawyer."

"It's a long story, but I'm a doctor too." Kevin's puzzled look made her laugh. "Guess I just couldn't make up my mind what I wanted to be when I grew up."

The sound of voices spared her from further explanation. She looked up to see Sean and two rangers come into view. "Sure glad to see you guys," she called. "Can you radio back to the station? We're going to need a medevac chopper."

"What happened?" asked Sean.

"Abby and I cut Sam's neck open so he could breathe."

The older brother looked skeptical, and the ranger with the radio paused in midsentence. "Stand by. What should I tell them?" he asked Abby.

"Tell them that we have a ten-year-old who required an emergency laryngotomy and has fractures of the right radius and ulna. We have a crude airway established, and the fractures have been splinted. Need priority evacuation!"

As the ranger relayed this information to the station, Abby turned back to Sean and Kevin. "I need one of you to go back and get your mom and sister and one to stay here with me in case Sam wakes up. He won't be able to talk, and we can't let him move his head. It will help for him to see someone he knows."

"I'll go," said Sean. "Mom's gonna freak."

"Scaring her and Katie before they get here won't do any good. I'll explain the whole thing when she gets here. Just tell her that Sam's hurt, but that the rangers are here, and it looks like he'll be okay. We'll head back to the trailhead to meet the helicopter."

Chapter 26

ABBY WATCHED THE HELICOPTER PASS out of sight. With the older boys and Katie on their way to Knoxville with the state troopers and the onlookers dispersed, Abby found herself alone at the trailhead. She stowed her pack in her own car and made sure the Sanders' car was secure until someone could come back to retrieve it. Arriving back at the campground store, she saw a familiar car in the nearly empty lot.

"Jeez, I can't leave you alone for a minute, can I?" said Jake as she got out her car.

"What are you doing here?"

"The better question is what have you been doing here? George tells me you've been out rescuing lost hikers again."

"I guess," she said, moving into his embrace. In the safety and warmth of Jake's arms, the fear and tension of the past few hours were suddenly released, and much to her chagrin, she burst into tears. When they didn't come into the store immediately, George walked out to see what had become of the couple. He found them in the parking lot, Abby's sobs subsiding into soggy sniffling against Jake's chest. For his part, Jake simply held her, looking damp and a little bewildered at her reaction.

"Hey, what's all this, gal?" said George. "You're the hero of the day. The rangers say the boy's going to be just fine, thanks to you."

"I don't know what's wrong with me," she said, taking the handkerchief that he offered.

"That's okay, gal. Don't think I've ever seen you cry. Not sure that I like it much either."

"Sorry, gentlemen. I don't know what came over me. It's been quite a day."

"You do look a little the worse for wear. How about we break camp and head back to town? You could use a little TLC."

Abby shook her head. "I'm okay, really. It's not like me to blubber like that—it just all hit me at once. And back to my question, what are you doing here?"

"I'm not sure, actually. I was minding my own business, working away in the attic, when I was overcome with the urge to see you." Seeing her expression, he quickly added, "No, not *that* kind of urge. I just couldn't shake the feeling that I was needed back here, so I packed up and headed back. Want me to leave?"

"No!" she said with more force than she intended. Blushing, she continued, "I know I came up here to be alone, but I'm really glad to see you. The TLC sounds good, but I'm not ready to go back to town."

"How 'bout you two coming down to the cabin for dinner?" said George. "I've got a couple of big T-bones in the freezer and a pretty good bottle of cabernet stashed away."

"That offer is almost too good to refuse," Abby said.

"Almost?" said Jake. "I detect a *but* there."

"More of a yes and no. What I'd really like to do right now is go to the hospital and check on Sam."

"Want me to go along?"

Abby considered this for a moment. "No, I think I want to do this on my own. Do you mind? I'll meet you at George's later."

"I guess that'll have to do."

She smiled and kissed him on the cheek. "Thanks. Did you by any chance pack your sleeping bag? I think I might know where there is a tent around here with a little extra room."

"Now that's an offer *I* can't refuse. One thing, though. You might want to wash up before you head into town. You look a bit rough."

Looking down at her dirty clothes and bloodstained hands, she replied, "I guess I do, at that. See you gentlemen later."

* * * * *

The palpable tension of the surgical waiting room hit her as a dozen faces turned toward her. When they realized that she carried no news of their loved ones, they resumed their anxious pacing, finger drumming and pretense at reading. Abby picked out Marilyn and a man she assumed to be her husband.

"Abby!" Marilyn greeted her with a warm hug. "Sam's still in surgery."

"John Sanders. Sam's father," the man said, extending his hand. "I understand we're in your debt."

Abby flushed, at a loss for words.

"Sanders?"

They turned to see a young woman in scrubs walking toward them. "I'm Amy Black. I assisted with your son's operation."

"Will he be okay?" asked John.

"Yes. It will be a few days before we're sure about his voice, but we're optimistic. The surgeon will be out to talk to you in a few moments."

"Thank you, Doctor. And thank you, Abby," said John. Marilyn, who until this moment had been so calm, turned and cried softly against his shoulder.

Turning to Abby, the young physician said, "They told us this happened up in the mountains, and someone opened an airway on the trail. Was that you?"

Abby nodded.

"Nice work," said an older man as he joined them. Tall and athletic, he removed his scrub hat to reveal a coarse thatch of still-dark hair that belied his sixty-something years.

"I had a good teacher. Marilyn, John, this is Dr. Richard Tucker," Abby introduced her former professor and mentor.

"Mr. and Mrs. Sanders, your son's surgery went very well. I think we were able to repair the damage to his vocal cords. It's still early, but I think his voice will recover, along with the rest of his injuries."

"When can I see Sam?" asked his mother.

"It shouldn't be too much longer. The orthopedic team is working on his arm."

"Thank you again, Doctor," said John.

"You're quite welcome, but from what I understand, if it hadn't been for Abby, he wouldn't have made it to my operating room."

Abby felt the red creep up her neck again as he continued, "This young woman had the makings of a fine doctor. Glad to see she didn't forget everything we taught her even if she has gone over to the dark side."

Abby laughed at his reference to the legal profession. "Well, at least I didn't go into malpractice."

"There is that, I guess. Any regrets?"

"How is Sharon?" Abby avoided his question by asking about his daughter, a former classmate of hers.

The two chatted for a few more minutes before Dr. Tucker was paged to return to the OR. Abby took her leave of the Sanders after promising to come back to visit Sam and headed back to the mountains.

The evening turned chilly after the warmth of the day. Back at the cabin, she found Jake in the kitchen putting the finishing touches on a salad and George seated in front of the fireplace. "How's the boy?" George asked as she sank gratefully onto the couch.

"It looks good. Turns out the surgeon was a professor of mine. I guess if it hadn't been for Dr. Tucker, I wouldn't have been able to do what I did. He's a good man. What's for dinner? That doesn't smell like steak, but it smells wonderful."

"We made an executive decision in your absence," said Jake as he brought her a glass of wine. "When it started getting cool, we decided spaghetti sounded better than steak. It's almost ready. Are you hungry?"

"Did you remember the sugar?"

"Yes, Ms. Fussbudget! I remembered the sugar."

Abby's favorite Italian restaurant had the best spaghetti sauce she had ever tasted. After two years of wrangling, she finally learned that chef's secret ingredient was a pinch of sugar. "But not too much!" the old lady had warned. Since that time, Abby always added it to her own sauce. The first time Jake caught her putting it in, he thought she was crazy but quickly learned to appreciate the barest of sweetness it gave to the aromatic sauce.

"Come and eat, you two," said George. "Or I'll have it all to myself."

After dinner, George insisted on cleaning up and sent them to enjoy the fire. Abby was already dozing against Jake's shoulder when the old man joined them. "What I can't understand," he said, "is how you managed to find him. What you did to save him was a wonderful thing, don't get me wrong, but there's many a man, woman, and child who have been lost in these mountains and never found."

"I was just lucky, George. He wasn't far off the trail, and someone would have found him."

"Maybe. But would they have found him in time?"

Abby wasn't sure she was ready to share the sightings of the strange man on the trail with George, but she was curious.

"Did you ever hear of anyone seeing anything strange on the trail to Abrams or up around the Elijah Oliver place?"

"Strange how?"

"Just strange. Has anybody told you about anything out of the ordinary?"

"Once in a while, some hiker will happen on a snake that's just eaten and swear it's swallowed a small child or claim to see a Sasquatch. Now back in the '70s, when those hippies were smokin' their wacky tabacky out there on the trail, we got a lot of wild tales. But not so much anymore. Why? Did you see something?"

"Not really," she said. Trying to close the door she'd opened, she continued, "Sam was hallucinating when I found him, and I just wondered if he might really have seen something. But he took a pretty good blow to the head in addition to everything else."

George looked skeptical but let the subject drop. After she dozed off for the third time, George suggested that they stay the night. "Thanks, George," Abby said. "But I'd just as soon head back to the cove. If I can get my buddy here up early enough, I thought we might go horseback riding in the morning. Maybe up to Spence Field."

"Haven't you had enough for one trip?" Jake laughed.

Later as they snuggled together in their sleeping bags, Jake once again mused at how amazing it was that Abby found the boy.

"I had help, you know," she said.

"Sure, you told me his brothers were looking too. But it was *you* that actually found him."

"I'm not talking about the boys, Jake."

"You mean the mystery man?"

"Uh-huh. Only this time, it was almost as if he knew who I was. I was down below the falls looking in entirely the wrong direction when he appeared and told me to turn around. He seemed to know who I was and who I was looking for. I never would have found Sam if it hadn't been for him."

"What do you mean?"

"Sam was down off the trail in some brush and fallen trees. Nothing really dense, but I couldn't see him from the trail. I'd been following the man or ghost or whatever he is for quite a ways, then he just stopped and looked toward the river. I couldn't see anything. I was scared and mad. Scared that I was off chasing a ghost when I should have been looking elsewhere, and mad that he didn't take me right to the boy. So I yelled at him."

"'Him, who? The ghost?"

"I know it sounds silly, but you know how I get."

"That old ghost is just lucky you couldn't hit him. So what happened?"

"I don't know exactly. I guess Sam must have been drifting in and out and woke up enough to call out. He wasn't that far off the trail. I just couldn't see him 'til he sat up. It was so strange."

"I wonder who this guy is, or was."

"Me too. That's why I was asking George if anyone else had reported anything. I hate to think I'm the only one who sees this guy."

"Well, if it is GG3, I've seen him too."

"That's right. I'd forgotten about your night visitor at Aunt June's. Do you suppose it really could be the same person? And I wonder why the heck he keeps appearing to me."

"I don't know, but we're not going to figure it out tonight. Besides, I didn't drive all the way back here just to discuss ghostly apparitions. Suppose a fella could get a kiss around here somewhere?"

Chapter 27

THEIR PLANS FOR AN EARLY morning went awry from the outset. When Abby finally succumbed to sleep, she did not awaken at first light as she normally did in the mountains. Jake tried to rouse her shortly after dawn but was greeted with only a muffled "Hrmmph." She was still sleeping soundly at 7:00 a.m., and Jake, unaccustomed to the confines of the tent, crawled out and set about making breakfast. The smell of coffee and bacon finally penetrated her sleep-fogged mind, and Abby poked her head out of the door of the tent.

"Morning, sunshine. Did you sleep well?"

"Too well, apparently. What time is it?"

"About eight-thirty."

"So much for a sunrise ride up to Spence Field."

"I figured you could use the rest after your adventures yesterday. Coffee?"

"Yes, please. But give me a minute, and I'll be out. Do I smell bacon?

"I'm not the campfire gourmet that you are. Bacon and eggs and hash browns is about all I can manage. George tells me you can make spoon bread in a Dutch oven, but that's way beyond me."

"It's not that hard. I'll teach you sometime. But what you've got there smells awfully good to me."

After they put the breakfast dishes in a pan, Abby sat back in a camp chair with a second cup of coffee and tried to clear the cobwebs. She couldn't remember the last time she had slept so soundly or so dreamlessly. Meanwhile, Jake fidgeted around the campsite until she finally said, "Is something bothering you? You're pacing."

Jake stopped and grinned. He took a seat near her on the picnic bench. "Are *you* okay?"

"Of course. Why?"

He took a deep breath. "I didn't tell you the whole truth about why I came back yesterday."

"That sounds a bit ominous."

"Ominous, no. Weird, yes. But then again, maybe not."

"Okay, spill it."

"I was up in the attic yesterday, poking around to see if sis had missed anything. Even though the letters and journals are starting to make a sense, I still feel like there is a big piece missing, and I haven't been able to find the link to the cove."

"Did you find anything?"

"Nothing new in the attic, but while I was up there—" He paused.

Abby noticed a flush of red creeping up his neck. "What?" she demanded.

"I think the place may be haunted."

Abby laughed. "What, you mean you've got your own ghost now?"

"I don't know, but there was something strange up there and then…well, I just had to come back and make sure you were all right."

"So are you going to tell me about it?"

"I was up there poking around yesterday morning when I heard a woman's voice calling 'Jacob.' At first I thought it was my sister. I hollered back but got no answer. I figured maybe I had heard someone outside looking for someone else. Then I heard it again. 'Jacob, I need you.' No one in the family calls me Jacob, so that alone was enough to raise my hackles. Anyway, I still figured it was my sister, so I went down to see what she needed. But when I got to the first floor, her husband said she'd gone shopping—there was no one in the house but the two of us."

"Okay, that is weird. Are you sure it wasn't your brother-in-law pulling your leg?"

"I wasn't at first, but when I went back to the attic, it happened again."

"Did you see anyone…or anything?"

183

"No, but the longer I stayed up there, the more I felt like there was something wrong with you, and I needed to come back. It wasn't thing specific...not like a premonition or anything. I just had to come back."

"Based on last night, I think I know what you came back for."

"That was nice, but seriously, that's not why I came back."

"Believe me, given the number of times I've gone off chasing GG3, I know exactly what you're talking about. But I've never been there. How could it be related to me? Did you tell Sarah about it?"

"Are you kidding? My sister would have me committed. Besides, a ghost might not be good for business. Well, if your ghost led you to me, why couldn't mine send me to you?"

"Point taken." Abby laughed. "So what are you going to do?"

"About the voice, nothing right now. But I found something new night before last in Aunt Sarah's diaries. A reference to a place called Wolf Mountain. I don't know if it refers to a town or a place. It appears that some part of the family may have come from there."

"Do you know where it is?"

"Sarah's diary doesn't say for sure, but I got out a North Carolina map this morning and found a dot with the name of Wolf Mountain. Don't know if it's the place or not, but seems worth a shot. Since you seem to be safe and sound, I thought I'd go back and check it out."

"Would you like some company?"

"I thought you wanted this week to yourself."

"I did, but I don't think I'm going to find my answers here. But if you'd rather go alone..."

Within the hour, they stowed away Abby's gear in her car. They stopped and made arrangements with George to leave her car at his cabin, and by noon they were on Highway 441 across Newfound Gap into North Carolina.

Chapter 28

WHILE JAKE DROVE, ABBY IDLY poked through one of the boxes of old documents he had in the back seat. "Have you gone through all of these?" she asked.

"Not all. Feel free to see if you can make any sense of what you find. So far I haven't been able to see any rhyme or reason to the way the papers are stored. I've been sorting them as I come to them and putting them in boxes by year and author. I haven't touched that one."

At first glance, the box appeared to contain only things of recent vintage: land records, car titles, and the like. She was about to close it and try another when she spied a small book. Pulling it out, she was disappointed to see that it simply contained notations about crops and plantings and seemed, like the other documents, to date only to the early 1900s. Before replacing it, she opened its covers wide and fanned the pages. A scrap of yellowed paper fluttered to her lap. Laying the other items aside, she held it to the window so she could read the faded writing.

"Jake! I think I've found something. Listen to this."

May 21, 1865

> *Today I will marry Luke Bartlett. It has been almost three years since I came to live in the company of his mother's people. Charlotte, or Sa-lut-tah as I have come to call her by her Cherokee name, has asked me often if I am sure about my decision. Koo-le-cheh, Luke's grandfather, too seems puzzled by my decision.*

"It fades out here, and there's something I can't read. Okay, it goes on…"

> *Sa-lut-tah tells me I was sick for many weeks after Luke brought me to their village. When I finally awoke from the deep sleep, I had no memory of what had taken place on the trail or before. When my past came back, it was like the pain of an enemy's knife thrust suddenly and sharply into my heart. For months, I was unable to even look at Luke. I was so happy that day back in the cove when I heard their footsteps on the porch. Jacob was home. and I could finally tell him about—*

"Jacob? Who's Jacob? Tell him about what?" Jake asked. "Let me see that."

"You just watch the road. There's nothing more to see…the page is torn."

"But she mentions the cove, right? This has to be the woman who came from there. Is there anything else in her writing?"

Abby took everything out of the box and shook each document before replacing it but found nothing else in the woman's distinctive handwriting. Frustrated with that search, she began scanning some of the land records for references to Wolf Mountain. Near the bottom of the pile, she found a paper that appeared to document some sort of land swap.

"Here's something else. Near as I can tell, it looks like a land deal of some sort. Let me see…looks like a Walter Jameson traded some land…"

Jake drummed his fingers on the steering wheel while Abby scanned the document.

She held up a finger to quiet him. Finally, she continued, "Okay, it looks like a Walter Jameson traded some land on Wolf Mountain for a lot in Asheville. But who the heck is Walter Jameson?"

"That would be Aunt Sarah's husband. He died back in the '30s, so we never knew him. What is the address in Asheville?"

"There isn't an address, just a land description. It does say that one side was bounded by the Old Post Road."

"That's Sarah's house, the one Gramps inherited from her. What does it say about Wolf Mountain?"

"Just a land description, nothing like an address or anything. It's dated 1900."

"Seems like that would have been around the time Aunt Sarah got married."

"Didn't you say she was born in 1867? Odd that she waited that long to marry. Did they have any children?"

"No, that's why she left the house to Gramps. Anything else of interest in there?"

Abby went back to her rummaging but found no other references to Wolf Mountain. "Where do you want to start when we get there?"

"I'm not sure since I don't know what we'll find when we get there. It doesn't look like it's very big, so maybe our best bet is to check out cemeteries and see if we can find any old Bartlett bones 'a moldering' in the ground."

After passing through the Indian reservation at Cherokee, they continued south on Highway 441. For a while, Abby contented herself by watching the ever-changing and yet ever-sameness of the misty blue mountains that surrounded them. What would have it been like to live in these mountains 125 years ago, she wondered? Even today, there were areas accessible only by narrow winding dirt roads. How would it have been when only game trails connected small settlements and remote cabins? Hard to imagine, she thought, but a part of her envied the pioneers that first inhabited this land.

When the tree-covered mountains started sprouting billboards and other signs of modern civilization, she opened the glove box and pulled out a map. "Where did you say this place was?"

"Somewhere south of a town called Tuckasegee, I think. It was hard to tell."

"I see Tuckasegee, but there's no Wolf Mountain anywhere around. Are you sure that's where it is?"

Jake pulled the car over to the side of the road. "Let me see that map. You must be looking in the wrong place."

"I beg your pardon! I believe I know how to read a map and—"

It was Jake's turn to raise a hand for silence. "But it was there this morning."

"What? So now you're telling me that we have ghost towns to go along with our people ghosts? Are you sure you weren't dreaming again?"

"Of course, I'm sure. I was looking at the map when you got up this morning. It was on *your* map."

"*My* map?"

"Yeah, I got the atlas out of your car."

"That old thing? I've had it since I first started driving. It's so old you can get lost just looking at it. I don't know why I hang on to it."

"It was a small dot on a secondary road, so maybe it just wasn't big enough to be put on the newer maps. It was between Tuckasegee and Glenville, so it's not like we can miss it."

When they arrived in Glenville, it was all Abby could do to keep from saying, "I told you so." The road from Tuckasegee was paved but winding, and there were few signs of civilization between the small towns. "Do you want to go back and see if we missed it somehow?" she asked as Jake slowed and pulled off the road at a small store.

"No. I'll go in here and ask if they know where it is."

Abby looked at him with mouth agape.

"What? Why are you looking at me that way? Haven't you ever had to stop and ask for directions."

"Will you marry me?" she asked and immediately had the child-like urge to clamp her hand over her mouth.

"Huh? What's wrong with you?"

"N-n-nothing." To her consternation, the word came out in a squeak. Clearing her throat, she laughed and continued, "I just always said if I ever found a man smart enough to stop and ask for directions when he was lost, I'd propose on the spot."

Jake shook his head and got out.

As Abby watched his retreating figure, her mind raced. *What on earth possessed me to say that? He did know that I was just kidding, didn't he? Didn't he? Surely he did. And I really was joking, right? Right. I was, wasn't I?* In truth, she wasn't sure. She sat a moment waiting for the inevitable panic to set in. When it didn't, she probed her mind further. *You do love him, don't you? And he loves you, doesn't he? Okay, so what if he takes it seriously and accepts? What are you going to do then?* Abby had absolutely no idea but realized that she was no longer afraid of the answer.

When Jake returned to the car, he had another map in his hand. "Okay, the good news is that I haven't lost my mind. There is a Wolf Mountain. The bad news is that we can't get there from here—at least not directly."

"That doesn't sound too bad."

"Well, there's a little more bad news."

"How bad?"

"I'm not sure. From the looks of the map, TVA or the Corps of Engineers has been busy over here, and the dot for Wolf Mountain is right on the edge of a reservoir. It's possible that we could get there and find that what we're looking for is underwater."

"So how far is it?"

"As the crow flies, not far, only a few miles. The way we have to go, maybe thirty miles."

"We better get going then. We don't have that much daylight left."

"Are you sure?"

"Well, this does look a little like where they filmed *Deliverance*, but as long as we don't see any cross-eyed boys with banjos, I guess I'm game."

Jake laughed, and they started out again. Shortly after turning onto the secondary road that would carry them to Wolf Mountain, they ran out of pavement. At first, it appeared that there was just repair work in progress; but after several miles on the rough and narrow winding road, Jake said, "Would you check the map and make sure we didn't miss a turn somewhere? Is this supposed to be a dirt road?"

Abby peered at the map and the legend. "Can't tell from the map, but I don't think so."

"We've got more than half a tank of gas. What do you think?"

"I vote we go on. We only made one turn, so how lost can we get? If we don't find it or hit paved road again soon, we can always turn around and go back."

The road got narrower and steeper as they went over one mountain down the other side. When they reached the bottom of the steep grade, the road immediately climbed out of sight again. Abby found her mind wandering again to how it must have been to live in this area in the 1800s. Except for the road they traveled on, the land appeared little changed from what it must have been like then. No power lines or microwave towers here; nothing but the road itself to indicate that man had passed this way before. She nodded yes to Jake's unasked question, and they drove on. Shortly after crossing the summit of the second mountain, they rounded yet another hairpin turn and found themselves back on pavement. Below them, they could see the late-afternoon sun sparkling off the water.

"That must be the reservoir down there," said Jake. "Maybe we're actually going to find this place."

But when they reached the lake, it appeared deserted. There were a few piers jutting out into the water on the far shore, but no sign of a town or indication that there had ever been one. Jake drove on slowly. A mile or so after crossing the small dam that created the reservoir, they saw a small brick church. The sign read "Wolf Creek Baptist Church." He pulled off the road as a man came around the side of the church with a pair of hedge clippers.

Chapter 29

"Excuse me," said Jake as he got out of the car. "We're looking for Wolf Mountain."

The man took off his hat, revealing a thick thatch of white hair. He took a handkerchief out of his overall pocket and wiped the inside rim of his hat and replaced it on his head. "The mountain or the town?"

"Both, I guess."

"The mountain's over yonder," the old man said with a gesture that took in quite a lot of real estate. "The town, or most of it, is out there in the middle of that lake."

Jake's shoulders slumped at this news. "Oh," was all he managed in reply.

By now Abby had joined them. "You said 'most.' Does that mean that part of the town was spared?"

"I wouldn't say *spared*. What exactly are you looking for?"

Jake shook his head as if to clear the cobwebs of disappointment. "My name is Bartlett, Jake Bartlett. I'm looking for some ancestors from around here back around the time of the Civil War and before."

"Bartlett, did you say?"

"Yes, sir. Are there any still around?"

"No, not anymore. Who were your kinfolk?"

"My great-great-grandfather was Luke Bartlett. I believe his wife's name was Abigail."

"Abigail? The medicine woman?"

"Gee, I don't know. They had a daughter, Sarah, who was my great-aunt. I don't remember hearing that her mother was a medicine woman. The story in the family is that she came from a place in Tennessee called Cades Cove, but that's about all I know."

"My name's Henderson, John Henderson. Actually, I think we're distant cousins of some sort. My great-aunt Priscilla was married to your aunt Sarah's brother. I remember Sarah, 'tho by the time I came along, she had moved off to Asheville and only came back for visits. She and my grandmother were friends when they were girls."

Jake's face lit with excitement as he fired off questions in machine-gun fashion.

"Slow down, young fella." The old man laughed. "Let's take a walk. I want to show you something."

Abby and Jake followed Mr. Henderson across the road and into the woods on a well-worn track. As they walked, his story unfolded.

"I don't know the whole story, but I'll tell you what I know. Some of this comes from my grandmother, and some is just local gossip, and not all of that is…" He paused, as if trying to decide how to proceed. "According to the stories I've heard, not all the Bartletts were what you'd call upstanding citizens."

"I guess every family has a black sheep or two. What were they, cattle thieves?"

"That, and maybe worse. That part of the story is pretty murky. A couple of questions for you. Did you know that your great-great-grandfather was half-Cherokee, and did you ever hear of bushwackers?"

"Yes to the first question. As to the second, just from Saturday-morning Westerns. I thought it was a cowboy term."

"I'm not sure how it got started either, but it was used in connection with some of the guerrilla fighters on both sides of the Civil War. I guess it's true that war brings out the best and worst in people. Anyway, the story goes that Joshua Bartlett, that would be Luke's older brother, was one of the latter. Seems he wasn't much for the real fighting but took to the raiding and looting that the Southern Army often had to depend on to keep provisioned. The farm over on Wolf Mountain was doing poorly, so he took to raiding over in Tennessee. Part of what he stole went to the army, but part of it he kept. Somewhere along the line, he took Luke on one of his raids, and this is where the story gets murky. Josh and his partner came back without Luke and said he'd been killed."

"But—" Jake started to interrupt, but the old man raised his hand.

"I'm getting to that part. A year or so later, seems like Josh must've got too lazy to go clear to Tennessee to do his stealing, and he was hung as a horse thief over in Macon County. The rest of the family stayed pretty much to themselves on the farm and waited out the war. Then one day long about 1872, Luke shows up with a wife and a couple of youngun's. There was a little boy named Josiah and a little girl."

"Aunt Sarah?"

"The same. She must have been about four or five then since she and my grandmother were the same age."

"But where did they come from?"

"Do you know the story of the Cherokees and the Trail of Tears?"

Abby and Jake both nodded.

"Then you know some of the Cherokee from Georgia escaped into the mountains of North Carolina when the rest of the Cherokee were herded up. Apparently, Luke's mother and her people were part of this group, and Luke's father went with them. James and Mary came to Wolf Mountain around the time Josh was born, and she died right after Luke was born some years later."

"But where was Luke all that time? And how did he meet Abigail?"

"As to the second question, I don't know that I ever heard tell. She was just with him when he showed up after the war. If anyone around here knew her story, I never heard it. Seems like I do remember my grandmother saying that she sometimes talked about that place you mentioned, some cove, wasn't it?"

"Cades Cove."

"That's it, but I can't remember anything specific other her saying it was over in Tennessee someplace. As to where they were for all that time, Luke and Abigail were off with his mother's people. I don't know how they got there or how long they stayed, but that's where Abigail learned to be a medicine woman. Weren't any doctors hereabouts back then, and my grandmother said she helped a lot of people in her time."

By this time, they had reached a small clearing in which stood a tall wooden cross. Just beyond it, on a spit of land jutting out into the lake, was a cemetery. Some of the graves were marked with headstones of polished marble or granite and bore dates in the 1900s while others were unpolished and worn. All the graves were well-tended and covered with a blanket of small white stones.

"You asked if part of the town survived. Well, here is what's left. The church was flooded along with everything else, but the cemetery was on a hill. A few of the graves had to be moved, but most of them were above the high-water line. The Bartletts' plot is over there," he said, pointing to a group of weathered stones.

Jake and Abby picked their way through the garden of stone and artificial flowers until they reached the collection of graves. "James Bartlett, 1810–1869," read the first stone.

"This must be Luke's father," said Jake. "Here's Mary's grave too. But here's another grave that says 'wife of James,' so he must have remarried after Mary died. And here's Luke and Abigail."

Nearby they found the graves of Josiah Bartlett, his wife, Priscilla, as well as Micah Bartlett and his wife, Polly. "These must be Aunt Sarah's brothers. I guess they stayed here on Wolf Mountain. Gramps was Josiah's son, and he went off to Asheville to work for Aunt Sarah's husband."

"Who does this one belong to?" Abby asked, pointing to a small stone partially obscured by flowers. "I thought it was the footstone for Abigail's grave, but it has writing on it. Looks like maybe they had a baby that died."

"I must have missed that one. Can you read it?"

Abby dropped to one knee, moved the flowers aside, and peered at the inscription.

"Well, what does it say, Ab?"

"Come see for yourself. Tell me if this says what I think it says."

Jake dropped down beside her and read, "Jacob Matthews Cutter."

1865

"Today I will marry Luke Bartlett..."

Abigail sat staring at the words. No wonder E-do-di and Sa-lut-tah questioned her decision. Seeing the words on paper, she realized how strange it must seem to them. Three autumns ago, he had returned to their village after a long absence with the wife of another man. A man dead at the hands of his brother and his partner. And the baby... She didn't want to think about it, but with the pen now quiet in her hand, she remembered...

By the time her memory returned, the snows had come, and travel was impossible. Abigail wanted nothing more than to get away from Luke and all that reminded her of him. But where would she go? Without Jacob, she had no reason to return to the cove. The cabin and their land had been a gift from Jacob's father, and with good land at a premium, she didn't think he'd allow her to farm it alone. A part her life and heart would always be at home there, but without Jacob... At the same time, she didn't want to return to her father's house. She had changed so much since she left Virginia; and after being the mistress of her own household, she knew she would feel like a stranger in her parents' home. Many months of winter lay ahead, and there was no urgency in her decision. Throughout the cold days and long nights, Abigail sat at Sa-lut-tah's side as the older woman taught her about the medicines she made. When it was time to gather the spring herbs and roots, Abigail went to Luke's grandfather and asked for permission to remain in the village.

Sa-lut-tah allowed Abigail to stay with her without question, and the younger woman became an eager apprentice as the medicine woman went about her business of tending to the sick and injured of the village. The two spent hours in the woods as Sa-lut-tah taught her the proper times to gather the plants and what ailments they were used for. Back at the cabin, Abigail helped place them on drying racks and later learned how to mix them in the proper proportions. Too little would not help, and in some cases, too much could kill. By midsummer Sa-lut-tah often sent her off alone to gather what was needed, and Abigail found herself at ease in the quiet dark woodlands surrounding the village. Back in the cove, it was not unusual to see the granny woman out in the woods in the mountains far from her home in the settlement, and now she knew why. Many of Sa-lut-tah's poultices and remedies were similar to those prescribed by the granny woman.

One day, Luke came to the cabin as they were preparing a batch of kanstatsi. Abigail had seen little of him in the past few months. After her memory returned, she refused to see or talk to him. His grandfather said it would be best if he left the village for a while. So Luke went deep into the forest to a place where their ancestors once wintered in caves. He remained there until spring. Since his return, their words had been few and tense.

"Would you come for a walk with me?" he asked.

"Why should I?"

"I'd like to show you something."

Suspicious but curious, she followed him to edge of the village. There in a clearing of freshly cut trees stood a new cabin.

"E-do-di says you have decided to stay here in the village."

Dumbfounded, she just stood there.

"I built it myself. It's not big, but it's snug. There is a spring out back, and Sa-lut-tah says the ground is good for growing herbs."

"You built this for me? But why? Surely you don't think…"

The anger and accusation in her voice hit him like a physical blow, and he faltered. "I don't think anything. It's just that…I just thought… I know you probably won't believe this, but I had no idea what Josh and Matt were up to when we left Wolf Mountain."

Unwilling to believe his words, she remained mute.

"Oh, I guess I knew they were bent on thieving, but I never imagined…Josh wanted to kill you."

His words released a deep anger inside of Abigail, and even though she knew she was making no sense, she was unable to stop the torrent of angry words and bitter tears that followed. All the months of pent-up rage and grief came spilling out. Luke stood there, head down but unflinching in the face of her wrath. When she finally ran out of words, he looked up at her, and the tears in his eyes matched those in hers.

"Do what you want with the cabin," he said quietly and walked away.

For a time, Abigail just stood there. Finally, stirred by curiosity, she found herself at the cabin door. What sort of man would kidnap a woman and then build her a cabin, she wondered? And what sort of cabin would that man build? Inside she found its one room contained all that she would need to make a home. A small table and chair stood in the center. The hearth was well-suited to cooking, and there was a sturdy mantle above. In one corner behind a curtain was a bedstead, and across the room were racks like those Sa-lut-tah used for drying herbs and roots. Herbs and flowers were already drying there, bringing their color and fragrance into the room. The cabin was well-built. In different circumstances, Abigail would have said that it had been lovingly built, but that was impossible. Unsettled, she closed the door and returned to Sa-lu-tah's where she found the old woman waiting with Luke's grandfather.

"What my grandson did was not right, but I think his heart is not evil like that of his brother."

"But what does he want, E-do-di? What should I do?"

"Luke seeks only to return, in some small measure, what was taken from you. He cannot bring back your husband or the child, but hopes that perhaps you will be able to make the cabin your home."

"I'm not sure, E-do-di."

"In time, my child," said Koo-le-cheh. "In time, your heart will tell you what to do."

Chapter 30

JAKE STARED AT THE STONE marker in disbelief. "Jacob Cutter...JC?"

"How could it be? Besides, this looks like a child's grave."

Jake shook his head. "Yes, but why would there be a Cutter grave in the Bartlett plot?" He turned to Mr. Henderson, who had busied himself tidying up some graves in another plot. "Do you know anything about this?"

"Afraid I can't help you there. I asked my grandmother if Sarah had ever mentioned it, but apparently they never discussed it."

"Looks like we're about back where we started."

"Oh, I don't know. At least we found Wolf Mountain and know for sure that Abigail came from Cades Cove. That's a pretty fair day's work from what I understand of genealogy," Abby replied.

"I guess you're right. I just wanted to know the whole story. And there's that grave. It just doesn't make any sense." Turning back to their guide, he asked, "Do you mind if we take a few pictures?"

"Go right ahead. They're your kinfolk, after all. Do you think you can find your way back to the church? I need to get back and lock up."

"Sure, no problem. Thank you for all of your time."

"My pleasure. Good luck on working out the rest of the story. If you're ever back this way, stop in and tell me what you've found."

They spent a few minutes photographing the Bartlett gravestones and walked back toward the car.

"So where do we go from here?" Abby asked.

"From a research standpoint, I'm not sure. Otherwise, it's getting late, and there sure as heck isn't much in the way of hotels around here. We're not that far from Asheville. How would you like to meet the rest of the Bartlett clan?

"As long as they're alive! I think I've had enough of ghosts and cemeteries for one day."

"I make no promises other than a good meal and a million questions from my mother." He stopped on the trail and stood looking at her.

"What's with the Cheshire grin?"

"I was just wondering how I should introduce you."

"What do you mean?" she asked in mock innocence.

"As I recall, you asked me to marry you a few hours ago."

"Yes, but I was only…" She stopped, took a deep breath, and said, "How should I know? You never answered."

"So what if I say yes? What would you say to that?"

"I guess I'd ask if you were sure you knew what you were getting into."

"And if I still said yes?"

Moving into his embrace, she took another deep breath and said, "Then I guess I'd say you could introduce me as your fiancée."

Chapter 31

ALL THOUGHTS OF FUTURE PLANS were quickly forgotten when they reached Sarah's. A petite woman with short blonde hair flung the door open at their knock and demanded, "Where have you been? Mom's been trying to reach you for two days."

The smile on Jake's face vanished. "What's wrong?"

"Nothing's wrong. Mom and Dan are fine. It's just that—oh my goodness, you must be Abby," Sarah said, giving her a hug. "We've been just dying to meet you. Does Mom know you're coming? We were so disappointed when Jake called and said you couldn't make it this trip. What changed your mind? Have you had supper?"

As they were bombarded with questions, Jake winked at Abby. "No sense in interrupting her. She'll run out of breath eventually."

Sarah sputtered into silence.

"May I say something now?" asked Jake. Without waiting for a reply, he continued, "Abby, this motormouth is my little sister, Sarah. And this gentleman who can't get a word in edgewise is her husband, Tom. And before you get wound up again, Sis, we're starved."

Sarah laughed, and introductions were made all around. In the kitchen, Sarah set about fixing a meal of cold cuts, cheese, and home-made bread, followed by apple pie fresh from the oven. The conversation was a lively mix of questions and the sort of tales that brothers and sisters love to tell on one another.

Two hours later, as Sarah cleared the table and set about making coffee, Jake asked, "I almost forgot. What did Mom want?"

"I'm not sure. Something about your genealogy stuff, I think. She was pretty excited when she called, but I never did find out what it was all about."

"Fat lot of help you are. Do you suppose she's still up?"

Sarah looked at the clock. "Not a chance. She and Dan have been on a health and exercise kick, and they go to the Y and swim every morning at five-thirty. They hit the sack about nine o'clock these days. Call her now, and you'll scare her out of her wits."

"I guess it'll have to wait 'til morning. Are you sure she didn't say what it was about?"

"I don't think so." Sarah paused, her brow furrowed in concentration. "She may have said something about a letter, but I wasn't really paying attention."

"You're no help whatsoever. What if it had been important?"

That remark was greeted with a swat from Sarah's dish towel. She turned to Abby. "Despite what my big brother thinks, I really am a responsible adult. I just don't get into all this family-tree stuff the way he and Mom do."

Abby laughed. "I know what you mean. But it does sort of grow on you. My mom and dad have been working on ours for the past year, but I haven't really gotten into it. But we found your great-great-grandparents' graves today, and that was pretty cool."

"Oh?"

"Aunt Sarah's and Gramps's parents," Jake said by way of explanation.

"Oh! Now that is cool. I'm named after Aunt Sarah, you know. I was only about four or five when she passed away, but she always told the neatest bedtime stories. My favorite one was about living in an Indian village as a child."

Jake bolted upright in his chair. "What? I didn't know that. Why didn't you tell me?"

"I don't know. I hadn't really thought about it in years. I guess I figured she told the same stories to all of us. Why, is it important?"

Jake told her about their visit to Wolf Mountain and the story John Henderson had told them.

"You mean Aunt Sarah really lived with the Cherokee? I always thought she just put herself in someone else's story. And what about her mother? Was she really a medicine woman?"

"Seems like it," said Jake. "I sure wish it wasn't too late to call Mom."

"Speaking of late," said Tom, "it's after midnight. Our first seating for breakfast is at seven-thirty, so we'd better get some shut-eye."

"Sorry," said Jake. "I forget this is a working household. Do you have room for us?"

"You're in luck. We've just renovated two rooms to increase our capacity. There is a bathroom in between. I hope you don't mind sharing," Sarah asked with a mischievous gleam in her eye.

"Subtle, sis, real subtle. I think we'll be able to manage."

Sarah was up early tending to the other guests the following morning, and by the time Abby and Jake showered and reached the dining room, she had already contacted his mother. "Mom and Dan will be here in about five minutes."

"What? Did you tell her that Abby was here?"

"Of course, silly, why not?"

"Abby, I have to warn you, Mom is a little more direct than Sarah. Be prepared for anything."

Abby just laughed.

Sarah handed her a cup of coffee. "Sorry, I guess I should have given you a little more warning. Hope you're ready."

As if on cue, the doorbell rang. Before Sarah could reach it, the door flew open; and a tall, spare woman entered, leaving her husband standing in the open doorway. Barely glancing at her daughter and son, she stopped in front of Abby. Ignoring her outstretched hand, the woman walked all around Abby, looking her up and down. Apparently satisfied with what she saw, she hugged Abby soundly and turned to her son. "So, Jacob, when are you going to propose to this young woman?"

Ignoring her question, Jake said, "Hello, Mom. Abby, this is my mother, Melissa. And the poor man she left outside is her husband, Dan Gallaher. Come on in, Dan."

"I'm so glad to finally meet you, Mrs. Gallaher. Jake has told me—"

"It's Melissa, please. And, Jake, you haven't answered my question."

"Mom—" Sarah tried to interrupt.

Jake looked at Abby, who nodded. "Actually, Mom, Abby has proposed to me."

"What? When? Why didn't you say something last night?" asked Sarah. "So what did you say? When? Where? Have you set a date?"

"Sarah!" Melissa said, silencing her daughter's barrage of questions. Turning to Jake, she continued, "I certainly hope you had the good sense to accept."

Jake laughed and nodded. "Of course. I just hope you haven't scared her out of it less than twenty-four hours later."

"Oh pooh. She doesn't look like the sort who would frighten easily. Besides, you've been mooning over this woman for months. I just wanted to make sure you didn't let her get away. Welcome to the family, Abby."

Breakfast was a merry affair with plenty of teasing questions. Protesting that they really hadn't made any plans, Abby and Jake were able to fend off most of Melissa's and Sarah's questions. Finally, in an effort to change the subject, Abby said, "Mrs.—uh, Melissa, Sarah said you found something related to Jake's genealogy research."

"I almost forgot. Remember your aunt Sarah was married to a man named Walter Jameson?" Seeing nods all around, she continued, "Well, even though Sarah and Walter had no children, apparently he had a sister who did. Jessica, her name was, and her son was married to one of the Wilkes...I think you or Luke might have been in school with some Wilkes boys, probably some of her grandchildren or maybe great-nephews. Sarah, weren't there some Wilkes kids in your class too? Or was it Alice?"

Exasperated, Jake interrupted, "Mom, stick to the point. What does any of that have to do with the Bartletts?"

"If you'll let me finish, I'll tell you. Anyway, as it turns out, Jessica's granddaughter is teaching the art course that I took last spring over at Brevard. I told her all about you, Jake, and your genealogy. Of course, this was before I knew about you and Abby. I'll have to remember to tell her you're off the market."

"Mom!"

"Sorry. Anyway, we got to talking about family, and that's how we found out that she's related to the Bartletts. I haven't seen her since last year, but she called me last week. Turns out her mother inherited one of those big old houses over by the college from her grandmother. When her mom passed away, the house passed to Susan. She was getting ready for the estate sale, and that's when she found the letter."

"What letter?"

"The letter from Aunt Sarah, silly. Haven't you been listening?"

"To every word, Mom. So tell us about the letter."

Chapter 32

As it turned out, Melissa had an entire bundle of letters in Sarah's distinctive handwriting. Jake thumbed through the bundle looking at the postdates that covered a span of some twenty years.

Melissa took the packet from him and extracted one letter from the middle. "There is a lot of history in these pages," she said, waving it overhead with a flourish. "But this is *the* letter."

"Okay, Mom, enough with the drama. What does it say?"

"Read it for yourself. I think this is the key you've been looking for."

Jake took the yellowed envelope from his mother, opened it carefully, unfolded the pages, and began to read:

November 1917

Dearest Jessie,

I am writing today with the saddest of news. Mother was more gravely ill than Father knew when he wired me. There was an outbreak of scarlet fever on Wolf Mountain, and for two weeks, Mother had been helping the families in the community nurse their sick. Unfortunately, the roots and herbs she used to soothe the fever and rash for others seemed to bring her no relief when she fell ill. By the time she allowed Father to summon the doctor, there was little he could do for her.

When I arrived, Mother was delirious with fever, and there was nothing Father and I could do except to try to keep her calm. At times, she seemed to know me, and that seemed to give her some peace, although she spoke to me as she had when I was a girl. For three days, we sat with her, and when the fever was at its worst, Mother began calling for someone named Jacob and fretting about "the baby." When this happened, Father held her hand and said, "Hush now, I'm here. Don't fret, the baby is sleeping." That seemed to be what she wanted to hear, and she finally drifted off to sleep. Father abruptly left the room, and when I was certain Mother was not going to awaken right away, I went to look for him. I found him sitting in front of the fire, tears streaming. When he looked up, Jessie, I've never seen such deep sadness as I saw on my father's face that night. Mother passed away in her sleep a few hours later, and for a while, I forgot about Jacob.

The next night, after all the visitors had come and gone and we retired for the night, I heard Father moving about in the bedroom where we had Mother laid. The funeral was scheduled for the morning, and I went to try and persuade him to get some rest. I found him sitting in a chair by the bed, murmuring to her over and over, "I'm sorry."

Thinking that he somehow blamed himself for her illness, I tried my best to console him. I told him there was nothing he could have done to prevent her from going out and tending to the sick; she's always done it. "No," he said, "not always." The story he told me was one that I could scarce believe. Mother and Father were married for more than fifty years, and no hint of the secret they shared had ever passed their lips.

I knew that Father had an older brother, Josh, who came to no good end; but his name was rarely mentioned and then only in hushed whispers when the adults thought no children were about. I'd truly *forgotten about him until Father started the story that turned into a confession. Uncle Josh, it seems, was more interested in stealing than in fighting for the cause and became a bandit. Times were lean in western Carolina, and most of the able-bodied men had joined, or been forced to join, the Confederate Army, leaving their homesteads undefended. Pickings were easy at first, but when their faces began appearing on sheriffs' notices near home, Josh and his partner found places over in Tennessee where folks had decided to ignore the war and continue farming.*

After a time, Father began riding with Josh and his partner. He said that at first it was an adventure. Like Robin Hood and his men, they would swoop down and steal what they could and ride off without hurting anyone. Then they would escape back across the mountains and share their plunder with the folks on Wolf Mountain. But as time passed, Josh became greedier and more brazen in his deeds. If a victim tried to resist, he would not hesitate to shoot, and more than one man had died at his hand. Father wanted to quit, but Josh threatened to kill him if he did. So they continued their raids.

One place that had proved easy pickings was a place called Cades Cove. Josh and his partner had been there several times. The menfolk were mostly absent, and the women and children put up little resistance. But on one raid, the lone woman they found in her cabin was not afraid to fight them. She caught Father unawares and managed to run away, but Josh chased and caught her. He was going to kill the young woman, but Father talked him out of it. Fearing the woman would raise an alarm, they took her with them.

Father broke down at this point in his story. His anguish was such that at times he was unable to talk. I tried to tell him that whatever had happened so many years ago could no longer matter, but to no avail. He soon regained his composure and continued with his tale.

One night, Josh got drunk and took the woman off into the woods. Father tried to stop him, but the other man knocked him over the head. By the time he came to, the woman had been beaten and used by both men. When Josh and the other man fell into a drunken stupor, Father took the woman and escaped deep into the mountains to the village of his Cherokee grandfather. There, the medicine woman nursed her back to health but was unable to save the baby she had been carrying.

Father paused again in his story, and for a long while, he just sat and looked at Mother with a sad smile. Then he looked at me and said, "The woman I rescued was your mother."

Although my mind was filled with dozens of questions, Father said that he was tired. He would answer all my questions in the morning, he said, but wanted to spend a few more moments with Mother before going to bed. I retired myself, although sleep was long in coming. And, Jessie, I have more sad news to relate. When I awoke the next morning, Father was not in his room. I found him still sitting with Mother, her hand in his. Sometime during the night, he had joined her in that endless sleep.

Jake let the remaining pages fall to the table. "Well, I'll be."

Chapter 33

THE ROOM WAS SILENT SAVE for the ticking of the grandfather clock in the corner. Finally, Sarah demanded. "Well, is that what you were looking for or not?"

"Seems like it might be. It certainly does tie Abigail to Cades Cove," replied Jake. "I wish we knew Jacob's last name, though, so I could trace his family. And what was her maiden name? Who were her parents? Was she born in the cove?"

"Geez, brother! Here, Mom finds something you've been trying to find for years, and all you can do is ask for more."

Turning to his mother, Jake said, "Sorry, Mom. I don't mean to seem ungrateful. This may be the key I've been looking for, but in genealogy, every door you open leads to a dozen more."

"That only makes sense," said Melissa. "There are parents and grandparents and so on for each of us. But this does help, doesn't it?"

"Certainly. Now I know for sure that Abigail lived in Cades Cove. I just have to figure out who she was married to so I can find a record of that marriage since I haven't been able to find one for her and Luke."

"Maybe you've uncovered a family scandal," said Sarah. "Maybe Abigail and Luke were never really married."

"Oh, they were married, all right, but maybe not in a church."

"What do you mean?"

Jake told them about the scrap of paper Abby had discovered. "Based on this letter, I'd guess they were married in a Cherokee ceremony."

Abby sat lost in thought as Jake and his mother and sister discussed the letter and its ramifications. Her mind kept going back to the cemetery on Wolf Mountain and the tiny grave. Could it be?

The thought was too preposterous to mention aloud. But what else could explain the name *Jacob Cutter* in a plot filled with Bartletts? The letter *did* say Abigail was carrying a baby when she was captured. And the scrap of her journal said she was waiting for Jacob. On the other hand, from what Mr. Henderson said, it sounded as if Luke and Abigail stayed with the Cherokee for several years. Surely the baby would have been long buried by the time they returned to Wolf Mountain. But still…why didn't Abigail try to return to Cades Cove after she recovered? Wouldn't she have wanted to get back to Jacob? And where was he when the bushwackers arrived? And why didn't he go after her?

"Earth to Abigail. Hey, Ab, you all right?" Jake said.

"Huh? What? Sure. What did you say?"

"I was just telling everyone about your Dad's mystery man."

"What? Who? Oh, you mean GG3."

"What are you taking about? Who is GG3?" asked Sarah and Melissa in unison.

"That's what my dad calls him. It's the only way he can keep all the 'greats' straight. Once he gets past great-great, he starts numbering them. It really helps when they have the same name."

"I think I'd like your dad," said Melissa. "Jake rattles off names like he knows these people personally, and the rest of us can't keep the generations straight. So tell us about GG3."

"As Jake said, he's a mystery. Apparently, he showed up on GG4's farm in Indiana after the Civil War. Somewhere along the line, he married GG4's daughter, Louisa. Dad was able to find military records indicating although he mustered into the Union Army in Kentucky, he came from Blount County, Tennessee, and that's the last I've heard. I was supposed to do some research for him, but since Christmas, I just haven't had the time."

"But how did he get to Indiana?"

"We're not sure, actually. He was mustered out of Chase Prison over in Ohio after a prisoner exchange, but last I heard, Dad hadn't been able to find out what drew him to Indiana. Jake, I've been thinking more about that grave we found."

"What grave?" asked Melissa.

Jake told his family about the cemetery on Wolf Mountain and of finding the tiny stone.

"The odd thing," said Abby, "is that GG3's name was Jacob Cutter."

1865

"Where is my son?" Ezra demanded as Jacob entered the kitchen.

"Ezra! Where are your manners?" said his wife.

"That's all right, ma'am. I'm sure you're all anxious to hear about Thomas."

She placed a steaming bowl of stew and plate of warm bread in front of him. "We know he's alive and well, and that's enough until you've had some food."

Jacob glanced at the steaming bowl of stew she placed in front of him and then at Ezra glowering at him across the table. "I think if I did, your husband would bust something. Let me tell you about the captain—uh, Thomas. I can't get used to calling him that. I guess he wrote you about most everything that happened after we were captured. When they first took us prisoner, he insisted that they take me to Libby Prison with him even though they mostly just took officers there. Reckon I would've died if he hadn't. After my arm finally healed, though, they sent me to Andersonville, and I didn't figure to see the captain again. Just before the war ended, I got sent to Chase Prison over in Ohio, and I hadn't been there but a day or so when I hear someone call my name, and lo and behold, it's the captain. Sure was good to see a familiar face."

"Yes, yes, but where is he now?" Ezra interrupted.

"Sorry—"

"Hush, now, Ezra," Rebekah said to her husband. "It's all right, Jacob. You just tell us the story in your own way."

"Yes, ma'am. Well, here comes the cap—Thomas, looking fit as a fiddle, like I said. They treated the officers pretty well over at Libby. Anyway, he took me to the barracks where he was staying, and there was this other fella there that had been out in the Indian Territories and California before the war started. He'd gone after gold with the forty-niners, but when he didn't find any, joined up with the army. Said he liked knowing where his next meal was coming from. Anyway, this fella, Buck Everett was his name, spent some time out in the New Mexico Territory and said he'd heard there was a lot more silver out there than they'd found over in Nevada at Comstock. Said he was going back out

there as soon as the Rebs let him loose. Seemed like the more he talked about it, the more the captain listened. When we finally got released, Thomas said he reckoned he wasn't cut out to be a farmer and thought he'd try his hand at prospecting. The last time I saw him, he and old Buck were boarding a train for St. Louis."

"Damn!"

Jacob's bowl and spoon rattled as Ezra's fist came down on the table. He stormed out, slamming the door behind him.

Abashed by her husband's behavior, Rebekah was silent.

"I'm sorry about Father," said Louisa. "It's been hard to find good help since the war, and he was counting on Thomas."

"I know what you mean, ma'am. Farming's hard work. I've spent the last two years trying to figure out what to do now I can't go back to it."

"What do you mean?"

He looked down at his empty sleeve, and she blushed. "But surely..." *Louisa faltered.*

"Nonsense," said Rebekah. "My grandfather kept a farm and raised six children after he lost his arm. You can do anything you set your mind to," she said as she left in search of her husband.

"She's right, you know," said Louisa. "I think Grandfather James was the strongest man I ever knew. We just need to fatten you up a bit. I bet you were a big man before they sent you to Andersonville." She stopped again, blushing. "I mean...uh, Thomas said..." She lapsed into silence.

"It's all right, ma'am. I guess the captain told you I was sort of a scrapper. Guess I had a pretty big mad on me when I joined the army and not just for fighting those Johnny Rebs..."

His voice trailed off, and his face took on a faraway look. Louisa sensed a deep sadness in this man. A hundred questions swirled in her mind. Sensing that this was not the time to unleash her curiosity, she got up and busied herself clearing the table.

"I baked an apple pie this morning. Would you like some?"

"Yes, ma'am, that would be fine." Jacob shook off the memories that the conversation had stirred. "The captain told me you were a mighty fine cook."

"Please, it's Louisa. When you say ma'am, it makes me feel like my mother. Besides, I feel like we already know you from Thomas's letters."

"All right, Louisa it is."

* * * * *

A year later, Jacob paused in his circuit of checking fences to gaze out at the herd of Shorthorn cattle. As he watched the cows grazing peacefully, his thoughts were on how he had come to be here. When he'd promised to go to his captain's family farm, he had no intention of staying this long. He was going to deliver the message that Thomas was not returning and then leave. Beyond that, though, he wasn't sure where he was going. While in Andersonville, he learned that his mother had died. Later still, he learned that Russell Gregory had managed to organize the old men of the cove, including his father, in a successful resistance against the bushwackers. But after years of protracted guerrilla warfare, the farm was in ruins. His father had abandoned their homestead and gone to live in Knoxville. With Abigail gone, Jacob had no taste for returning to the cove. He'd had no taste for farming either, or so he thought. But here he was, far from the mountains of Tennessee, farming nonetheless. He still couldn't believe it.

At first, he'd stayed because he was just too weak to argue with Rebekah Shepard. She was a very determined woman, and since her own son had not returned from the war, she poured all her energies into nursing Jacob back to health. Andersonville had not killed him as it had so many of his comrades, but it had taken all of his strength just to survive. Before joining the army, Jacob stood six foot two and was well-muscled and strong. The man who arrived at the Shepard farm all those months ago was little more than a shell. Weak and tired, the seduction of sleeping beneath clean sheets and eating food that was not crawling with vermin was too powerful to fight. And aside from these enticements, there was Louisa.

Although he had accepted Abigail's death as a fact, Jacob couldn't imagine life with another woman. When he lost his arm, he became convinced that he had nothing to offer a woman and resigned himself to a life lived alone. But as he regained his strength, Jacob found himself *drawn to this spirited woman. The pity that he saw in most people's eyes was missing from hers. Within a few days of his arrival, she began a subtle campaign to help him regain his strength. At first, it was simply asking him to accompany her on a walk around the farm; then it was a request to help her with a task that only required the use of one arm. As the days and weeks passed, the walks became longer, and the tasks became more difficult. When he protested that he couldn't do this or that—that it took two arms—she helped him find a work-around to accomplish the task with one.*

Like chopping wood. One day, while her father and the hired hands were out in the fields, Louisa asked Jacob to chop some kindling wood for the stove.

"Takes two hands to wield an axe," he said.

"But not a hatchet. Come along now. I have to get dinner started. Father and the men will be back soon."

"I don't think—"

"You think too much. Just do it. Come on, I'll steady the log while you split off the kindling."

"But what if I miss and hurt you?"

"I'm willing to take that risk. And you'll never know what you can do until you try it."

And so it went. Whenever Jacob started to say "I can't," Louisa was right there telling him he certainly couldn't unless he first tried. Soon Ezra and Rebekah joined their daughter in challenging their guest to push himself. As they pushed, he pushed back; and within a few months, he'd gained back all the weight he'd lost and developed more strength in his one arm than some men had in two. He began looking upon each new task as a challenge rather than an obstacle, and finding a way to do it was as rewarding as the doing. He fell asleep each night tired to the bones from honest labor, and it felt good. In his heart, he knew that he had Louisa to thank for his recovery. But gratitude was not the only emotion growing in his breast; Jacob was coming to the realization that he had fallen in love with Louisa. And much to his amazement, it appeared that she returned that love. Last night, he'd had a long talk with Ezra, and tomorrow after church, he planned to ask Louisa to marry him.

Chapter 34

ABBY WAS DISTRACTED. ORDINARILY, SHE attacked her work with a single-mindedness that irritated and sometimes worried her friends and family, to say nothing of Jake. To date, their only serious disagreement had been over a forgotten dinner date. But a week after returning from North Carolina, she still couldn't concentrate on her work. Fortunately, despite the stack of pink message slips that had covered her desk Monday morning, most of what needed to be dealt with was minor. Her secretary, bless her, was the soul of organization; and with her help, Abby managed to stay on task. But by Friday afternoon, even Sandra was beginning to cast questioning looks in her direction. Abby sat in her office trying to understand the source of her distraction.

Jake? No, and much to her own surprise, it was not her decision to marry Jake that was troubling her. Although her proposal was made half in jest, Abby soon realized that her heart had belonged to Jake almost from the beginning. She had never met anyone with whom she was so immediately at ease, and she could not imagine not having him in her life. On the drive home from Asheville, they had discussed the matter at some length and decided that they would wait until the end of the semester to make any formal announcement or begin making plans. They agreed that neither could see the advantage of a long engagement, but left things at that. She would, of course, tell her parents; but otherwise, they would keep things low-key for a while. Abby had at least one major felony trial coming up, and Jake had a full schedule of classes. Neither, they decided, needed the additional stress of planning a wedding.

No, it wasn't her relationship with Jake that was troubling her. And it wasn't her professional life. Almost without conscious thought, she had made a decision about that as well. Monday afternoon, she placed a call to Dr. Tucker. He was on ward service and on call until the weekend and unable to get away but agreed to meet her for drinks after work next Tuesday. When he asked if it was a business or personal call, Abby had simply replied, "A little of both."

In truth, she realized, her distraction had nothing to do with her own life but that of two people long dead—GG3 and Abigail. Abby could not get them out of her mind. Was it really possible that they had been married? The logical part of her brain told her that this was just a fanciful notion brought on by the romance in her own life. At the same time, it made a certain sense of things. She now accepted the fact that the apparition that she kept seeing was GG3. Why she knew this, Abby wasn't quite sure, but she knew it nonetheless. And accepting that, it brought other happenings into focus. Why, for instance, had GG3 appeared in Jake's room at Christmas? Did he somehow sense Jake's relationship to Abigail? And hadn't she been following GG3 when she found Jake injured at the cabin ruins? Even Steven seemed to understand the connection. Abby smiled to herself. *Maybe I am losing my mind...I'm sitting here accepting as a fact that I've been having conversations with not just one but two ghosts. And what's worse, it all seems perfectly normal to me.*

Taken together, there was too much to accept just as a series of coincidences. Last night, she had even gone so far as to call her father to see if he had learned any more about GG3. Abby was ready to spell out all her theories for him, although she was far from certain what his reaction would be. The machine answered her call, and she felt a flood of relief. No, she thought, I'm not ready to share this with Dad and Mom. I certainly can't tell them about Steven; that would certainly convince them that I've gone round the bend.

Okay, she said to herself, *I've figured out what's bothering me. Now what am I going to do about it?* Finally she pulled out a legal pad. When she was building a case for prosecution, Abby made chart of the facts in evidence. She put the names of the parties involved in separate boxes on the page. Then using the evidence collected by the detectives, Abby sought possible links between the victims and suspects. Where the connections were clear and uncontroverted, she drew heavy lines and arrows between the parties. When the evidence was merely circumstantial, she used broken lines. The detectives she worked with routinely were familiar with her diagrams and dreaded the broken lines, which meant more hours of investigation. But knowing that Abby had a better-than-average record at trial, they seldom grumbled.

Across the top of the page, she wrote *GG3*, *Abigail*, and *Cades Cove*. Thanks to the letter Jake's mother had provided, she was able to draw a heavy line between Abigail and Cades Cove. But although she knew that GG3 was from Blount County, she had nothing to tie him directly to the cove, and she reluctantly made the connection with a broken line. Abby continued making boxes on the page—the initials *JC* and *AM* on the cornerstone at the cabin, Abigail's diary reference to Jacob, Luke's deathbed confession about the kidnapping, and the tiny grave on Wolf Mountain. She sat staring at the jumble of boxes and lines. There was more supposition and conjecture than fact. But how did she go about proving or disproving her theories? Obviously, the easiest solution would be to enlist Jake's help. When her father first found out that GG3 was from Blount County, he had volunteered to help her track him down and even raised the possibility that GG3 could be the "JC" on his great-great-grandmother's locket. But on the trip back from Asheville, Jake had been less than enthusiastic about her theory about a connection between GG3 and Abigail. While he didn't dismiss it out of hand, he gave her a handful of reasons why her theory was likely incorrect.

Abby found herself wishing that she'd paid more attention when Jake and her father discussed their research techniques. The references and resources for her legal research were readily at hand, but genealogy was an entirely different matter. She knew that her father did a lot of his research at the Allen County Library in Fort Wayne and that her mother had become adept at mining the resources of the internet. Jake must be using whatever resources were available through the university, but what about the local library? Did it have a genealogy section? She started a list of possible resources: libraries, county records, and the internet. All good sources, she thought, but surely there must be some quicker way to find out if she was on the right track. On a whim, Abby logged on to her computer and did a search for the name *Cutter* in Maryville. There were seven.

She dialed the first number on the list and quickly put the receiver down before anyone answered. *What am I going to say?* she wondered. *These people are likely to think I'm crazy. I can just hear the conversation now: "Hello, I'm a perfect stranger, but I'd like to know about your family history."* Abby picked up her pad again and jotted down a script that she hoped would prevent any potential "cousins" from hanging up before they heard what she had to say. She picked up the phone and dialed again. Forty-five minutes later, she sat staring at the list again. The first three numbers had been disconnected. There was no answer at the fourth, but Abby used her script and left a message that she hoped didn't sound too bizarre. An elderly gentleman answered her next call. Apparently, the only word he heard from Abby's scripted spiel was *history* because he launched off into tales of his days at the Oak Ridge National Laboratories back in the '40s. When she was finally able to get a word in edgewise, she learned that he was the first Cutter of his line to come to Tennessee. Abby thanked him politely for the history lesson and rang off. The last two calls put her in contact with Cutters whose parents or grandparents had moved to the area in the early 1900s to go to work at the then new Alcoa company.

I guess that would have just been too easy, Abby thought as she gathered up her papers and put them in her briefcase. *Guess I'll have to hit the library and do this the hard way.* She picked up the phone again and dialed Jake's number.

"How about a blockbuster night?" she asked when he answered. "I'll stop and get a couple of movies if you'll get the pizza."

"Sounds like a plan. I have a stack of papers to grade this weekend, but tonight I'm all yours."

"What sort of movie are you up for? Something new or a classic?"

"How about one of each?"

"What do you want on your pizza?"

"Anything but anchovies. I can't stand those furry little fish! Just surprise me."

"I can do that. Your place or mine?"

"Mine. I know you well enough by now that if you can see that pile of papers, you won't pay any attention to me or the movie."

Jake was waiting on the front steps to her apartment when she arrived. Picking out a movie had been more difficult than she anticipated. The new releases were picked over, and she hadn't known Jake long enough to know what he'd seen in the past few years. When she finally settled on one, it was too late to go browsing through the classics. They went inside and were soon settled in front of the television with their dinner. Two hours later, Jake stood up and stretched.

"That's the last time I let you pick out a movie."

"You didn't like it? I thought it was wonderful."

"You would."

"What do you mean?"

"Chick flick, big time."

"Oh, I don't know about that. I thought it had a sort of symmetry about it."

"See what I mean? Chick flick. All I got out of it was some pretty scenery and ample opportunities to show off Brad Pitt's backside."

"But it's such a nice backside. Okay, so you get to pick next time. One question, though. Whose backside will we be watching then?" she said, ducking the pillow Jake threw at her.

"So what else did you get?"

"Nothing, actually. I ran out of time. But I was thinking of *The Quiet Man*, and I have a copy of that."

Abby opened the cabinet under the television to find the movie. Jake moved to stand beside her and laughed and shook his head as he browsed through the collection. "I knew you were a fan of the Duke, but I never realized you had all these."

"Dad's a big fan, and Steven and I were raised on John Wayne movies. I guess he wasn't the greatest actor of all times, but there is something about the black-and-white, right-or-wrong simplicity of his movies that has always appealed to me."

"I've always liked this movie," he said, and they watched the opening credits. "Besides, maybe I can learn something about dealing with a hardheaded woman." It was his turn to duck the pillow.

* * * * *

The phone rang the next morning while Abby was in the shower. When she came out, Jake asked, "Who is John Cutter?"

"What? Who?"

"You had a call while you were in the shower. The man said his name was John Cutter and that you'd know what it was about."

"Oh, him. Just running down something Dad asked me to check out for his genealogy," Abby fibbed, unwilling to tell Jake what she was up to. "Want some breakfast?"

"No thanks. I've got to get home and start on those papers before the sight of you in that towel distracts me any more."

"Flatterer," Abby said and kissed him. "See you later?"

"Probably. What have you got planned for the day?"

"Nothing special, just all those lovely Saturday chores that don't get done all week."

"Don't forget to call that guy back. Let me know if you find anything interesting."

Chapter 35

AN ELDERLY-SOUNDING WOMAN ANSWERED THE phone and, when she learned Abby's name, called her husband to the phone.

"Cutter here."

"This is Abby Edwards. Thanks for calling me back."

"Your call was intriguing. What can I do for you?"

"I'm helping my father with some genealogy research. Cutter is a family name. In fact, it's my middle name."

"Where are your folks from?"

"'Indiana, but—"

"I think you've got the wrong Cutters. We're all from Tennessee. Sorry I can't help you. Goodbye."

"But we think my great-great-great-grandfather might have been from Blount County," Abby said quickly before the man had a chance to hang up.

"Blount County, you say? Where?"

"We're not exactly sure, but when he mustered into the Union Army in 1863, he listed Blount County as his county of residence."

The man's voice became animated. "Eighteen sixty-three, did you say? What was his name?"

"Jacob. Jacob Cutter. Why, do you know the name?"

"I know the name. Do you know who his parents were?"

"No, I'm afraid not. He's somewhat of a mystery in our family."

"But you're sure he was from around here?"

"Pretty sure. Do you know who he was?"

"I can't be sure, but I think he may have been my grandfather's half-brother."

Abby felt her own excitement growing. "Mr. Cutter, was your grandfather by any chance from Cades Cove?"

"No, he was born in Knoxville."

"Oh," said Abby, her hopes dashed.

John Cutter continued, "But his father was from the cove. Like many others, his farm suffered during the war. After his wife died, he moved to Knoxville, remarried, and started a second family."

"How much do you know about Jacob?"

"Not much. He never came back from the war."

"Was he married, do you know?"

"Oh yes. The letter speaks about a woman, and we're pretty sure it was his wife."

"What letter?" Abby was beginning to understand how Jake felt trying to tease information out of his mother.

"Didn't I tell you about the letter? No, I suppose I didn't. Forgive me, I'm getting a little forgetful these days—turned eighty-three last winter. We found the letter in an old family Bible after my father died. He was just shy of one hundred when he passed on. We Cutters live a long time."

On the other end of the line, Abby tapped her foot and made a rolling motion with her hand. She didn't want to offend Mr. Cutter but wished he'd get on with his story.

"Anyway, the only thing we really know about Jacob comes from a letter he sent to his father after the war. Reading between the lines, it's pretty clear that he must have run into some other soldiers from the cove while he was a prisoner. He knew that his mother was dead and that his father had moved out of the cove."

"And his wife, what does the letter say about her?" Abby tried to mask her growing impatience.

"He seems to be explaining to his father why he isn't coming back to Tennessee. He says now that...darn, I can't remember her name. Rowena, do you remember the name of that woman in the letter from Grandpa's brother?

Abby couldn't understand the muffled reply.

"That's right," he said. "The woman's name is Abigail."

"Abigail? Are you sure?" Abby interrupted.

"That's what the letter says. Why, is that important?"

"I think so. Mr. Cutter, would it be possible for me to get a copy of the letter?"

"Certainly. I'll get my grandson to take it to town and make a copy and send it to you."

"I appreciate that, but would it be possible for me to come and see it. Today?"

"Well, I guess. What's your hurry?"

"It's kind of a long story, but I think your letter may solve two family mysteries. Would it be too much of an imposition? I'll tell you everything I know."

"If it means that much to you, sure, come on over. Do you have a pencil? I'll give you directions."

After jotting down the directions Abby thanked him again and started to hang up. "Mr. Cutter," she asked, "do you mind if I bring a friend?"

Chapter 36

"THIS BETTER BE GOOD, AB," said Jake as they drove down the dirt road to a rambling white farmhouse. "I really have to get those papers graded this weekend."

"Trust me on this, will you?"

"But can't you even tell me what it's all about? I mean, you just show up at my door and order me into your car."

"Just trust me, please."

Mr. Cutter was sitting on the front porch dozing in the afternoon sun when they arrived. The sound of the car doors startled him out of his nap, and he stood up stiffly.

"You must be Abby."

"Yes, sir. Mr. Cutter, this is my fiancé, Jake Bartlett. I think he's going to be as interested in the letter as I am."

"Letter? What letter?" asked Jake.

"Come on in the house, children, and I'll show you. Rowena," he called, "those young folks are here about the letter."

After introductions had been made and they were seated at the Cutters' dining-room table, Jake turned to Abby. "Okay, you've got me here. Now will you tell me what's going on?"

He listened in growing amazement as Abby explained how she'd come to speak with Mr. Cutter and learn about the letter from his great-uncle. She then explained to the Cutters about Jake's great-great-grandmother and her theory that the two might be related.

"Could we see the letter, Mr. Cutter?"

He pushed a plastic-covered paper across the table to them. Together, they read slowly through the penciled scrawl.

Ohio, 1865

Dear Pa,

Reckon by now yall give me up for dead. I thought I was dead for sure but the good Lord must not be done with me yet. Dont reckon I'm much good now but Ma always said God has a plan for all his critters. After George got killed our regiment saw a lot of action. Most of us got captured at a place called Rogersville over in Hawkins County. I got shot and they cut off my left arm. My captain got hurt in the same battle as me. He talked the Rebs into taking me to Libby Prison with him instead of shipping me straight off to Andersonville. They tell me I'm lucky and I reckon its so. Did get sent on to Andersonville a while later and it sure was an awful place. Ran into old Jeb Fuller there and he told me that Ma died. I sure hope she went peaceful like. Didnt know there were so many bad ways of dying but I reckon I seen most of them there. I hate to think of Ma suffering like some of them fellas there. I hear tell most of them that was with me never made it home. Not sure how I lived. Or why. They sent me up here to Ohio a few months ago, and I seen my old captain. He's going west to hunt for silver and wants me to take word to his folks that he aint coming home. I owe him for taking care of me when I got shot so I reckon I will. Don't know what I'm gonna do then. With Abigail gone I dont have much belly for farming. I just wish I coulda caught them that took her. Take care of yourself and the rest of the family that lived through the war. If I dont see you before I will see you one day on the other side.

Your son
Jacob

Abby sat back in her chair and waited for Jake's response. He reread the letter and finally turned to Mr. Cutter. "Sir, I think I can clear up the mystery of what happened to Jacob's Abigail. It's a long story, but as near as we can tell from old letters in my family, my great-great-grandfather was one of a group of bushwackers who kidnapped her from the cove."

"Do tell."

"We found a letter from my great-aunt a few weeks ago, and she tells about how her father confessed to the kidnapping right before he died. Although he was with the men who took her, he seems to have been cut from a different cloth. He rescued her and eventually married her."

"But what about GG3?" Abby interrupted, no longer able to contain herself.

"Sorry, Ab, this puts us closer, but I can't say for sure that this Jacob is GG3."

"But—"

"Let me finish, woman. I think he may be GG3 since I think it's unlikely that two Jacob Cutters joined the Union Army in Blount County. On the other hand, this letter doesn't tie him to your grandmother Louisa."

"But what about all that stuff that Dad found?"

"That tells us about GG3, but it doesn't definitely tie him back to this Jacob. For instance, has your dad found anything in his research about GG3 having another wife?" Jake turned to Mr. Cutter and continued, "How did you come by this letter? Are there any more from him, maybe earlier in the war?"

"Sorry, son, that's the only one. We found it in the old family Bible some years back."

"Does the Bible have any other family information in it? A record of marriages, baptisms, burials, and the like?"

"I'd almost forgotten about that. It does. In fact, my son made a sort of family tree using the information he found there. The pages are pretty fragile and the writing is faded, so he spent a lot of time copying down what he could decipher."

"Does it mention Jacob and Abigail and their marriage? Was she from the cove too?"

"Rowena, bring me that other paper from the desk. The one with all the family names on it."

For the next half hour, Abby and Jake pored over the list of names, dates, and places. Jake finally looked up and said, "This is fantastic. Could we get a copy of it as well as the letter?"

"Sure, you can. Did you find more of what you were looking for?"

"Yes, indeed. All I've ever known of my great-great-grandmother was that she came from Cades Cove. But I didn't know anything of her family. According to this, she was born up in Virginia, around Lynchburg, and now I know her maiden name, so I can see if I can trace her family back any further."

"And no matter what Jake says, *I* think the Jacob who wrote the letter is my great-great-great-grandfather. Now we just have to figure out how to prove it. I can't wait to talk to Dad."

When Abby stopped the car in front of Jake's apartment, he sat looking over the documents and shaking his head. "I still can't believe that you found the link I've been looking for all this time. Or that you did it by just picking up the phone."

"Just playing a hunch. Guess I've spent too much time with cops. I'm happy it paid off for you, but I'm still really bummed that you don't think it's a solid connection to GG3. I really wanted to tie it all up. Guess that was pretty naive of me."

"Maybe a little. You never know where you're going to find just the right bit of information to tie things together. I sure never would have thought of making cold calls, though."

They spent a few more minutes discussing their plans for the remainder of the weekend and upcoming week. Both had separate plans that would require all their time for the next few days. After some discussion, they agreed to meet for dinner after Abby's meeting with Dr. Tucker.

Chapter 37

ABBY DRUMMED HER FINGERS ON the table as she waited for Dr. Tucker. Now that the time for their appointed meeting had arrived, she was nervous. She switched from drumming her fingers to tearing a napkin into tiny pieces. Her decision to try to return to medicine would change nearly everything in her life. Was it the right one?

"Sorry I'm late," Rick Tucker said as he folded his long frame into the booth opposite her. "I got called in on an emergency."

"I guess that's why I didn't decide to become a surgeon. Your life is never entirely your own."

"Is it really any different for an attorney? By the way, how goes it in the halls of justice these days?"

"Oh, you know, sometimes you get the bear, and sometimes the bear gets you."

Dr. Tucker grinned at the reference to a poster that one of her classmates had posted in the surgeons' locker room during their rotation. "And who is winning?"

"So far this week, it's lawyers 2, criminals 0, but it's early. You just never know. How's Sharon? And the rest of the family?"

"All fine, but I suspect you didn't invite me here to be regaled with family doings? You said this was partly business and partly personal." He peered at her intently. "Are you feeling okay?"

Abby laughed. "Quite fine. I just need some advice...and I guess it will impact both." She paused, suddenly uncertain as to how to go on.

"Well, are you going to tell me, or do I have to guess?"

"Sorry. I, uh, I..." She took a deep breath and searched the faces of the happy-hour crowd for inspiration or another diversion.

Finding neither, she plunged right in. "I think I want to go back to school and complete a residency."

Dr. Tucker sat back in his chair and blew out a low whistle. "Are you sure?"

"Pretty sure. I know it's a big step, but I really think it's what I want to do."

"Before you start down this road, you'd better do more than just *think* it's what you want to do."

Abby felt herself blush under his gaze, feeling like a first-year med student again. She was relieved when the waiter interrupted to bring their drinks. When he left, Abby squared her shoulders. "I've been thinking about this for months in an abstract way. But that thing on the mountain really tipped the balance. Since then, it's been on my mind all the time. Can I do it?"

"You can do anything you set your mind to, but this is huge undertaking. Are you sure you aren't letting one incident color your judgment? You got lucky on the side of that mountain. You don't just wake up one morning and decide you want to play doctor again. You haven't practiced in, what, almost ten years? What about your license and your continuing education hours?"

The bustle of the busy restaurant fell away as Dr. Tucker's rapid-fire questions and stern manner took Abby back to her early days in medical school. More than one hapless student had fallen victim to the barrage of questions he threw at them. "A doctor has to learn to think and act decisively," he told them. "There's no time in the OR to look things up. You have to *know* what you're doing."

No longer totally in awe of her former teacher, she shot back, "Actually, I've been working at least one weekend a month in a free clinic over on the south side for more than eight years. My license and CMEs are all up-to-date."

Another whistle. "You're just full of surprises. I guess you *have* given this some consideration. Aside from surgery, have you given any thought as to what you want to specialize in?"

"I'm leaning toward pediatrics. For someone with no children of her own, I seem to do pretty well with kids."

"That's right. You were that way in med school as well."

"So can I do this? Will they let me back in?"

"I take it you mean at UT?"

"Well, yes. I'd like to stay here in Knoxville if I could. I'm sort of engaged."

He raised an eyebrow. "Sort of engaged?"

"Well, we haven't set a date or anything, but I've met someone, and we're talking about marriage."

"And how does he feel about you changing careers?"

"Actually, he's all for it." Abby laughed, remembering their first meeting. "Jake was another of my rescue efforts. I met him up in Cades Cove when I found him in the woods with a nasty bump on the head and a broken ankle."

"You have an uncanny knack for being around when folks get hurt. Does he have any idea what being married to, or even involved with a resident is like?"

"Probably not. But Jake's encouraged me to get back into medicine almost since the first day we met. And you haven't answered my question. Do I have any chance at all of getting back in?"

"Given what you've told me, I'd say you have a pretty good shot at it. In fact, you probably have a bit of an edge over the younger students. Schools are looking harder at older students these days. The attrition rate is much lower in that population."

"I guess anyone crazy enough to even consider medical school at my age is pretty certain that they really want to be a doctor when they grow up," Abby said with a grin.

"Something like that."

"Guess I really just wanted to hear you say that I haven't lost my mind."

"Definitely not. I always thought it was a shame when you didn't come back after losing out on the Vanderbilt residency. How about if I give the dean a call?"

"Oh, you don't have to do that."

"I know I don't have to. I want to. When are you going to apply?"

"Soon. I'm sure I'm too late for the June class, but I want to get my name on the list early for next year. It'll take a while to wrap my cases. Don't want to burn that bridge too soon in case I don't get in."

"I don't think you have to worry about that."

They talked a while longer about the admissions process and then rose to leave. Jake met them as they stood in the doorway saying their goodbyes. After introductions were made, Rick said, "The next few years will be an exciting time for you."

Jake raised his eyebrows a notch and murmured a puzzled, "Thanks."

"Our engagement," Abby said quickly, trying to steer the conversation away from a reference to their residency discussion. "I know we're not telling most people, but Rick's an old friend. His daughter was one of my best friends in medical school."

"I'd better run," said Rick. "My wife is waiting dinner. I'll get back to you once I've had a chance to talk to the dean. I think you're making a wise decision."

Jake's eyebrows raised another notch, and he started to speak but closed his mouth when he saw Abby's expression. To his credit, Jake waited until they were seated to pounce. "What decision? And please don't say marrying me. The man doesn't even know me."

"Could we at least order first?" Abby asked as the waiter approached.

Jake rattled off their order, and the waiter departed. He turned back to Abby. "Again, what decision?"

Stalling for time, she replied, "Since when am I not able to order my own dinner? Suppose I wanted something different for a change?"

"Do you?"

"Well, no, but—"

"So what decision?"

Unable to stall any longer, Abby squared her shoulders and dropped the napkin she'd been twisting in her hands.

"I really wanted to wait until I was sure it really could happen before I told you. I met with Rick this evening to see if I can get back into a residency program."

"What? Are you sure?"

"As sure as I am that I want to marry you one of these days. Assuming, of course, that you still believe you can live with a woman crazy enough to change careers in midstream."

"You know the answer to that one. When will you know for sure?"

"No idea. I'll have to reapply and then wait. Rick's optimistic that I'll be able to get into next year's class."

"What are you going to do until then?"

"I haven't sorted all that out yet. I really just made up my mind a few days ago."

"For what it's worth, I agree with Dr. Tucker. You're making the right decision. Is there anything I can do?"

"Just put up with me. I may not be the easiest person in the world to live with for the next few months."

"You got it. Now, a toast to *Dr. Edwards.*"

* * * * *

A few weeks later, Abby was sitting at her desk when Sandra buzzed and said she had visitors. Seconds later, Sam and Katie burst through her door.

"Sam, Katie, when are you ever going to learn to knock?" said Marilyn Sanders as she followed her children into the office. "Sorry, Abby. Are we interrupting?"

"Nothing that can't wait. It's so good to see you. I've been meaning to call, but it's been a bit hectic around here." Turning to the children, she continued, "And how are my two favorite hiking buddies?"

Katie beamed, and Sam, his voice still raspy, said, "I'm going to play Little League this summer. Will you come and watch?"

Abby shot his mother a questioning look. Marilyn shrugged her shoulders. "I'm afraid there will be no slowing him down once the cast comes off."

"Sam, if the doctor says you can play, I'd love to come see you play."

"Abby, will you come to the party too?" asked Katie. "Tell her about the party, Mommy."

"We're throwing a little party to thank all the wonderful people who helped when Sam was hurt," said Marilyn. "It wouldn't be compete if you weren't there."

"Wow, Abby, are all of these books yours?" Sam interrupted as he and Katie flitted around her office, peering at the walls lined with bookshelves.

"They're not exactly mine."

"Have you read them all?" asked Katie.

"Not quite all, but a lot of them." Turning back to his mother, she continued, "A party sounds like a wonderful idea. When will it be?"

"Sam wants to wait until the cast comes off. It will probably be sometime shortly after Memorial Day. I haven't worked out all the details yet, but that's my target."

"As far as I know, I'll be in town."

Certain that Abby would attend the party, the children returned to their circuit of her office, pausing here and there to look more closely at the books, photographs, and other items on the walls and bookshelves.

After an admonishment to the children about not touching anything, Marilyn said, "There are a couple of people that I haven't been able to track down yet, and I was hoping you could help."

"Sure, if I can, although I'm not sure I know any of them. Have you checked with the rangers' office and the hospital?"

"I don't think they were rangers or paramedics. Sam said you were talking to one of them, so I took it for granted that you knew them."

Abby looked doubtful. "There was no one around when I found Sam. Maybe he heard me talking to Kevin. But now that you mention it, he did say something about a man in a green suit chasing a bear away. I just thought he was hallucinating."

Just then, Sam stopped in his circuit around her office. "It's him. It's the man in the green suit. You must know him, Abby. You have his picture."

The boy was staring at a photo on a bookshelf—a photo of Steven. He was standing next to his jet dressed in a flight suit—a green flight suit.

Shaken, Abby searched for a reply. She moved to Sam's side and knelt beside him. "I believe you saw a man, Sammy. But it couldn't have been this man. This is a picture of my brother. He died in a war before you were born."

234

"But I saw him," Sam insisted. "He even had the same suit on."

"You had a really bad fall, honey," his mother said. "We believe you saw someone, just not this man."

"But what about the farmer? I saw you talking to him."

Abby looked bewildered, and Marilyn smiled. "He has such clear memory of both of them. I was sure you would know who they were."

"A farmer?"

"Maybe he wasn't a farmer, but he had on old-timey clothes," Sam interjected.

"I guess this will sound strange," his mother continued, "but the way Sam described him reminds me of some of the old photos I've seen of the cove's early residents. Some of those old farmers up around Townsend don't look much different today, and I just assumed he must have been a local. Do you know who he was?"

Abby realized that the man Marilyn described sounded an awfully lot like the apparition she'd begun referring to as GG3. It was one thing to admit to Jake that she'd been having conversations with her long-dead ancestor and more recently dead brother, but admitting it to anyone else was out of the question.

"I didn't see anyone except Kevin and the rangers when they arrived," she fibbed. "I honestly don't know who it could have been."

"But I heard you yelling at him, Abby. You wanted him to help."

Abby just sat there. Could Sam have really seen GG3? Or Steven? She racked her brain for a sane response. "I was so worried about you that I was probably talking to myself. And like your Mom said, you had a nasty bump on your head. I'm sorry, Sammy. I really don't remember seeing either man."

"That's that then. I'm sorry, Sam. If Miss Abby doesn't know who the men are, I don't know where else to look. It'll be a good party anyway. Everyone else who helped you is going to be there."

Sam didn't look entirely convinced at her story, but with a final look at Steven's picture, he said, "I guess I could have been dreaming."

Abby sought for a way to change the subject. "Sam," she asked, "is it okay if I bring a friend to your party?"

Chapter 38

ALTHOUGH THE INITIAL PLAN HAD been to host the party at their home, Marilyn Sanders had called a few weeks after their visit to say that Sam had insisted that the party be held in the cove.

"I'm afraid that going back there would be traumatic for him, but he is adamant," Marilyn explained when she called Abby.

"Kids are amazingly resilient. I'd be more worried if Sam *didn't* want to go back. Besides, the picnic area is a wonderful place for a gathering."

The day of Sam's party dawned sunny and warm. When Jake arrived to pick her up for the drive to the mountains, he was driving a rented red Mustang convertible. "I thought we might drive the loop after the party," he explained.

Abby leaned back in her seat and soaked in the warmth of the sun as Jake drove. The weeks since she'd received the invitation, life at work had been hectic. Two weeks ago, she broke the news to her boss that she would be leaving.

"When?" Tim Banner asked pointedly.

Abby smiled at the man who was, in effect, responsible for her becoming an attorney. An assistant when she'd met him, Tim was now the district attorney for Knox County.

"You always cut to the chase, don't you?" she replied. "I'm not sure, actually. Are you in a hurry to get rid of me?"

"Quite the contrary, but it will take some time to replace you and bring them up to speed on your cases."

"I realize that. That's why I decided to tell you now. Aren't you going to ask where I'm going?"

Tim finally smiled back at her. "I'm guessing you've finally come to your senses and are going back into medicine."

Abby's mouth flew open. She closed it again. Tim's sharp mind was one of the things that had attracted her to him all those years ago. "With anyone else, I'd wonder how they knew that, but not you. You're right. I'm too late for this year's program, but I'm anxious to move in that direction. My options are limited, but if something comes up, I want to be able to take it."

"Fair enough. Let's schedule some time next week to review your caseload."

Abby thanked him, rose, and went to the door. As she reached it, Tim's voice stopped her. "As your boss, I should tell you that you're throwing away a promising legal career."

"And as my friend?" she teased.

"You've made the right decision. Get out there and cure cancer or something!"

Jake's voice interrupted her reflection. "So now that you've told your boss, have you given any more thought to what you're going to do for the next year?"

"You know it's really disconcerting when you read my mind like that," she replied, punching his shoulder lightly.

"Just call me Carnac," he said, referring to the turbaned character played by Johnny Carson.

"Okay, Carnac, find me a job. Seriously, though, I don't have huge range of options. Much as I want to get back into medicine, I can't just hang up a shingle. I could work full-time at the clinic, but they couldn't pay me, and I've grown accustomed to having a roof over my head."

"You could move in with me," he said with a Groucho Marx leer. "Or," he sobered, "I could help you out financially. You're probably a good investment."

"Oh, so that's why you're marrying me...for the investment potential." She laughed.

Abby had been giving the whole matter a lot of attention. She would get a stipend during her residency but would have to supplement it with her savings. Her goal was to come out of her residency without incurring any debt. As enticing as both of Jake's offers were, she couldn't accept either. Her independent streak ruled out the latter, and her rearing made the former unacceptable. She knew that her parents at least suspected that she and Jake "played house," as her mother would put it, but they would not be happy if the couple moved in together before being properly married. And Abby didn't want that either. She wasn't certain why, but she didn't.

A fair-sized group was already gathered in the picnic area when they arrived. When Sam recognized Abby, he ran up to greet them.

"Great car," he said as he ran his hand along the sleek side of the sports car.

Abby laughed. "Well, that proves a theory of mine. Men, even very young ones, have a car gene. I really think you guys would rather look at a flashy car than a pretty girl."

"Girls, yuck! They have cooties," said Sam.

"I'm a girl, Sam, and I thought you liked me."

"But you're different, Abby. You're old, like my mom."

"That'll teach you." Jake laughed.

"Teach her what? Who are you anyway?" Sam asked.

Marilyn Sanders arrived at that moment. "Sam! Where are your manners? I'm Marilyn," she said as she extended her hand. "Honestly, I don't know what gets into him sometimes."

"Jake Bartlett. And I'm sure my mom said the same thing about me on more than one occasion!"

Katie spied them and ran up as they walked toward the rest of the group. She gave Abby a hug and then stood back to look at Jake. "Who are you?" she demanded.

Her mother blushed anew as Jake knelt to the child's level. "You must be Katie," he said. "I'm Jake. Abby tells me you're really good at finding wildflowers."

"Uh-huh. But you can't pick them," she admonished. "I found some rotor flowers. Come see," she said as she took his hand.

"Rhododendron," Abby answered Jake's unspoken question. "But how did you know, Katie? They weren't blooming when we were here before."

"I 'membered the leaves," she said, taking Abby's hand as well. "Besides, you said it looks like where the dwarfs put Snow While 'til the prince found her. Come see." Katie led them to a large group of shrubs covered in shell-pink flowers. They were, indeed, rhododendron.

After receiving their praises for correctly naming the plant, Katie danced off to join the other children. Abby and Jake joined the other adults where Marilyn introduced Jake to the rangers, paramedics, and others who had assisted in Sam's rescue. Rick Tucker and his wife arrived to join the party a short while later. John Sanders, wearing a chef's hat, presided over the grill. The hat, in the university's traditional orange, sparked a lively debate about football. Although most present were UT grads, there were enough "foreigners" to keep the discussion interesting.

As some of the group began to drift off to hike or drive around the cove, Rick pulled Abby aside. "Do you have a few minutes to talk?" he asked.

"Sure, what's up?"

"Actually, I have a proposition for you."

Abby grinned at her old friend and mentor. "A proposition? Why, Rick, you're a married man," she said in mock dismay.

The older man grinned back. "You're as bad as my daughter. But if you can behave for a minute, I'll explain."

Abby placed her hands on her lap like a dutiful child.

Rick continued, "My physician assistant is resigning. Her husband has accepted a fellowship in orthopedics at Duke, and for some strange reason, she'd rather go with him than stay and work for me."

"Imagine that. But what—" She stopped as he raised his hand.

"The scope of practice for a PA is pretty broad these days. Jamie does just about everything I do except surgery. She even has limited prescriptive authority. As a licensed physician, you'll be able to do all of that and perhaps more."

Abby fought to comprehend what Rick was offering. She had been overwhelmed by his offer to speak to the dean of the College of Medicine on her behalf, but this was beyond belief. Working with someone she admired and respected as much as she did Rick Tucker was a dream come true.

"Are…are you sure you want me?" she finally sputtered.

"I wouldn't offer it if I didn't. You were one of my most promising students. It's way past time that you started acting like a real doctor, and if you work for me, I'll see that you do."

"I don't know what to say. It's too good to be true."

They stood as Jake came toward them. "How about you come to see me one day next week, and we'll discuss the details. I may not be able to meet your salary demands."

"You forget that I'm a lowly civil servant. My expectations are not all that grand."

"What's this about expectations?" Jake asked. "Sure hope you're not talking about me."

"Rick's just offered me a job."

"Judging from the grin on your face, you must have accepted."

"Abby, call me Monday, and we'll see what we can work out. Jake, good to see you again," Rick said as he took his leave.

"Nothing is set yet. I'll tell you all about it tonight," Abby explained as they moved back to where the Sanders family was seated. "Right now I say let's take that shiny car of yours for a spin around the cove."

"Can I go, Abby?" Sam asked. "I've never ridden in a convertible before."

"Me too," chimed Katie. "I want to ride in the 'vertible too."

"Maybe Abby and Jake would like some grown-up time," said John Sanders. "I think they've given up enough of their Saturday for you. You can ride with us. Sean and Kevin have already started around on their bikes."

Abby was about to tell the youngsters that they would be welcome to join them when Jake said, "Abby and I need to talk about something for a little while. How about we meet you and your folks at the Cable Mill, and then you can ride the rest of the way around with us."

Chapter 39

"So what is it that we need to discuss?" Abby asked as they headed for the car.

An enigmatic "later" was Jake's only reply. Puzzled but content to wait, she relaxed in the passenger seat and breathed in the clear air. The early summer sky was a brilliant blue, and there was life everywhere. The lush green of the cove floor was punctuated by the orange blooms of the butterfly weed and brilliant red cardinal flowers. The white petals and bright yellow center of the oxeye daisy were another familiar sight along the roadside, and many of the fences were adorned with the blossoms of the white potato vine. *I hope Marilyn or John has a good wildflower book*, she thought to herself as she imagined Katie's nonstop barrage of "what's thats."

"What are you grinning about?" Jake asked as he pulled the car to a stop near the Elijah Oliver cabin.

"Just thinking about Katie and all the flowers. Bet she's driving her mom crazy."

Jake opened the door and said, "Let's take a walk."

Despite the crowd in the cove that day, Abby was glad to see that the trail back to the cabin was fairly deserted. Remembering the last time she'd been on this trail, she wondered if GG3 would make an appearance. Thinking about her encounters with this friendly spirit, it occurred to her that most of his appearances coincided with trouble. Gazing around at the placid surroundings, she felt it unlikely that he would appear on this carefree day.

Preoccupied with her musings and content just to be in Jake's quiet company, Abby lost track of where they were and didn't realize that they had turned off the main path until she saw the ruins of the cabin in the clearing ahead.

"What made you turn off here?" she asked. "I thought you wanted to go back to Elijah's place."

"We need to have a serious talk, and this is a nice, quiet place, assuming the resident rattlesnake is not in attendance."

Searching Jake's serious face, Abby felt a knot form in the pit of her stomach. Words like that seldom boded good news, but she resisted the urge to ask if something was wrong.

Jake threw back his head and laughed out loud. "I wish you could see yourself," he said when he was finally able to contain himself. "Sorry, I know how you hate to hear 'we need to talk.'"

He brushed the leaves and dirt off the top step of the ruins and told her to sit down. Puzzled by his mood and his behavior, she sat without comment. Apparently discomfited by her compliance, Jake strode around the clearing. Abby watched his pacing but managed to remain quiet until he joined her on the step.

"I just want this to be perfect," he said. "I had it all planned in February, and we ended up having a fight. Then you had to go and jump the gun on me. So let me say my piece before you argue with me, will you?"

Abby saluted smartly and said nothing.

When he spoke again, his words came out in a breathless rush, as if he were afraid she would interrupt. "I know we agreed not to rush into marriage. And you're nervous about your residency. You think residency and a new marriage is a recipe for disaster. And you're worried about finances. I'm sure you could come up with a dozen other reasons why we should wait to get married, but here's the deal." He paused and drew a long breath.

"I love you. I think I have since the day you found me here dazed and confused. And I don't want to wait until you're done with school or all the bills are paid or I've reached tenure or any of those things that will happen someday. My dad always promised my mom a mink coat and a trip to Europe 'someday,' and then one day he didn't come home from work. I don't want to put our life on hold for someday."

He paused long enough to reach into his pocket and take another deep breath before he went on. "Abigail Cutter Edwards, will you marry me? Tomorrow, next week, I don't care, just as long as it's soon."

While he spoke, the knot in her stomach melted away, only to be replaced by a lump in her throat. Her remaining composure was washed away by the tears that filled her eyes. Unable to speak, she could only nod her yes as Jake slipped a ring on her finger then took her into his arms.

When her happy tears finally subsided and Jake released her, Abby looked down at the ring. The perfect blue sapphire flanked by two diamonds was seated in delicate platinum filigree.

"It's beautiful," she whispered. "Where—"

"It was my great-grandmother's. My father gave it to Mom. She gave it to me when we were there in April."

"It's perfect."

"So now that you've said yes, when?"

Watching his earnest face, it was Abby's turn to laugh. "You're really serious about this, aren't you? Is August soon enough?"

"What day?"

"I have a day in mind, but can you wait 'til I make sure it's the right one?"

"Oh, I guess so. Promise?" he said in a childlike whine that sent Abby off into another fit of laughter.

"Cross my heart," she said when the giggles subsided. Taking his hand, she pulled him from his perch on the step. "Now that our future is settled, we'd better head for the mill before Sam sends out a search party."

When they arrived at the visitors' center a short time later, they found the Sanderses in the small outdoor museum that included the working gristmill, as well as a blacksmith's shop and sorghum mill. A man dressed in period garb was giving a demonstration at the blacksmith shop. Katie stood in rapt attention as the man hammered the white-hot metal on the anvil. He finished the piece, dipped it in cold water, and handed it to her as Abby and Jake walked up.

"Look, Abby. It's a horseshoe nail. Did you know that horses have to have their shoes nailed on?"

"Uh-huh. Aren't you glad you're a little girl instead of a horse? Where is Sam?"

"He's over there by that pole thing. He said he wanted to talk to someone, but whoever it was must be gone," she said, pointing toward the sorghum press.

Abby turned to look where Katie pointed, only to see Sam deep in conversation with a familiar figure. "Stay here with Jake. I'll go get Sam so we can go for that ride."

As she arrived at Sam's side, he turned to her and said, "Abby! This is the man I saw the day I got hurt." He turned back to the now empty space and said, "Where did he go? He said he's your…I forget how many, but he's your great-grandfather. I thought you said you didn't know him."

Abby took Sam's hand and led him to a nearby bench. "If I tell you something, can you keep it a secret just between you and me? You can't even tell Katie."

He held up three fingers and said, "Scout's honor."

Ignoring the fact that he wasn't yet a Boy Scout, Abby looked into his serious blue eyes and accepted his pledge. "Have you ever known someone that died?"

"Just the old lady that lives across the street. She smelled funny and had a lot of cats."

Abby suppressed the smile the image evoked. "Anyone else."

"Well, Dad says that my Grandpa Sanders died in some place called Vietnam. I only know about him from pictures. And Andrew, my best friend from kindergarten."

"What happened to him?"

"He got sick in first grade. His hair all came out, and he couldn't come to school anymore."

"I'm sorry. Do you know what happens when someone dies?"

"They go to heaven, silly. Everybody knows that."

"That's right, but I think that sometimes their spirits can come back here."

Sam's eyes widened with understanding then disbelief. "You mean you believe in ghosts?"

Abby shook her head. "Not like Halloween ghosts. But I believe that sometimes when we're in trouble, the spirits of the people we love can come back to help us."

Sam pondered that idea. "You mean like a dream or something?"

Abby nodded.

"When I was in third grade, I lost the lucky rock I found when we went to the Grand Canyon. I looked for it everywhere. One night, I had a dream about Andrew and me. He told me my rock was in the tree house. The next day, I found it in the tree house like Andrew said."

Sam looked at Abby for a sign of understanding. She wasn't sure where he was going with his story, so she simply nodded again.

"Andrew never saw that rock. We went to the Grand Canyon in the second grade. Do you think that was Andrew trying to help me?"

She paused, before going on. Explaining her beliefs to a ten-year-old was more difficult than she'd thought. "Yes, I do. You said Andrew was your best friend, and that's what best friends do." It was now Abby's turn to search Sam's young face for comprehension.

"So your grandfather was trying to help you find me when I was hurt?" the boy asked doubtfully.

"I think so. And my brother too. I know it seems strange, but it's the only explanation I have. I would have walked right past you and never seen you behind that log if he hadn't made me stop."

Sam sat quietly, and Abby could almost hear the wheels turning inside his head. What was going on his mind? she wondered.

After a time, he must have reached some unspoken conclusion. He stood and took her hand. "I'm just glad you found me," he said and paused. "Will I ever see them again?"

"I don't know," Abby said and meant it. "But tell them I said hi, if you do."

"I will," he said solemnly. "Can we go for a ride now?"

Chapter 40

ABBY AND SAM MOVED OFF to find the rest of his family and quickly found them seated in the shade of the visitors' center's wide front porch. In keeping with the historic theme of the outdoor museum, the center was a large log cabin. Katie and her mother were just coming out of the door with several packages when they arrived.

"I always have to get some honey and cornmeal when we come up," Marilyn explained.

"I know," Abby agreed. "For some reason, the stone-ground meal just tastes better."

"Sam, Katie, are you ready for your ride?" Jake asked.

After retrieving the children's sweaters from the Sanderses' car, they set off. The shadows had grown long in the late afternoon, and the deer had begun to come down to feed in large fields that still remained in the cove. Abby could remember when a few farmers still had cattle in these fields and evenings when the cows and deer grazed together. And like Abby had as a child, Katie begged to stop so she could count each cluster of the feeding animals. Jake dutifully stopped each time the child spotted one, and by the time they arrived back at the entrance to the cove, it was nearly dark and growing chilly. After delivering the children back to their parents and raising the convertible roof, Jake and Abby set off for Knoxville.

In the dim glow of the dashboard lights, Abby gazed at the ring on her hand.

"Penny for your thoughts," Jake offered.

"Just thinking," she replied. Although Jake wasn't entirely convinced, Abby knew in her heart that GG3 was married to Abigail. During those brief moments when she let her fanciful nature take

246

over, she could almost imagine that she and Jake were destined to complete the life that Jacob and Abigail were denied.

"I could tell you were thinking. Want to tell me what about?"

"About that date you want to set."

"Okay, you've got my attention. What about it?"

She hesitated, uncertain of Jake's reaction to her idea. "Well, I know we don't have proof yet, but even if you aren't, I'm convinced that GG3 is the Jacob that was married to Abigail. I can't remember the day for sure, but they were married in August, and I was thinking that it might be a good date for our wedding."

Jake grinned. "I like it. Sorta fits with an idea of my own. What would you think about getting married here in the cove?"

"You must be reading my mind, but I thought use of the churches was restricted to descendants of the cove's inhabitants."

"Nope, that's just for the cemeteries. I already asked George about it and found out what we have to do."

Abby punched him lightly on the arm. "And just how did you know I'd say yes?"

Jake leaned over to steal a quick kiss. "I didn't know for sure but wanted to be prepared. I figured I'd better have a plan ready so we could do it before you got cold feet."

Abby smiled back at him. "Not this time. I'm sure."

Back at Abby's apartment, they pulled out the page of dates John Cutter had given them. Jacob and Abigail were married August 24, 1861.

Jake pulled a small calendar out of his wallet. "Hmm. The twenty-fourth is on a Wednesday. Not very practical, is it?"

"Not for a big formal wedding, but I don't really want that, do you?

"I've had my heart set on one since I was just a little boy. You should see my hope chest," he said, throwing up his hands as she reached for the sofa pillow.

"Our parents are both retired, so I don't think it will matter to them. The days are long in August. What if we have it in the evening? That way, your brothers and sisters would only have to take about a day and a half off. Suppose they could manage that with enough notice?"

"The girls have been trying to marry me off for years, so I think they'll manage. James is his own boss, so he can come and go as he pleases. Yep, works for me. Speaking of folks, suppose we should let them in on the news?"

Calls were made to both sets of parents and Jake's siblings. Their news was met with lots of well wishes but very little surprise from either set of relatives. Abby commented on this when they finally reached her parents later that evening.

"We've been waiting on this call since you brought Jake home for New Year's." Madeline laughed. "What has taken you so long?"

"That's what Jake's mom wanted to know. I guess it just took me a while to figure things out."

Steven Cutter came on the phone and, after offering his congratulations, said, "We were going to call you this evening anyway. We just got back from Wyoming."

"Wyoming?" Abby asked. "Whatever possessed you to go to Wyoming?"

"Your mother located a distant cousin of mine on one of her internet searches, and we've been corresponding for some time. He's a descendant of your Thomas Shepard, your great-great-great-grandmother's brother."

"The black sheep you mentioned?" Jake asked.

"The very same. Seems he went out west after the Civil War to hunt for silver. Apparently, that's the 'blot' on the family name. His father never forgave him. Anyway, this cousin and I have been writing back and forth, and he and his wife invited us out for a visit."

"Silver prospecting in Wyoming?" Jake asked. "I thought the big silver mines were farther south."

"They were. He first went to Nevada, and although he made a small strike, it quickly played out. By this time, he knew he couldn't go back to Indiana, so he went to Wyoming and used what money he had to buy a small ranch."

"But it grew," added Madeline, who had been listening on the other extension. "The ranch has been in the family ever since, and they now have several thousand acres. Abby, you would love the house. It has a veranda that runs all the way around the house, and the view is—"

"But that's not the best part," Steven interrupted. "Fred had a whole bundle of letters from Louisa. Even though the old man never forgave him, Louisa and Thomas seem to have been quite close."

At the mention of Thomas and silver, Abby had retrieved the letter they received from John Cutter and now could contain herself no longer. "I've been meaning to call you. We—I mean I think GG3 was married to Jake's great-great-grandmother before the Civil War."

"*Really?*" her parents spoke simultaneously.

"We don't have concrete proof," said Jake. "But Abby found a letter that is really intriguing. A Jacob Cutter was writing to tell his family he wasn't coming home—"

"Tell them about the captain who was going prospecting," Abby broke in. "It must be Thomas. Jacob saved his captain's life, and when the captain decided to go to Nevada, he asked Jacob to break the word to his family."

"How does this tie back to Jake's ancestor?" Steven asked.

Jake explained, "In the letter, our Jacob speaks of his wife Abigail being kidnapped by Confederate bushwackers. My mom found a letter from my great-great-aunt that told how her father took part in a kidnapping but later rescued the woman and married her."

They talked on about the letters and wedding plans and finally rang off with promises to fax each other their respective letters the following day.

September 1, 1876

Dear Thomas,

It was so good to get your letter and know that you arrived safely home after Father's funeral. I couldn't bear the thought of losing both of you. The papers have been full of the news of General Custer's battle and the Indians' unrest. It relieves me to know that the Natives in Wyoming seem to be content on the land set aside for them. It meant so much to Mother that you were able to come home. I'm just sorry that you and Father were never able to talk before he died. In spite of everything, I know in his heart he was proud of you and what you've accomplished. It still seems funny to me that you left Indiana because you didn't want to tend to farm full of cows and ended up owning a ranch in the West— tending even more cows. I wish Father could have met Emily and the boys as well. She is a wonderful woman, and you should be proud of your sons. Do you suppose that they will rebel against the idea of being ranchers? I guess all we can do is raise them the best way we know how and hope for the best.

For the most part, we are well. The girls are busy with school and excited with the prospect of a new addition to our family. Yes, brother, you will be an uncle again in the spring. And after three girls, Jacob, of course, is hoping for a boy this time. We'll just have to see what the good Lord has to say about that and just be grateful for a healthy baby. So far, I am feeling well, and that is a blessing since Jacob was taken ill shortly after you left. After all these years, he still has lingering bouts with the malaria that he contracted during the war. The fevers weaken him so that he can barely stand, let alone tend to the cattle. It is fortunate that we have enough good hands

CPSIA information can be obtained
at www.ICGtesting.com
Printed in the USA
FFHW022128030719
53380992-59074FF